A LETHAL LEGACY

P.C. ZICK

DEDICATION

I remember those who came before me and dedicate this book to
them.
You are not forgotten.

.

OTHER FICTION BY P.C. ZICK

Behind the Love Romances

Behind the Altar Book One – All seems perfect in Leah's life until tattoo artist Dean rides his Harley into her heart in this story of forbidden love.

Behind the Bar Book Two – Reggie and Susie almost lose each other as they struggle to overcome the past.

Behind the Curtain Book Three – Lisa returns to Victory with a reality TV crew, and Tommy and she struggle to remain friends despite a growing attraction.

Behind the Door Book Four – Sally Jean as she struggles to find true love even though she believes she doesn't deserve it. Dr. Brett helps her discover her true inner beauty.

Rivals in Love Series – Follow the Crandall family siblings as they find love and navigate careers, the political aspirations of their father, a U.S. Senator, and their mother, heir to a Chicago meat corporation.

Love on Trial – Oldest Crandall sibling, Jude, is on opposite sides of the courtroom with Malik, a slick lawyer with an Iranian mother who pushes to bring Jude and Malik together. She's helped by Sofia Mancini Crandall, Jude's mother. But it's two dogs that fall in love first and show Jude and Malik that love crosses all boundaries.

Love on Board – Rock Crandall is a pilot who is surprised by his new female co-pilot. He must change his view of the world as Sabrina shows him a whole different side to life than what he's known.

Love on Track – Race car driver Stone spends his life on the track with precision like focus. It's never left time for romance until his childhood friend who happens to be Jude's best friend forces him to step out of the driver's seat for a different kind of ride.

Love on Air – Diamond or "Mond" Crandall stars in this story about a rising star on a cable news show. When Hope Colson shows up on his show, their on-screen presence sizzles while off-screen it simmers with unease.

Love on Course – The youngest sibling, Turq, works as a chef in one of Chicago's finest restaurants, but he's tired and lonely after his girlfriend Cindy moves away. Trips to Italy and Ireland and questions from Cindy bring him to decisions about his priorities.

Love on Stage – Ruby, the only other female Crandall sibling, seeks stardom in Hollywood, but is drawn home for a family crisis and ends up finding a love that might change the course of her career.

Love on Holiday – Celebrate the fortieth wedding anniversary of the couple who started the whole thing. Nolan and Sofia face some struggles as the rest of the family plans a surprise anniversary celebration for Christmas Eve.

Florida Fiction Series

Native Lands – A novel rich in intrigue and history as a tribe of Native Americans, thought to be extinct, fight to save their beloved heritage.

Tortoise Stew – Politics, murder, and chaos in rural Florida reign supreme in a story where love triumphs over it all.

Trails in the Sand – Family secrets, an oil spill, and redemption create a roller coaster ride for journalist Caroline Carlisle.

Smoky Mountain Sweet Romances

Minty's Kiss – A sweet Christmas novella set in the foothills of the Smoky Mountains in Murphy, North Carolina. Two childhood sweethearts, one lonely little girl, and a smart kitty hope to find happiness as Christmas approaches.

Misty Mountain – The characters from *Minty's Kiss* return as Lacy and George struggle to overcome the heartbreaks from their previous relationships.

Mountain Miracles – David and Cecelia—two new folks and strangers to one another—come to town to start businesses. He wants to reconnect to his past and she wants to forget hers.

A Merry Mountain Christmas – Fran, the mother to everyone, finds herself alone and wondering how she can make a difference. When her first love returns to town he brings more than romance to her life.

Montauk Romances

Love on the Wind, A Montauk Romance, Book One – Six years of traveling for her television series has left host Kiley Nelson longing for a place to call her own. Spending a weekend at her girlfriend's beach house is the perfect reprieve until she smashes into a car containing the sinfully sexy and infuriated passenger, Jeff Hammond, who immediately melts her heart.

Jingle Bell Love, A Montauk Romance, Book Two – Denny and Jill find themselves lustfully drawn to one another. When friends disapprove, they hatch a pact to be friends with secret benefits.

Other Works of Fiction

A Lethal Legacy (Psychological Suspense) – A fascinating study of human expectations, failings, and redemption filled with lust and forbidden lovers.

Live from the Road (A Magical Route 66 Novel) – The reader heads out on an often humorous, yet harrowing, journey as Meg Newton and Sally Sutton seek a change in the mundane routine of their lives.

Third Base – When Adriana Moretti meets baseball star Tomas Vegas, she's surprised by his kindness. While Tomas puts all his energy into winning the World Series for the Pittsburgh Pirates, he's thrown off his game by the brilliant and beautiful Adriana, who owns a multi-million-dollar business she started with her late husband.

CHAPTER ONE

THE FOG ENVELOPED ME for the first time on that Thanksgiving in 1986. I remained trapped in it for an entire decade.

I married, made love, had children, and buried my relatives, but I did it while covered in a shroud of heavy moisture laden with coldness and despair. The years of my youth caught up with me, and my penchant for saving the world served as a guiding light as I fought to break through the deepening depression.

Trying to live and love and feel with a deep foreboding never leaving my consciousness proved to be a challenge. I knew I couldn't see the road before me. My actions came from instinct because the path in front of me lacked directions.

On that Thanksgiving eve, I drove over the bridges connecting the bayous and swamps that lead into New Orleans. The evening, warm for November, rained humidity, leaving everything in its wake damp. As I came closer to the city, the fog surrounded my car, swallowing it in one bite. I drove on, not sure where the road would take me, but still happy that I had decided to spend Thanksgiving with my cousin Gary Townsend who had moved to New Orleans almost ten years ago.

"Hey, Ed, don't you think it's time to get together?" Gary asked when he called the week before to ask me to spend Thanksgiving with him.

"It's been awhile, hasn't it?" I said.

"Why don't you come here? Then we can enjoy ourselves without our mothers' fussing over us and Philip growling at me."

"Who's going to tell them?"

"Well, you of course, Cuz! Tell them they'll have us both at Christmas. That should be enough for one year, right?"

Gary and I had grown up in Michigan, but in 1977 when both of our second marriages ended, Gary, an advertising executive, transferred to New Orleans. I was teaching high school English in Ann Arbor for ten years by then, but I aspired to be a novelist. When my mother moved to Florida after my dad died, I began considering a move there. She moved after my father's death in 1977 and joined Gary's parents in retirement heaven near Ocala.

By 1979, with two novels published, I quit teaching to write full time, and occasionally offering writing seminars through local community colleges.

In 1980, I moved from Ann Arbor into an apartment south of Gainesville, the home of the University of Florida, near the flat, yet powerful landscape of Paynes Prairie, and within a half hour's drive to my relatives in Ocala. I left my teaching career in Michigan with little regret and concentrated on my third novel that was a departure of sorts for me. After some research, I began writing about Florida's role in the Civil War.

Previously I wrote contemporary works with some autobiographical material. More accurately, those books contained Gary's life within their covers. I never wrote about myself, but I certainly had insight into Gary and could pontificate about his shortcomings and insecurities with ease. Gary, forever the faithful cousin, never minded. Or if he did mind, he never let me know.

North Florida's landscape lured and inspired me unlike anything I had experienced in the industrial regions of southeastern Michigan. The expansive branches of the majestic oak and towering pine trees calmed my senses and allowed me to enjoy the coldest January night and the hottest August afternoon. Either the Atlantic Ocean or the Gulf of Mexico was an hour's drive from my apartment. I found myself yearning for the sound of the waves upon the flat, white beaches of a north Florida coast if I went more than a month without a visit. The coasts boosted my creativity, and the beauty of the rolling hills of the horse farms kept me grounded.

On one of my first visits to the Atlantic coast, I went to Amelia Island just inside the state line but with a view of Georgia's Cumberland Island across a strait at the northern end of Amelia. I camped at Fort Clinch State Park, where one of the protective fortresses built by the British in the 1800s still stands. On my picnic table, someone had placed a sea oat branch. The sea oat, a highly protected plant that grows on the dunes, consists of a long slender reed with wispy threads coming off the seeds of the plant. It is at once beautiful and fragile looking.

I took it home with me and placed it in a tiny vase near my computer. A friend saw it one day and asked in horror why I had a sea oat on my desk.

"I didn't pick it. It was on a picnic table," I said.

"I'd keep it hidden. You were supposed to leave it there so it could reseed itself," my friend said.

I found it doubtful that such a wisp of a weed could offer much to the shore, so I read about the sea oat soon after and discovered that although it looks fragile in nature it actually performs an important but unseen duty on the dunes. It has a very long and deep root system that keeps the sand in place and helps prevent erosion.

I still keep the sprig of sea oats next to me as I write. The plant reminds me of myself. It doesn't look like much with its tall thin stalk, but it provides an unseen service to the world around it.

People often refer to me as having a lanky build. My sandy brown hair has always defied conventions. During my high school years, Brylcreme kept it in place. During the '60s, I let it grow long, but now it is a respectable length, rather short, but manageable. Standing beside Gary, I look like the sea oat next to his Live Oak tree. His sturdy build, enhanced by the weights he had lifted since high school, and his dark hair, always manageable, provided a contrast that kept most people from ever guessing that we shared some of the same gene pool.

But I kept the family together. I ran interference with Gary and his family, and since I lived so close to my mother, Gary's parents, and our fathers' sister, Aunt Susan, I became the family's anchor. I didn't mind. In fact, for once in my life, I felt that I was doing something important. Since my own father had died before my mother moved to Florida, I didn't have someone constantly criticizing my every move.

So, like the sea oat, my outward appearance drew little attention, but I had deeply buried roots that helped keep our family in place.

When Gary called suggesting that I come to New Orleans for this visit, I didn't hesitate. We had gone too long without seeing one another. Even though Gary and I were cousins, we had a relationship closer than brothers. Born only months apart, we both faced the burden of being only sons of two very different, yet complicated fathers.

As the fog deepened, I began to feel uncomfortable with my decision to make the twelve-hour drive from Gainesville. It didn't help that I had decided to take the less-traveled roads into Louisiana instead of I-10. Usually the view relaxed me and prepared me for the carnival atmosphere that is New Orleans no matter what time of year. However, the heavy mists on this evening left me feeling uneasy about the holiday that lay ahead. At times, the road disappeared, filling me with the sense that I might also disappear into the fog.

I settled into a confused state, unsure of why I now dreaded this visit. Gary always gave me a connection with my past and with myself.

However, I wanted to see Gary and touch base once again with my best friend. We talked on the phone, but the distance in miles kept us from visiting each other as often as we would have liked.

Where I remained reluctant to become involved with anyone after my second divorce, Gary forged ahead with new relationships after his move to New Orleans.

Gary knew he disappointed his father, but only in recent years had he stopped trying to please my Uncle Philip. Although I suspected that if Philip would ever offer Gary that much-needed acceptance, Gary would jump off cliffs, swim oceans, and fight wild boars to bask in the glow of his father's love.

Philip Townsend played football at the University of Michigan in Ann Arbor during the late 1920s, gaining a celebrity status as the team's star quarterback. He continued his hero status in the southeastern Michigan area by coaching football teams to two state championships while a coach at Pioneer High School, also in Ann Arbor. As a young boy, Gary didn't show much inclination toward athletics, and his father criticized him regularly for it.

"What's wrong with you, Gary," became an often-heard comment at the Philip Townsend house.

To make things tougher on Gary, I did perform well on the playing field. My lanky form might not have attracted girls, but it served me well in basketball and football.

When Gary didn't make the junior varsity basketball team his first year in high school, Uncle Philip quit talking to Gary for weeks. He wouldn't even look at his son. Although Gary agonized over it, Uncle Philip's probably saved Gary from further anguish.

The Junior Varsity coach, who didn't choose Philip Townsend's son for his team, left his position the following year. Philip's previous reputation still allowed him a certain amount of power within the school community even though he left coaching and teaching several years earlier to take a lucrative sales position with a large pharmaceutical company out of Detroit. He made a small fortune selling vitamins.

The JV basketball coach, new to the area, probably hadn't realized the mistake he made by not putting Gary somewhere on the team, no matter how badly he played. Gary himself only tried out because his father made him.

When Gary called me the afternoon that the final cut for the team was posted, he seemed relieved, but he dreaded telling his father. Gary's mother, my Aunt Claire, suggested he invite me for dinner to help soften Philip's attacks, which we were all certain would occur. Even his wife was powerless under his abuse.

We had just finished eating when Claire gave Gary a meaningful look. She waited to clear away the dishes while Gary cleared his throat. The three of us held our breath.

"Dad, I didn't make the basketball team," Gary said as his father took the last bites of his apple pie.

"What do you mean you didn't *make the basketball team?*" Philip shouted. In his world, a son of his would never "not make the team."

"I don't know. Coach didn't put my name on the list." Gary hung his head while he waited for his father's explosion.

"Gary, what's the matter with you? Everyone in this family has played sports. Get out there and apply yourself. Look at Ed, for chrissakes. Now there's a true Townsend," Philip said.

"Philip, stop. . .," began Claire.

"Sorry, Dad. But I'm going to run for class president."

"Class president? What kind of pansy runs for class president?" Philip asked.

"Philip!" Claire repeated. "Leave the boy alone. He'll be the most greatest fantasticest president ever. Right, Ed?" Claire always made up silly-sounding superlatives whenever she most wanted to cover up her true feelings. Mostly she did it when Philip acted stupidly. No matter her reasons for making the words up, it always made me feel close to her when she did it.

"You bet, Aunt Claire. Gary's the most popular guy in his class. You should see the girls chase him around when we go to the movies."

Gary and his father both stopped arguing. Philip brought the sports section up in front of his face, and Gary walked slowly down the hall to his bedroom. I looked at Aunt Claire and shrugged. She motioned with her hands for me to follow Gary.

"I guess I'll call Dad to come and get me, OK?" I said when I entered the bedroom.

Gary was sprawled across his bed. "I'm not a pansy," he said.

"Gary, you know how your dad is. Even if you had made the team, things wouldn't have worked out. Remember how he was when we played ball when we were kids? You don't want to go through that again. He doesn't know anything about being a class president, so you'll be safe."

"Hey, that's right, buddy! To hell with him! Let's walk downtown and get some ice cream. Then call home." Gary always rebounded quickly from one of his father's rebuffs, and in his typical pattern, he would usually do something stupendous in an attempt to win back his respect.

He won his election by a landslide, not because he had any outstanding qualities for class president, but because he was popular with both females and males. He served in this role for the next three years while doing very little work for his class. He had plenty of girls around to organize everything, while he received all the glory.

Gary lived right in the heart of the French Quarter. Many of the establishments along Royal Street rented apartments when not using the upper floors as art galleries. I found his place easily, but uneasily parked my car on St. Louis Street a block away. Gary assured me that New Orleans was safe, but I doubted his wisdom especially on this eerie night. The feeling of foreboding remained with me as I locked the car and walked toward his apartment.

"Cuz! You made it! Finally!" Gary said as he held me at arm's length to give me a long look.

"Hey, who ordered that fog? How can you live in a place where you can't see the road in front of you?"

Gary was as handsome as ever. My ex-wife Kelsey said he reminded her of Rock Hudson, but to me, he was just Gary.

"This is my friend Rick," Gary said as a young man in his twenties approached from the hallway.

"Hello, Ed. Heard a lot about you." He grabbed my hand before I could think of a response. I'd never heard of Rick before this moment. The last time I talked to Gary he had been living with someone else.

We walked into the living room just as the phone rang. Gary answered it.

Rick and I tried to start a conversation, but both realized that our whole reason for being together in this apartment revolved around the person on the phone. We tried to talk about the view of Royal Street from the balcony, but both of us failed as we kept our ears finely tuned to the voice emanating from the other side of the room.

"Yes, this is Gary Townsend. Who's this?" Gary asked.

"Kristina? Kris? My daughter?" Rick and I looked at one another in astonishment as we heard Gary's questioning voice. It had been fifteen years since Gary had any contact with his daughter from his first marriage.

"Of course, I want to see you. I've thought about you every day for the last fifteen years. Yes, yes, really. I want to see you." he repeated. There was silence for a moment. "Sure, don't worry, I'll make the arrangements tonight. Give me your phone number. Right. OK, got it. And Kristina? Thanks for calling." He hung up the phone.

Gary turned toward us. "That was Kristina."

"What did she want?" I asked. The feeling of dread I that left when I entered the apartment, suddenly returned.

"She wants to fly here this weekend, if I can arrange it." Gary said.

"That's wonderful, Gar," Rick said as he embraced him.

Gary shrugged off Rick's embrace. I could tell he was embarrassed by the open affection in front of me. Rick must have sensed it too because soon afterwards he made his excuses and left for his own apartment for the night.

"How did she find you?" I asked after Rick left.

"We didn't really discuss it. Maybe Pam?"

"Pam? Have you kept in touch with her?"

"No, but it wouldn't have been hard to trace me. Who cares about all that? She sounds great and wants to see me. That's all that matters."

"Are you going to call Claire and Philip?" I asked. Claire's heart had been broken when Pam took away her only grandchild so abruptly years earlier.

"No, I think I'll wait until after we meet. Be sure everything's OK, you know. Besides if it's not, Dad will find some way to blame me." Gary plopped his body down on the couch.

"What's wrong, Gary?" I asked.

"Nothing, really. Just a little overwhelmed. It's been a long time. Who knows what Pam has told her?"

He looked down at his hands as his forefinger began digging into his thumb. "Geez, I haven't done this in a while," he said in amazement as his fingers remembered the old ritual. So far, he hadn't drawn blood.

"Maybe she hasn't told Kristina anything. Gary, I probably should tell you something," I said.

"What?"

"I never told you this, but I promised Pam and I..." I paused as I searched for the words to explain.

"Come on, Ed, just say it."

"Pam used to call me after the divorce. But she would never tell me where they were. When I left Ann Arbor, she didn't know how to reach me anymore, so I haven't heard anything for ten years or so." I looked at Gary to get his reaction.

"I wish you'd told me before now," he said.

"I wanted to, believe me, but I promised Pam."

"Yeah, you take your promises pretty seriously, don't you? That's something we don't have in common. What do you think about Rick?" he asked.

"Rick?" I hadn't expected that question. "He seems like an all right guy, I guess. We only talked for a few minutes. What happened to John?" John had been Gary's partner for the past several years, and I had been waiting to ask Gary where he was.

"I guess even when I'm living like you always said I should, I still can't keep my promises. John got fed up just like everyone else and left." Gary stared at the floor. "I can't seem to be faithful for very long."

"Even Rick?"

"It's too soon to tell, Cuz." Gary dug deeper into his thumb pulling back skin at the edge of the nail. "Sorry, Ed; but I need to go to bed. Make yourself at home. The guest room is quite comfortable." Gary patted me on the shoulder sadly, and then turned to walk down the hallway to his room at the end.

I sat for a long time with the lights low. I thought about Kristina's call and what Gary said about his inability to remain faithful. My mind began to drift back through the years. I wondered if Pam told Kristina why they left Gary. My uneasiness with Kristina's arrival was reinforced by something I remembered Pam telling me when she left Gary back then.

I asked Pam if she was certain that she wanted sole custody of Kristina since she had never been very maternal with her young daughter.

"You bet, Eddie. She'll be my trump card if I need one in the future," she said.

Gary tried to book a flight from Las Vegas to New Orleans the next day, but since it was Thanksgiving, it was impossible. The best he could do was book a red eye flight leaving Las Vegas at midnight, arriving in New Orleans around 8:30 Friday morning.

Gary cooked a gourmet Thanksgiving meal unlike anything we'd ever had growing up in Michigan. Instead of turkey, we had roast duck, and instead of pumpkin pie, we had a pumpkin soufflé. The Townsend women would have been clucking and buzzing over this meal, for sure.

He and Rick invited several friends over for dinner. During the meal, a festive atmosphere reigned. Gary participated and told jokes, and to everyone but me, it looked as if he was having a carefree time. But I noticed the distant look in his eyes while the others talked. And he continued to pick at his thumb until it was raw.

Late in the afternoon while Rick and the others cleaned up Gary's fanciful mess, I asked Gary if we could go out and walk around Bourbon Street. Whenever we spent time together with both our families when we were younger, a walk around the block became our ritual. Usually at the Townsend gatherings, we left to escape our fathers. Today, we just wanted time alone.

"So how do you think Kristina found you?" I asked as we stepped out into the late afternoon shadows and headed down Royal.

"Pam must have told her something. I didn't really think to ask when she first called, and when I called her back about the flight, I forgot. I'll be honest with you, I'm a little uneasy about her visit, even though I'm anxious to see her."

"Is Rick going to the airport with you?"

"I don't think so, Ed. I thought it'd be better if you came. If you're there, we might get through those first awkward moments a little more easily. You're family, and you were friends with Pam. Something no one else in the family managed. Do you mind?" Again, he turned to me.

"No, I suppose it would be better to have a third party. I'm honored. By the way, did she mention a stepfather?"

"No, we really didn't talk about her life. Why?"

"In one of Pam's last calls, she mentioned that she was getting married again to an Oscar Timmons."

"Maybe Oscar could make her happy."

"Or maybe no one could," I said.

We turned onto Bourbon Street still keeping up our usual pace.

"I'd take you to my favorite bar, but it's not open on the holidays. All those gay boys go home and play normal on Thanksgiving, you know," Gary said without bitterness, and then he winked at me. "Instead I'm taking you to the classiest joint on Bourbon Street."

"And the girls will still come and dance just for you." I poked his ribs. He threw back his head and laughed heartily.

"That's right, Cuz. Wacky world, ain't it?"

We spent the next hour in a strip club drinking beer and reconnecting. It never took Gary and me very long to go back to that relationship we had always shared. The strippers did pay more attention to Gary than to me. We finally decided that we had given the others enough time to get the place cleaned up, so we downed the last of our drafts. With a wink in my direction, Gary slipped a bill into the G-string of the stripper performing just for him before we walked out the door and into the nightlife of Bourbon Street.

As I did every night before falling asleep, I wrote in my journal, not about my life, but about ideas for my next novel. This night in

New Orleans where the uneasiness remained on my shoulders, I pondered several ideas before settling on one that I had tossed around on a previous visit to New Orleans.

When he stepped down from the stage, groping hands reached to possess him. He smiled warmly, looking in the audience for that one person whose opinion mattered. Finally, he spotted him walking away toward the exit, sadly shaking his head.

CHAPTER TWO

THE NEXT MORNING, I could hear Gary moving around the apartment before dawn. Once I smelled the rich chicory coffee brewing, I knew sleep would be impossible for me, too. We left for the airport earlier than needed but waiting there for an hour seemed easier than pacing in the apartment.

Gary told me that he'd given Kristina a detailed physical description of both of us so it would be easy for her to find us when she came off the plane. Gary need not have wasted his breath. The minute we saw Kristina, we both knew her. She looked exactly like a female version of Gary with her dark hair and chiseled jaw line and high cheekbones. She had Pam's blue eyes and the beginnings of her voluptuous body, but that was the only resemblance between mother and daughter. However, no one would doubt the familial relationship of the father and daughter as they walked toward one another.

At first, they shook hands, but then Gary saw how ridiculous that gesture seemed. He reached out with both arms to embrace his daughter. Kristina returned the hug. Then Gary held her at arm's length looking into her eyes.

"I can't believe it, Kristina. No matter how many times I tried to imagine you, I just couldn't," Gary said.

"Please call me Kris."

"OK, Kris, this is my cousin, Ed Townsend."

"Kris, it's good to see you again, although the last time I saw you, I was a little taller." I tried to keep my tone light, although seeing a female version of Gary left me shaken.

"Nice to meet you, Ed." Kris reached out to shake my hand. "You know I think I have a vague memory of talking to you on the phone once. Is that possible?" She reached up and touched the side of my face as she had done sixteen years ago when she was just two. I shuddered.

"Good memory. Yes, we did talk once when you were about seven. I tried to explain who I was, but I don't think you understood." It surprised me she remembered and seemed so little changed when she made that one gesture with her hand.

The next few minutes were taken up with the incidentals of traveling. Kris certainly wasn't traveling light. We picked up four suitcases off the carousel before heading out to the car.

"Have you ever been to New Orleans?" Gary asked Kris as we settled into his Prelude.

"No, I've never been this far east before," Kris answered.

"You have; you just don't remember. There's time for all that later though." Gary seemed unsure of what to say next, and Kris didn't offer anything more.

For the rest of the trip, I talked about my drive from Gainesville, my writing, my mother, Claire, Philip, Aunt Susan, anything to permeate the silence. Both Kris and Gary responded or asked questions, probably relieved that I was filling up the dead air.

Once back in the apartment, Gary and I helped Kris settle into the guest room. Since I planned to leave on Sunday, I moved my things out of the spare bedroom to make room for Kris' baggage. I left my luggage in Gary's room to give Kris as much privacy as she needed.

We gathered back in the living room. Gary filled us in on some of the happenings in town during the weekend, trying to get a feel for what Kris might want to do. She wasn't interested in art, but the mention of some of the old cemeteries in town seemed to get her attention.

"I'd really like to walk down the famous Bourbon Street tonight," she said. We looked at her with surprise.

"Bourbon Street really isn't for young ladies with two old men," I finally said.

"Come on, Cousin Ed, you're not old." The way she said "Cousin Ed" made it sound like she was flirting with me.

"Why don't we just go out tonight for dinner and then see what happens," Gary said. "And I guess it wouldn't hurt anyone if you saw your first strip club while visiting New Orleans."

"I hate to break the news to you, but it won't be my first strip club. I grew up in Las Vegas, remember," Kris said.

"What was it like? Growing up in Vegas?" I asked.

"It's all I know; I guess it's not a typical environment from what I've seen on TV and in the movies."

Kris then told us something about her childhood. When she mentioned her mother, her face turned into a hard mask, and the eyes glistened. Her jaw became like the rocky edge of a cliff and gave away her bitterness. A nerve twitched at the back of her jaw, near the ear.

She talked mainly to me, occasionally touching my arm and looking at me with wide eyes during some of the more poignant moments. She touched my heart as she used to when she was only two. Back then, I would pick her up in my arms, and she would gently touch my face. I felt the same way I had then; I wanted to protect her. When Pam took her away, I lost my opportunity. Now I had a second chance. Through much of her story, I forgot about Gary.

When she wasn't looking at the floor, her eyes met mine. Gary sat beside her on the couch also looking at the same spot on the floor, shaking his head from time to time. He looked as guilty as the little boy caught with his hand in his mommy's penny jar. He wouldn't leave his thumb alone. I wondered briefly if he would get an infection in the now open wound.

Pam never made it to California as she planned. Kris said she didn't remember anything about Michigan. She only remembered living in Las Vegas. At first, Pam worked as a stripper, but her heavy drinking and smoking finally took its toll on her body and face. She began dealing blackjack then. Kris often came to the clubs with her.

She could remember the other strippers babysitting for her while her mom did her show or dealt cards. Then when Kris was around seven, Pam began dating Oscar Timmons, owner of the club where she worked. The year Kristina turned eight, Pam and Oscar were married. Timmons adopted her soon after, giving Kris his last name.

"What name had you gone by until then?" I asked.

"My mom's maiden name," she said. "Oscar never liked me when I was a kid so I'm not sure how Mom convinced him to adopt me. Probably a fifth of vodka had something to do with it." Kris clenched her jaw and looked at the floor before continuing.

Oscar liked to slap Pam and Kris around some, we learned as she continued. Nothing that Kris did was ever right according to her stepfather, and Pam mostly sided with Oscar. After a year of marriage, Pam became pregnant and when their son was born, Kris ceased to exist for both Oscar and Pam. Oscar didn't even bother to slap her anymore.

Kris became a child of the streets by the age of twelve. Around that time when she did come home, Oscar often came into her bedroom at night, she told us. He mostly liked to watch her. Sometimes he would try to kiss her, but Kris said she managed to hold him off with insults to his manhood, and he'd leave angry. However, the older Kris got, the more he pushed.

Her eyes filled with tears at the memory of those times. She refused to tell us anything more about Oscar. Instead, she told us about the streets of Las Vegas for a young, good-looking girl.

"Didn't your mother have a curfew for you?" Gary asked as the tales of Kris' exploits became more and more unbelievable.

"Are you kidding? She was just glad I wasn't around to cause problems with Oscar and Oscar Junior. She was jealous of Oscar and me. She knew he visited my room sometimes. But most nights when I did come home, she'd be so smashed that she didn't even know who I was. One night she even tried to get into bed with me, calling me 'Gary.' That's when I got curious about my real father. That and the night that Oscar . . ." She stopped, and we both looked at her. I didn't want to hear anymore. I doubt Gary did either. Neither of us asked for details.

I had no idea what to say to her. I only had a burning desire to kill this Oscar Timmons jerk, wherever he might be. Instead, I put my arm around her shoulders and held her close until she found the strength to continue.

She said Pam never told her anything about Gary. When Kris asked about her father, Pam would say, "He's dead. Now shut up about it." But Kris had a sneaking suspicion that her father was alive, especially after the incident in the bedroom. She knew she didn't look much like her mother except the eyes, so she began wondering whom she did look like.

She began by snooping through her mother's things. Finally, after weeks of going through the house when Oscar and Pam were either out or passed out, she found a cigar box tucked away in the top of her mother's closet. There were wedding pictures of a much younger version of Pam with a young man who looked very familiar. Then she found some newspaper articles about Miss America of 1974 and a wedding announcement from 1975 for Elizabeth Jackson, former Miss America, and Gary Townsend of Ann Arbor, Michigan. The article gave Gary's place of employment, parent's names, and just enough information for Kris to begin searching for the man she was beginning to believe was her father.

"I called a couple of places like General Motors. The article said you were an ad exec there. I told personnel I was an old college girlfriend. They bought it and told me you had moved to New Orleans, but they said they couldn't give out any other information. Luckily, your number is listed in the New Orleans directory. So, you were married to my mother and had a daughter named Kristina?" she asked needlessly, although she looked as if she did need this final confirmation.

"Yes. When we divorced, she forced me to sign some papers she had drawn up. One of the conditions for her to keep quiet about my personal life was having me give up my parental rights." Gary paused not sure how to justify or apologize for his actions, which seemed cowardly in light of the life that Kris had been forced to live for the past fifteen years.

"Why did you do that?" Kris asked as she turned to look directly at Gary for the first time since she had begun her story.

"I don't expect you to comprehend, Kris. I just ask that you try to understand. Times were different then, you had to know my parents . . ." Gary stopped and began his vigil with the floor again.

He seemed incapable of continuing, so I gave Kristina a bit of our early history. A memory from 1959 stood out in particular.

I remembered running down the field clutching the football under my arm. The shouts in the stands sounded like one loud roar. I crossed the line to make the touchdown that put Ypsilanti High School in the state championship game. I knew cheering loudest would be Gary who attended all of my games. He was my biggest fan.

Even though it meant that he had to suffer through the painful accusations from his father whenever I excelled on the athletic field, he still came to applaud for me.

My parents and I lived in Ypsilanti, just down the road from Ann Arbor, but miles apart socially and economically. Ypsilanti, whose motto was, "The town that works," housed several automobile factories on the eastern or Detroit side. Eastern Michigan University formed the boundary on the Ann Arbor side. In between lived the blue-collar class created in the years just before and following World War II.

On the other side of the tracks, Ann Arbor housed the white-collar professional class that had grown out of the large medical and scientific research facilities at the University of Michigan.

As a senior, I was finishing the football season with a bang, but I was happy my career as an athlete was ending. I preferred gentler pursuits such as reading and writing. However, I kept my preferences private from the rest of the family because they wouldn't understand. Gary already received his share of abuse and ridicule for not having the athletic abilities and inclinations of his father and now me. However, he made up for those deficiencies by becoming a leader at Pioneer High School and dating all of the prettiest girls in his class, although he refused to tie himself down to just one steady girlfriend. He also managed to look the part of the athlete by lifting weights obsessively, even when he and I just hung out in his room after family dinners. Philip always approved of that and kept buying him more and more equipment. It was the only thing the two of them had in common.

I looked up into the stands where I knew my father and Uncle Philip would be sitting side by side each analyzing and criticizing my every move while bragging to those around them about their star athlete. Uncle Philip would be trying to take all the glory by saying I had inherited his genes, and my father, quieter and grumpier, would make sure everyone knew I was actually his son. Aunt Susan, their sister, would be trying to referee as Aunt Claire and my mother ignored them.

When I came out of the locker room after the game, they all waited to take me out for a victory dinner. It looked like I wouldn't be going out with my girlfriend after all. I wouldn't put her through a dinner with the whole family just yet. We hadn't been dating long enough. Besides, I wasn't ready for her to meet Gary. Without even trying, Gary attracted every girl I ever dated and left me wondering if they only went out with me to get a little closer to the handsome and elusive Gary Townsend.

My father, Stanley, and his brother, Philip, stood side-by-side waiting for me to join them after I had received congratulations from all of the other families waiting for their sons. The contrast between the two brothers was as different as Ypsilanti and Ann Arbor, their respective homes.

Their personalities always clashed, but I had never really noticed the physical differences. They shared some similar features, like the receding hairline and the sandy blonde hair turning a dusty gray; just enough features in common for someone to know they were related. However, over the years, those similarities had taken different courses.

Both were tall men although Philip was slightly taller now, as my father seemed to be shrinking before my eyes. Philip wore a dark sports jacket with a pressed white shirt and bright red tie. His polished loafers provided a stark contrast to the dull working shoes that covered my father's feet. My father had worn his best flannel pea coat for the occasion, but it looked old and worn next to Uncle Philip's flashy attire.

I noticed the different expressions on their faces as I approached them. My uncle carried the smile of victory while my father looked at me through squinted eyes and curled lip. I imagined he would have rather been out with his cronies sucking down a few beers and bragging about his son than actually being there in person with me.

My father had never gone to college and began working in the automobile factories right after high school. Eventually after the Willow Run plant between Ypsilanti and Detroit began making automobiles instead of bombers after the war, Stanley managed to make it as foreman. However, my parents had never known the kind of success that had come so easily for Claire and Philip. My father didn't know how to manage his money, or he would have moved us from our small boring tract house years ago. Instead, he ended up squandering many paychecks at the racetrack and local bar.

"What a game, Ed!" My uncle slapped me on the back heartily. "You really showed those bastards who's boss."

"Philip!" Aunt Claire said. "Watch your language! People are listening."

"Really, Philip, keep your voice down," Aunt Susan said.

"Who cares? My nephew here just played the greatest game ever played in this town, and I'll say what I want. Right, Stan?"

My father just grunted and begrudgingly held out his hand to me. "You did all right, son. I still say you're crazy not to take that scholarship." My father could never pay me a full compliment.

"Dad, please." I didn't want to discuss my future right there in the lobby of the school.

"Stanley, leave the boy alone," my mother said while reaching up to give me a kiss on the cheek. "I'm very proud of you, Edward."

"Thanks, Mom." I smiled down into her hopeful face and winced when I noticed the moth hole on the collar of her best winter coat.

"You're the bestest and mostest, Ed." Aunt Claire overshadowed my mother's small frame as she came into view and grabbed me for a big bear hug. The collar of her fur coat brushed my nose causing me to sneeze.

"Bless you," she said.

"Whadda ya say, Cuz!" Gary came out of the crowd toward me with two girls on his arm. "Great game!"

"Thanks, Gar." We shook hands grinning at one another. Even though Gary would have to suffer through Philip's remarks about my game during the next few days, Gary was genuinely proud of me. We always banded together against the idiosyncrasies of our parents in order to survive.

"Bye, Gary. See ya later, I hope." Gary's girls went off giggling and whispering as we walked outside toward Uncle Philip's Cadillac parked in front of my father's plain black Ford.

After our celebratory dinner, the two families came back to our house for coffee and cake. Philip and Claire rarely visited us because of our small, cramped home, but tonight we went to a restaurant in Ypsilanti, so it only made sense that we come back to our house instead of driving into Ann Arbor to the large sprawling home of the other Townsend family.

Gary and I took a long walk around the neighborhood to get away from the badgering of our parents. Since both of us were only children, in our presence our fathers wouldn't leave us alone. When

Philip and Stanley began drinking whiskey, we both knew the assault on our shortcomings would be substantial.

"Have you ever gone all the way?" Gary asked me when we had been walking only a short while.

"With a girl?" I asked.

"Of course, with a girl, dummy, what else?" Gary punched my shoulder while smiling at me.

"Have you?" I wanted to avoid answering as long as possible.

"I asked you first, but yeah, last weekend."

"Who?" I asked.

"Just some girl from school. Cindy's her name. Been all over me all year long, so I thought, what the heck. What about you?"

"Not all the way," I said.

"But close?"

"Well, I guess. I know I've wanted to go further, but it never happened. So how was it?"

"That's the thing." Gary paused and looked at me sideways. "It wasn't any big deal," he said.

"What do you mean?"

"I mean I can't figure out what the big deal is. I never really cared if it happened or not. I was just curious, and it seemed to mean so much to Cindy, but then nothing."

"You mean you couldn't do it?"

"No, I could do it, I just didn't feel much of anything."

"Well, maybe it's just Cindy. You're not in love with her or anything like that, are you?"

"No, of course not. She's more persistent than most of the girls I know. Ed, it's like I . . .," Gary let out a long sigh and then began sprinting the rest of the way back to my house.

I followed him wondering what he had been about to say. When I arrived home, I didn't dwell on it for very long because Philip and Stanley, both drunk, had begun arguing about their parents. Aunt Susan decided to drive back to her home in Grosse Pointe before we got back from our walk, disgusted no doubt with the behavior of her brothers.

"You're the bastard that put our mother away," my father yelled at Philip.

"Someone had to; she was nuts," Philip yelled back.

Stanley tried to grab Philip's collar, but the whiskey was stronger, and he couldn't lean forward enough to take hold.

"Let's go, Philip; you can't settle this tonight." Claire urged her husband toward the door. "Gary, give me a hand, your father's been celebrating a little too much tonight. Thanks, Marge, for having us over. I'll call you," Claire yelled over her shoulder as she led her husband out the door.

"Leave me alone. Let that pansy of a son do something for a change," Philip yelled as they stumbled to the car.

"Gary, drive us home," Claire said as Gary took the keys from her hand.

He quietly slid behind the steering wheel of his father's large vehicle. "My pride and joy," Philip often called it. I looked out the back door and waved to Gary who looked straight ahead, not noticing me. He waited for his mother to secure his father in the back seat before putting the car in reverse and backing out of our driveway.

I tried my best to give Kristina a sense of what it had been like growing up with a father like Philip Townsend during the 1950s without revealing everything. Gary remained silent.

"Kris, try not to blame your father. He did what he thought was right at the time," I said.

"What are you talking about? How can I not be pissed off knowing my father signed away his rights to an alcoholic mother who hated me?" Kris jumped up from the couch and walked deliberately to the balcony doors with clenched fists.

Gary woke up from his trance and followed Kris, and I watched as the father and daughter, so alike physically, yet worlds apart emotionally, went out onto the balcony. I saw Gary speak quietly to Kris. She jerked her head back to look at her father. Then she shook her head with a sardonic grin looking for a split second just like her mother.

Gary continued to talk while Kris listened. I didn't want to intrude on this scene, even though I couldn't hear what they were saying. I let myself out of the apartment quietly and took a long walk around the block getting lost in a few art galleries and antique stores along Royal Street.

When I finally returned, Gary let me into the apartment. He told me Kris decided to take a nap and recover from her flight. I thought she had a lot more from which to recover, but I kept that thought to myself.

"I think we made a truce. Fortunately, she knows her mother and knows how unreasonable she can be at times so that made it easier for her to understand some things. I think she might be able to forgive me," Gary said with the first grin of the day.

"I'm glad about that, Gary. I'm still worried about Kris though."

"Why?"

"She's your daughter but remember Pam and this Oscar guy raised her. Things might not always go smoothly now that she's back in your life," I said.

Actually, I didn't tell Gary nearly half of what I was feeling. I didn't tell him about the nagging dread I felt ever since I arrived. The feeling had only intensified with Kristina's appearance. I kept my mouth shut because admitting it even sounded nutty to me.

"She's going to stay here through Christmas, and then we're both going to Florida for the holidays." Gary, in his usual manner, decided to ignore my words of warning.

"Can you imagine the celebration Claire and the rest will plan? We better warn Kristina about the Townsend women," I said as I put my arm around his shoulder and gave him a squeeze.

"It's going to be all right now, Cuz, I know it. I'm going to get the chance to make it up to her, you know?" He looked at me as if asking a question, but soon Gary's old confidence appeared.

"You'd better get ready for a night on the town with an eighteen year old girl. Are you sure you're up to it, old man?" Gary asked.

"I can manage just fine," I told him as I sank down into the couch brushing aside my fears about Kristina for the moment. "It's you who might be out of practice."

Gary wasn't the only one hoping for a second chance. It's just that I wasn't sure what it was I needed to take care of during this second go around with Kristina.

I had a new topic for my journal that night before I fell asleep. A character based on Kristina's life seemed too tempting to ignore.

She grew into a young woman never knowing what it meant to be loved. Many looked at her, many held her, many touched her, but no one ever broke through her hardened shell into her heart. It would take someone with patience and strength to give her what she had never known.

CHAPTER THREE

DURING THE NIGHT, I heard something near my head as I lay on the couch in the living room. At first, I thought I had been dreaming so I lay there listening with my eyes closed, and then I heard it again. I reached for the lamp next to me. As light flooded the room, my eyes made an uneasy adjustment while focusing on Kristina standing in front of me with my pants in her hands and her hands in my pants. She quickly dropped them to the floor.

"What are you doing?" I asked.

"I thought these were mine. Sorry."

"You thought your pants were in the middle of the living room floor next to where I'm sleeping?" I needed a moment to clear my head before dealing with this confusing story.

"I said I was sorry. Go back to sleep." She started back down the hallway.

"Wait a second, Kristina. What were you looking for?"

"Nothing. I told you. I thought they were mine." She turned to leave once again.

"And I don't believe you," I said in a voice I hadn't used since I left teaching.

"What're going to do? Arrest me?" She held her wrists out toward me.

"I just want to know why you tried to rip me off."

"Look, forget it; I said I was sorry, didn't I? I'm short on cash, that's all, OK?"

I looked at her bowed head and half believed she felt contrition for her attempted theft.

"You know if you need the money either your father or I would gladly give you some."

"I'm sorry, Ed, really." She looked at me once again with that trapped sense of fear – the deer caught in the headlights look – not guilty, just scared and frozen.

"Listen, I've forgotten it already. OK, Kristina?" Somehow, even though she had been trying to steal from me, I felt the need for her approval and acceptance as I became mesmerized by her deep blue eyes. "Here, take this," I said as I handed her a fifty-dollar bill.

"Thanks, Ed. You're all right." She came closer to accept the money.

She looked so pitiful that I couldn't help but hold out my arms to offer comfort and assurance. She pressed herself against me until I could feel her breasts molding themselves into my chest. I forgot everything except for the sensation of a beautiful woman persistently pushing against me.

"Ed, hold me, please. I get so scared sometimes," she softly mumbled into my neck. It felt as if she was trying to climb inside of me.

I held her, caressing her back and rubbing her neck all the while becoming aware that her closeness to me had begun to create confusing sensations within me. She turned her face up to mine and began kissing me. When I felt her tongue slide inside my mouth, I came to my senses.

"Kristina, stop. We can't do this, stop." I pushed her away from me. I looked at her in dismay as she brought her hand to her mouth and rubbed her lips.

"You can't say you didn't like it, though, can you? I guess you don't have the same problems as Gary, huh? And, Ed? It's Kris, not Kristina." She had become the tough street kid once again, more like her mother than ever.

"You will always be Kristina to me. I can't call you Kris. Sorry," I said.

Her eyes filled with tears, and she turned away from me. She sat down on my makeshift bed and wiped her eyes.

"Kristina, can you answer a question for me?" She looked up at me. "Just tell me one thing. Why did you come here?"

"To meet my dad."

"Yes, I know that's what you told Gary. But it's just you and me now. Why did you come?" I asked.

"I came because I got kicked out of the house and there was a warrant for my arrest for breaking and entering, and I didn't have a dime to my name. But if you tell Gary, I'll deny it and say you're crazy. He's so happy that I've come here, I could sell him the Brooklyn Bridge, don't you think, Cousin Ed?"

Her tone changed from a frightened seductress into a tough con artist right before my eyes. She still looked like Gary, but her physical demeanor had changed along with the tone of her voice. She tossed her long black mane behind her and held her head at a defiant angle. I tried to ignore the ample breasts she thrust out for my attention.

"Listen, Kristina, drop the act with me. I'm not going to hurt you, but I'm also not going to let anyone hurt Gary."

"Are you going to tell Gary what happened tonight?"

"What happened tonight?" I asked as I sat down next to her. I playfully tugged at her hair, and she slapped at my hand.

"That's the way you want to play it, huh?" She reached over and touched my face and looked at me trustingly.

I leaned down and kissed her longingly and thoroughly. Shaken by the sudden emotion overpowering me, I lost sight of everything but this lovely, vulnerable woman sitting next to me so obviously in need of love. She returned the kiss with equal passion. When our lips finally parted, we sat and held each other, spent from the outburst that moved me to forget our age difference, our relationship, and our reason for being in this apartment.

"Ed, have you ever been married?" Kristina finally asked me.

I pulled away slightly and looked at her. "Yes, twice."

"You're not married now?"

"No, I've been divorced from my second wife for almost ten years."

"How could someone as good as you not stay married?"

I searched her face for a hint of sarcasm in her last words, but I found only a sincere woman asking a question that puzzled her.

"Let's just say I'm not as perfect as you might think."

"Gambler, womanizer, drunk? I don't think so."

"No, it's much more complicated than that. Funny thing, I've never thought about it much. Sometimes I think I just didn't care enough," I said more to myself than Kristina.

I pulled her close to me once again, and I thought about my first experiences with the opposite sex.

Ypsilanti High School did win the state football championship in 1959, and I received many offers to play football at the biggest schools in Michigan, but I refused all of them.

"Are you crazy?" my father would shout night after night.

"Don't you want to be a success like your Uncle Philip?" my mother would ask. This question would send my father into spasms of coughing and yelling and spitting while fire engine red color rose from his collar to his forehead. It was the most emotion I had ever seen my father display.

"Like his *Uncle Philip*! What the hell is that? He's going to be better than my brother. He's nothing compared to my boy." That was the closest I ever came to receiving praise from my father.

Most of these discussions about my future ended then because my mother would spend the next hour assuring my father that she had meant no harm when she inferred that Philip had reached a level of success beyond his brother, Stanley.

But compared with my parents, Philip and Claire had achieved tremendous prosperity, and I wanted to be nothing like either of them. With their bridge games and country club memberships, Philip and Claire's lives reeked of superficiality. In a way, their lives were even sadder than my parents' lives. At least Claire had some character and personality.

Gary and I talked during our senior year of many things, but we never talked about the opposite sex again. Gary continued to date many different girls even though Cindy still pursued him relentlessly. She gave up her virginity to him, and she needed something in return for her sacrifice.

Even when I managed to go all the way with my steady girlfriend, Sally, I didn't confide in Gary. My experience had been something very different from the description of his first time, and somehow, I knew telling him about my own moment of ecstasy would make matters worse for him.

After my first experience, I wanted to shout from the mountaintops, if there had been any in Michigan, that I had the most wonderful girl in the world. I had already given her my ring that she wore with strings of Angora holding it in place. We had talked about marriage; otherwise, Sally wouldn't even have considered allowing me to become so intimate with her. I certainly felt something for her, and I wanted to feel it again as soon as possible.

When Gary and I did get together during our busy senior year, we mostly talked about the future. I decided I wanted to go to Eastern Michigan University in Ypsilanti. It had one of the state's best teacher preparation programs. I knew I really wanted to be a writer, but I was realistic enough to know I would need to do something else to support myself. By default, I pursued an English degree in secondary education. I had already applied for a few scholarships and planned on working. Unlike Gary, I had to figure out a way to pay for my education. And if I stayed in Ypsilanti, I could still live at home and at least spare myself the expense of a dorm.

On the other hand, Gary wanted to leave the area as soon as possible. His father's attacks became more and more vicious after my triumph in football. Gary really did need to get away from him. Claire's intervention between father and son sometimes made things worse so she began to encourage Gary's desire to leave home for college.

He decided to pursue criminal justice, and with luck, he hoped to attend law school. His father had no use for a career in law, probably for the simple reason that Gary wanted to pursue it. When his acceptance to Michigan State came, Gary decided East Lansing was far enough away, yet close enough to come home when he wanted to see his mother and me.

My feelings for Sally began to change within a few months of our first sexual encounter. I found myself only wanting to be with her if I knew we could be intimate. She thought we would marry as soon as we graduated from college. It became apparent to me that I had to break it off with Sally before she left for college, but I dreaded the encounter. She was what we called a "good girl" in those days, and she only gave into my pressure because I made vague promises to her during the heat of my passion.

She bored me intellectually so conversations were limited. She didn't want to talk about ideas, except if they had to do with setting up house in four years. She talked endlessly about the style of houses, color of paint, thickness of carpets, and type of appliances. At eighteen, none of these things remotely interested me. In fact, whenever she started her litany of things she wanted when we married, I felt as if a noose dropped around my neck, and with each mention of her list, the rope tightened.

Sally was going to Northern Michigan University in Marquette, 400 miles away in the Upper Peninsula or U.P., as any true Michigander would say. In my teenage mind, having a girlfriend so far away was intolerable. If she went to a school nearby, we would at least have our sexual relationship to enjoy, but the combination of her uninteresting personality and no sex held no appeal for me. And I was beginning to feel like a cad for only wanting her for sex. Even through the fog of my intense hormones, I knew I wasn't being fair to her. And I didn't even think about the possibility of seeing other girls while she still wore my ring.

I didn't need to worry for very long. One night, just before leaving for Marquette, Sally made a remark about how far away she would be. Much to my surprise, she gave me a reprieve.

"You know, Eddie, I'm going to be awfully lonely up in the U.P.," she began.

"It's a long way, that's for sure," I said.

"You probably won't be able to visit, and I won't be able to come home except at Christmas."

"That's true."

"I've been thinking, Eddie, honey. You know that I want to join a sorority, and there will be lots of dances and socials, and I'd hate to go to those things by myself." Her voice began rising to that high-pitched resonance I had begun to hate.

"I agree, Sal."

"What do you mean?"

"I agree that you shouldn't go to those things by yourself."

"So, are you saying, I should date other boys?" She turned to look at me.

"I would hate it, but I think it would only be fair to you. I'll manage, but it will be difficult."

"Oh, Eddie, I knew you'd understand! When I come home for Christmas, we can see how we feel about one another. You're really the only one I love, but I couldn't stand being home all alone on a Saturday night when everybody else is out having a good time."

"I wouldn't want you to sit home alone, Sally."

I listened to her go on and on about the new social life she would have and wondered how I ever thought I could marry this girl who was rambling on about what color she should wear to the first formal dance. At least, she wasn't decorating our house any more.

"How about one last fling before you go off?" I nuzzled her ear. I would do anything to get her to shut up.

"Oh, Eddie, I'd love to, but you know now that we're not going steady, we can't do that anymore. I'm going back to being a virgin," she said as she began unraveling the Angora wrapped tightly around my class ring.

"It doesn't work like that, Sal. And just one more time, who would know?"

"It will work like that for me, and I would know. I just can't, Eddie."

"OK, OK, I'll take you home." I put the car in gear and slowly backed out of our private parking space off Carpenter Road.

That summer I worked at Nick's, the student hangout across the street from EMU. The place had pool tables, pinball machines, and a jukebox. They served sandwiches and beer. I loved the atmosphere, and when it wasn't busy, I met people who had interesting life stories and some who didn't. But every night I would rush home and fill my notebooks with pages of stories about these characters that just happened into Nick's after their summer school classes.

One night in late August, Gary and a group of his friends from Pioneer High School decided to meet at Nick's for a farewell party before they all left for college. Gary and I hadn't seen much of one another since I had started working. Within a few weeks, he would be going off to East Lansing, and I knew he wouldn't be home much after that.

"Hey, Cuz, how goes it? You know just about everyone, right?" Gary asked when I came over to the table.

"Hey, everyone," I said. Luckily, it was a slow Wednesday night, so I sat at the table for a few minutes.

I did know everyone sitting there except for the girl at the end of the table. When I looked down at her, I felt like someone had just punched me in the gut. She smiled slowly.

"Do you know Allison?" Gary asked. "She just started at old Pioneer last semester, and graduated with us in June."

"No, I-I-I..." I said.

"Nice to meet you, Ed," she said so quietly I had to lean closer to hear. She casually brought a hand to her softly curled brown hair to brush it back away from her perfect face.

Later, after my boss let me off for the night, I pulled a chair up next to Allison and even managed to speak.

"Where will you be going to school?" I asked.

"Right across the street! How about you?"

"Me, too," I answered, happy that this wouldn't be the last time I would see her.

"Great! I know someone! My family moved here in January from Chicago. My dad's company transferred him. Can you believe it? In the middle of my senior year!"

"What's your major?"

"I'm interested in philosophy and world religions, but my dad won't tolerate a major in either of those areas. In fact, I'm only allowed to major in education, and then choose an acceptable field for teaching. And you?"

It took me a minute to answer. A girl who was interested in philosophy and talked like an angel and looked like a brunette version of Sandra Dee? Unbelievable.

"I want to be a writer, but figured I better get a teaching degree first so I can at least support myself when I get out of college."

"A writer! How romantic! What do you write?" She seemed really interested. No one had ever asked me that question before.

"I write about things I hear and see. When I leave here tonight, I'll write about all the people I met, and the conversations I heard."

"Will you write about me?" She lowered her voice and inclined her head closer to mine.

"All night long," I replied very softly as *Teen Angel* began playing on the jukebox.

"And so Allison was your first wife?" Kristina asked when I finished talking about my life in Ypsilanti.

"Yes, when we finished college, we got married. We didn't stay married for very long."

"What happened?"

"That's a long story with a strange ending. How about we save that for another time?" I ran my hand through her hair. It was so soft and luxurious I wondered how I would be able to keep my hands away from it when we had to face Gary in the morning.

She reached up and touched my hand. With her other hand, she reached for my face once again. "You know, Ed, you're all right. My mom told me that before I left. She said, 'If you're going to see your father at least try to hook up with Ed. He'll be a friend.' I don't believe my mother half the time, but this time I think she might have gotten it right."

I kissed her on the forehead before she stood up to go into her bedroom. "Good night, Kristina."

"Hey, Ed, will you write about me tonight?"

I smiled, and she turned and left me on the couch unable to do anything but think of her, remembering what it felt like to have her in my arms. I forgot all else and relinquished myself to the memory of her vulnerability and obvious need of me.

I stood and looked out from the balcony to no avail. The fog had rolled in once again, and I stared out into a white blanket of mist unable to see even the closest detail of the street below.

Her beauty crept up on him approaching without warning. She took it for granted when he told her that she was beautiful. She wanted him to make her feel whole; her looks served as the tool to achieve her goal.

CHAPTER FOUR

WHEN I FINALLY TURNED out the light to sleep after Kristina left me, the memories stirred by talking with her would not rest. I could remember Allison and our marriage, but I couldn't write about it. I could write about her, Allison, but not my part in her life. I let my thoughts wander back to the time when Gary and I both entered into our first marriages.

Not only did I write about Allison the night I met her, but I also wrote about her during the next four years of college while we dated and when we became engaged. When we both decided to go for our masters' degrees before getting married, her parents offered to buy us a house as a wedding and graduation present. That gave us two years during graduate school to decide where we wanted to live and teach.

I moved out of my parents' house during my senior year of college and rented an apartment across the street from campus and within view of the tall, phallic water tower that greeted all visitors to Ypsilanti. My small abode faced Cross Street and the admission's office for EMU. With its dark wood and one main room, my apartment provided comfortable living quarters for one person. Although cramped when Allison stayed over, the bathroom with its claw-foot tub and skylight made it livable.

Allison lived with three other girls two blocks away in a large rambling house soon to be replaced by one of the new modern apartment complexes. However, she still spent many days and nights at my place where the smallness of the apartment sheltered us from the outside world.

We would lie on the day bed and read poetry to one another while the snow fell outside and the radiators hissed inside. Sometimes winter storms stranded us for days in the small space. Luckily, the apartment was right above a small pharmacy that carried a limited amount of groceries for the convenience of its college student neighbors.

During these years, I saw little of Gary. We talked on the phone occasionally, and we saw each other on the major holidays. Other than that, he never came home because when he did his father harangued him about finding a girlfriend.

"Look at Ed! Already engaged to marry when he completes his masters," Uncle Philip said during Christmas break, the winter before my wedding.

"I'm so proud of you and Allison for getting your education first before settling down. Plenty of time for that," Aunt Claire said.

"But what's he going to do with a degree in *literature*, for God's sake," my father said.

"He's going to be a teacher, right, Ed?" my mother said. "And coach."

"I'm going to teach, Mom. I'm not so sure about coaching. I'm still writing, remember? And you and Aunt Claire will be the first to get autographed copies of my first novel."

My father snorted and picked up his beer before walking into the living room to watch football.

"At least you've got your future set," Claire said. "Allison's a fine girl, Ed. She'll be the most wonderfullest mother around."

"Wait a minute, Aunt Claire. Allison and I planned on waiting a few years before starting a family."

"All I can say is, at least you're man enough to get a girl and pin her down, hey, Ed." Uncle Philip came around the table and slapped me on the back before heading to the buffet for another shot of whiskey and then into the living room to watch the game with his brother.

I looked over at Gary who had been listening to these exchanges with a strange look in his eye. When his father made the last remark, Gary shoved his chair away from the table and put on his jacket.

"Where you headed, Gar?" I asked.

"Out. You can come or you can sit here and receive more praise from the great Philip Townsend about your manhood."

"Gary, please, not today," Claire said. Forever the peacemaker, Claire just wanted us all to get along.

"Let's go." I reached for my jacket, and we headed out into the cold, bleak day.

We began our ritual walk around the neighborhood with no particular destination in mind. Gary walked faster than normal, and I kept slipping on the ice in an attempt to keep up with him. He was determined to put space between us. Gary had never gotten angry with me before when his father used me as his prime example to humiliate him, so I couldn't figure out why today should be any different.

"Gary, come on, talk to me. What did I do to make you so angry?"

"Do you have to do everything so damn perfect?" he finally said.

"What? Me, perfect?"

"Yes, you. The perfect decisions, the perfect girl, and now you'll probably have the perfect marriage, perfect house, perfect children, perfect job, the perfect . . ."

"Wait a minute, Gary. That's not fair." I wouldn't let him go on taking it out on me. "You're the one who's perfect! Good looks, personality; I've had to fight for everything in my life. Everything has always come easy for you."

"Looks can be deceiving, Cuz. Nothing comes easy for me, especially girls."

"What do you mean?"

"Nothing. I can't seem to find the right girl, like you did. So, no girlfriend, and I'm not really interested in finding one except that Dad, Mr. Perfect Townsend, has to make such a big deal out of it. I wish he'd just leave me alone, for chrissakes."

"Gary, you're only twenty-two years old. You haven't met the right girl yet. I was lucky to find Allison, but that's all it is, luck. It hasn't got anything to do with what kind of man I am."

"Maybe." Gary paused and stopped walking for a moment. He looked at me. "Ed, remember when I told you about my first time?" He began walking again with his head down, and his chin nearly pressed into his chest. I had to struggle to hear him.

"Yes, so what?"

"So what, is that it's never changed for me. I never feel anything and believe me, I try. Sometimes I . . ." He was struggling I knew, but I was at a loss to help him.

"What is it, Gar?" I asked.

"Nothing, nothing. You're probably right, I haven't met the right girl yet." He patted me on the back and changed the subject.

Allison and I were married one month after receiving our degrees in the summer of 1966. As her parents had spared no expense, we were married in a flashing, sometimes blinding frenzy of activity. I walked around in a daze for almost a month wondering how I had gotten myself into this mess. Allison reveled in all the activities and social events, dragging me along by her side. I felt numb.

We had both taken teaching jobs at Pioneer High School in Ann Arbor and decided to let her parents buy us one of the older homes on the west side of town. We finally agreed on a place badly in need of fixing up, which we began in the months prior to our wedding.

Allison wanted a new home at first, until I convinced her that our two-story colonial would be a challenge and a showpiece once we refinished the wood floors and removed the paint from the hardwood banisters and woodwork. Most of the homes around us were much simpler in design so our home would stand out from the others once we made all of the improvements. I didn't realize at the time the appeal this facade held for Allison.

Gary served as my best man and performed his duties to perfection. All of the bridesmaids fell a little in love with him as he treated each one with a friendly respect. When I watched him so effortlessly flirting, I wondered why he couldn't find someone to make him happy.

He was living in Chicago working for an advertising firm since his graduation from MSU the year before. Sometime during his second year of college, he decided that advertising suited him much better than law. For once Uncle Philip agreed with his decision.

We had little time to talk with all of the festivities, but Gary did manage to throw me a great bachelor party. Two carloads of us drove to Detroit to a couple of strip clubs. At one of them, Gary and the guys paid for my own private show. Even the callused strippers seemed to gravitate toward Gary though. Throughout the night, I would watch as he juggled one and sometimes two girls on his knees and wondered once again when he would find happiness.

At the reception, Uncle Philip congratulated me loudly, making broad hints about the wedding night. Allison told me later that Philip was nothing more than a dirty old man.

"What do you mean?" I asked.

"He had his hands all over me while we were dancing. He kept pulling me closer; I had to fight him all the time."

"He was drunk. He always does stuff like that."

"No matter what you may believe, don't ever leave me alone in a room with him. If he does that in public while I'm in a wedding dress, then imagine what he'd do if we were alone."

"Ally, he's harmless." I laughed to think of Uncle Philip and my new bride together.

"OK, laugh, I'm just warning you."

Gary came home for Christmas of 1966 with a new girlfriend named Pamela. We managed to see each other daily during the weeklong visit. Allison and I tried our best to become acquainted with Pamela, the first girl Gary ever brought home to meet the family, but she was distant and thoroughly devoted to Gary, except when flirting with Philip.

Pamela looked like a movie star with her bleached blonde hair poofed out around her face. Her pouty lips and high cheekbones didn't attract attention because of the generous figure that strained the sweaters and tight skirts that seemed to be her uniform during the visit. It was difficult for me to keep my eyes off her. She and Gary made a striking couple, which Allison pointed out to me almost immediately.

"They look perfect together, don't you think, Ed?" She asked as we drove home on the first night of their visit.

"She's a looker all right," I said.

"Gary better watch his father around her. Honestly, why your Aunt Claire puts up with him, I don't know. And your father wasn't much better tonight."

"They were just trying to make Pamela feel comfortable."

Allison snorted as we pulled into our driveway, ending further discussion for the night.

Allison was right about one thing. My father and Uncle Philip had fallen all over themselves to assist Pamela that holiday season. After a few drinks, they became quite comfortable around her. Philip, in particular, took every opportunity to put his arm around her shoulders or touch her backside, not caring who saw.

One night, we were having cocktails in the living room just before dinner when Philip made a particular fool of himself.

"Philip, how about another drink?" Pam asked as she made her way to the side buffet to make herself another one.

"Why, thanks, little lady," Philip said as he handed her his glass. Then he patted her behind as she walked away. She turned and gave him a slow grin while the rest of us watched uncomfortably from our chairs.

"Listen, Pam, if that boy of mine doesn't treat you right, you let me know, OK?" Philip said when she had returned with two freshened drinks.

"You bet, but you don't have to worry. Gary treats me just right." She turned to Gary and winked.

"He better. He's never shown much good taste until now," Philip said.

Gary got up from the couch and silently went to find his mother who had disappeared after Philip's thoughtless behavior moments before. Just like Allison, I also wondered why Claire put up with his behavior. I found it difficult to believe that she still loved him.

Gary called me on a January evening in 1967. Gary and I hadn't talked since Christmas, but we never went too long without keeping in touch. We even managed to visit each other twice a year either when he came home or when Allison and I drove the five hours to Chicago for a weekend.

"Old man, are you ready to return the favor?" Gary asked.

"What do you mean?"

"I need a best man in April. Since I did it for you, I was hoping you'd do it for me."

"You and Pamela? April?" I was astounded. When the two had been together at Christmas, Gary never seemed to touch her or even pay much attention to her, especially after one of his father's public passes.

" I'm waiting, Ed." Gary jolted me back to the moment.

"Of course, Gary. What do you think; I'd let you down? Tell me where and when and I'll be there." I'd finally gotten back my voice.

"It's going to be small, right in Ann Arbor at Mom's and Dad's. By the way, do you think Allison would mind playing matron of honor?"

This question surprised me. Allison and Pamela had only met once. Allison hadn't really liked Pam. She referred to her as "cheap," a euphemism for what she really thought. Allison hated the way Pamela flirted with Philip so outrageously. Now I wondered why Pam didn't ask a sister or cousin or friend, but I decided it was none of my business.

"Allison can answer that better than me. I'll talk to her tonight, and then call you back. And, Gary? Congratulations, I hope you and Pamela are as happy as Ally and I."

"Thanks, Ed. That means a lot," Gary said just before hanging up.

Claire and Philip Townsend held the small wedding in the back yard of their house on Bydding Street. The sprawling house could have raised three or four children instead of just Gary, but that had not been in the cards for Aunt Claire and Uncle Philip.

At Gary's request, they kept the ceremony small, but his parents insisted on inviting more than a hundred people from the Ann Arbor community for a reception immediately afterwards.

Both Gary and Pamela looked like models for the bride and groom wedding cake toppers except that Pamela wore a short ivory lace gown with no veil, and Gary wore a good black suit instead of a tuxedo. However, they both glowed from the excitement and champagne.

I offered my congratulations both privately to the couple and in a prepared toast in front of all of the guests. I once again mentioned that I hoped they would be as happy as Allison and I. When I went to kiss Pamela, she seemed very drunk and stumbled as she reached out to embrace me.

"Thanks, Eddie, you're a sweetheart. Are we kissing cousins now?" she asked seductively while her hands traced the outline of my shoulders.

"Not quite. Take care of Gary. He needs to be loved," I said while pulling away from her embrace. I also felt the need to warn her about something, but I wasn't quite sure about what.

"You'll be my friend, too, won't you, Ed?" She asked.

"I am your friend. Just don't hurt Gary, ever, OK?" I looked straight into her blue eyes, and she glared back defiantly.

"Don't worry, I'll take care of your precious Gary," she said before she staggered away.

After a honeymoon in Las Vegas, Gary and Pamela settled back into life in Chicago, and I didn't hear anything from them for a very long time. Aunt Claire kept me up to date on their life, but usually she just told me what they had bought, how much it cost, and how successful Gary was becoming as an advertising executive.

Gary finally found a way to please both his parents by wearing the right wardrobe, acquiring the most possessions, buying the perfect house, and marrying the proper wife.

I attempted to get comfortable on the couch in New Orleans as I thought about the way both of our marriages ended. Mine with little fanfare, Gary's with a huge explosion. I finally fell asleep in the early morning hours with my mind back twenty years ago.

We managed to spend the next day showing Kristina the sights of New Orleans. She entranced both of us as we took the cemetery tours, rode the riverboat, and ate crawfish pie at Cafe Beignet. I had almost forgotten the feelings that Kristina had evoked in me the previous night, almost but not quite. There were moments when Gary left us alone to order food, go to the bathroom, or buy tickets that we would look at one another, and I would remember. I fought to keep my hands away from her hair, away from any part of her.

As soon as Gary returned to us, the atmosphere changed, and Kristina became the doting daughter. I had never seen Gary so happy and so eager to please anyone else. I even noticed that he stopped bothering his thumb, maybe because he wore a band-aid over the raw part he opened during the past few days. After a leisurely dinner in the courtyard at the Court of Two Sisters, we headed back to the apartment. We all decided it had been a full day, and we were all settled in our beds before eleven. I fell asleep almost immediately.

Sometime around dawn, I woke with a start. Raucous laughter made its way down the hallway of the apartment. Suddenly, I realized that the rhythmic pounding came from whoever was in the guest room.

Gary walked into the living room still in his underwear rubbing his eyes and looking as if he was still sleeping.

"What's going on?" He motioned toward the guest room.

"Not sure. The noise just woke me up, too. I guess I slept pretty soundly last night."

"Who'd she bring here? Doesn't she realize how dangerous this town is?"

"I guess not. Should we go investigate?" I began pulling on my abandoned pants and running my fingers through my hair.

The noise continued in the other room, and I tried not to imagine what the stranger might be doing with Kristina. "Should we do something?" I asked again. Gary stood immobilized in the center of the room.

"You bet we do something. We throw whoever's in there with her out on his scrawny ass." He headed for the bedroom and knocked loudly several times before the noises stopped.

"Kris, please come out here."

Gary waited by the door for a few minutes before Kris appeared.

"What?" she asked, standing in the doorway stark naked with her hair wildly surrounding her face.

"Who's in there?" Gary pushed past her into the bedroom.

There I stood facing Kristina, attempting to look anywhere but at her body. I finally turned away but not before absorbing the sight of her body into my memory bank.

I could hear Gary give some commands and soon a scruffy-looking boy came bounding out of the room, zipping his pants and carrying his boots.

"See you around, baby," he said as he leaned down to plant a loud smack on Kristina's forehead.

Gary and his daughter stood glaring at one another even after the door slammed.

"Don't ever bring slime like that into this apartment again," Gary said. "Your mother may not have had any rules for you, young lady, but you will follow my rules as long as you stay under my roof."

Kristina started to protest, but when she looked up into Gary's face and saw the anger blazing from his eyes, she shut her mouth and slammed back into the bedroom.

"Gary, how long is she staying here?" I asked when he came back into the living room.

"We haven't really discussed it, but we've talked about going to Florida for Christmas, remember? I assumed she would stay at least until then."

"Has she asked you for money?"

"Not really. I noticed yesterday that she didn't seem to have cash, so I offered her some spending money. She seemed reluctant to take it. Why?"

"I gave her some money the other night, too," I said.

"Really? Why?" He seemed puzzled.

"She said she was broke, and I felt sorry for her, that's all. But I wonder why she needs so much cash."

"Not sure, but I'm not footing her bills to play the slut in New Orleans, that's for sure. Even if I do feel responsible for how she got this way." Gary turned to go into the kitchen.

"I think you need to be wary. She may be your daughter, but you don't really know her. Remember, keep in perspective, for fifteen formative years you had no input into her life," I said as I followed him into the kitchen.

"Ed, I know you mean well, but let me handle this my own way, OK?"

"That's all, Gary, just be careful. I'm going to head back today. I think you and Kristina will be all right, and I've got some work to do."

"You're going back today? I thought you were leaving Monday."

"I thought you and Kristina should have more time alone before you go back to work on Monday." I did think they should have some time alone, but mostly I needed to get out of there.

"You're probably right. I may not always show that I appreciate it, but you're a real friend, you know?" Gary grinned at me before turning back to make the coffee.

I got up to finish packing before breakfast and tried not to feel guilty. If I was such a good friend to Gary, why did the image of Kristina as she stood naked in the doorway of the guest room keep popping into my mind and why did it take longer each time to brush it away? It remained as the only clear image in my mind of the whole weekend.

He dreamed about her last night. He hoped that the creature of his imagination would become a reality. This apparition, his angel and vision of the perfect woman, walked toward him when he awoke, and he reached for her certain that his future would be secure. When his arms tried to embrace her, she disappeared into the mists, and his arms remained empty.

CHAPTER FIVE

WHEN THEY CAME TO Florida for Christmas, Gary and Kristina spent large amounts of time socializing with the family since Claire and Philip made quite a fuss over the returning granddaughter. One night they insisted on throwing a bash for all the country club folks to introduce their own little princess.

And a princess is exactly how they treated her. Kristina seemed quite at home with all of the attention and played her role to the hilt. I watched from the sidelines and even began to enjoy myself in her presence, although I made sure to avoid any alone time with her. That was fairly easy because between my mother, Claire, and Aunt Susan, Kristina had plenty of chaperones.

I wondered if Kristina would get tired of the attention lavished on her. She certainly never received anything like it as a child except for maybe when she was a tiny baby before Pam took her away.

Claire and Philip gave Kristina plenty of money to spend, and the women took her shopping nearly every day.

"My car will only hold so much, Mom," Gary told Claire one afternoon when the "girls" returned from a shopping spree at the mall.

"Maybe Kristina will have to stay here. How would that suit you, Mr. Selfish?" Claire reached up and gave him a peck on the cheek.

"Do you really think she needs all this stuff?" Gary asked.

"Look who's talking. How many suits and ties do you own? Why shouldn't I enjoy spoiling her for a little while?"

"OK, Mom, have your fun, but remember you created this monster."

"Are you calling my granddaughter a monster?"

"Not a chance, not a chance."

I loved to watch Claire and Gary together like this without Philip around to spoil things. They enjoyed a casual relationship that I had never been able to establish with my own mother. Partially it had to do with Claire. She had an easy-going, accepting style with just about everyone. She was confidant and outgoing, whereas my own mother had always felt inadequate particularly around Claire. It showed in my mother's relationships with others; she couldn't let down her guard because I sensed she felt she might give away some inadequacy or character flaw if she let anyone get too close.

One night between Christmas and New Year's, Gary and I had the opportunity to talk alone in the kitchen at Claire and Philip's house. The night, a chilly one for Florida, kept us transplanted southerners at the kitchen table instead of taking our traditional walk through the neighborhood.

"What will she do now?" I asked.

"I'm not really sure. She hasn't talked about going back to Las Vegas, and I don't think she's even called her mother since she arrived. I've decided that she'll be welcome to stay with me under certain conditions."

"And, they are?"

"First, a job. She needs a job. I'm not going to foot her partying bills."

"Have you told her this?"

"In so many words."

"How many words, Gary?"

"Now, come on, Cuz, I'll tell her. It's not easy since I haven't had her around. At least she doesn't bring scum home anymore."

"And you feel guilty?" I asked.

"Maybe, I don't know." Gary shrugged his shoulders and held up his hands. "I worry though."

"About what?"

"She's a little wild, not like we were in college. Sometimes I don't think she's aware of what she's doing. It's like she doesn't have a conscience." Gary whispered this last sentence and looked over his shoulder as if someone might walk in on him and overhear.

"But maybe with your influence?" I left the question hanging in the air.

"Maybe, but she seems to make fun of me sometimes. Like I'm stupid or something. It's usually when I'm trying to show her some affection. It's a little scary."

"Sometimes she does the same thing with me. She changes into this tough little street kid and tries to be hurtful."

"When I bring up topics that seem like I might be criticizing her or suggesting that she might change in some way, she becomes defensive. That's why we haven't really discussed a job yet."

"You need to put your foot down, Gary, really. If she wants to stay, she's got to work or go to school. You shouldn't feel like you owe her. Maybe you can get her to take some college courses?" I really couldn't imagine Kristina going to school and taking it seriously, but maybe I hadn't seen that side of her.

"I know, but I'm a little afraid." He hung his head and rubbed his hands together.

Aunt Claire walked in the kitchen at this precise moment.

"What are you afraid of, Gary?" she asked.

"Nothing, really. I was just talking to Ed about Kris," he said.

"Kris? What about her? Isn't she the beautifullest, most stupenderific granddaughter, ever?" She looked at us as if challenging us to disagree.

"Yes, Mom, she's the best, but I think she needs to get a job."

"Sure, sure. There's time for that. Give her time. Remember you boys weren't all that great at life and relationships when you first started out either. And you had my fine influence all the time you were growing up!"

Claire had a point there although she didn't know half of it. Gary and I made messes out of our first marriages. The shame of it was that we never tried very hard to save either of them and were swept up into the relationships without considering our partners' feelings or needs. We just went along with the course of our life without thinking. And we both paid dearly.

My toast and wishes for Pam and Gary at their wedding turned out to be horribly ironic. Almost from the beginning of my marriage to Ally, something went wrong. At first, we were busy with the decorating and refinishing of our new home. We did little else in our spare time. Both of us settled into comfortable positions at Pioneer High School. I taught creative writing and elective literature courses that I designed myself. Allison taught history and became an advisor for several service clubs bringing her into contact with the socially prominent Rotary and Kiwanis Clubs in Ann Arbor.

When the house was finished, Allison began throwing elaborate dinner parties. At first, the guests consisted of her parents and some of their friends and their children who were our age. I didn't enjoy these events, but Allison thrived on making four course dinners and showing off her china, crystal, and gleaming house. She began scouring the antique markets and making rather substantial purchases for our home. She insisted that all of the pieces come from the same era as our house. Soon our dwelling began to look like a museum for antique American furniture and design.

When she had the house exactly the way she wanted, she began working on me. I'd rather she kept piling up our debts while purchasing furniture. When she looked at me, I could tell she felt differently about our relationship. Our sex life, at first, didn't suffer, but the more she harped on my shortcomings, the less I wanted her sexually.

"I don't understand why you won't apply for the position of vice principal," she said one Saturday morning over bagels and coffee. This position suddenly became available at PHS when the current vice principal was fired.

"I'm happy where I am," I said, not for the first time.

"But the money, Ed. It would mean $5,000 more a year."

"I'm not interested. If I took that job, I'd never get my novel done."

"*Your novel* You're never going to go anywhere with that."

"Ally, I don't want to talk about it anymore."

In recent months, she taken to ridiculing the one thing that kept me alive, my writing. No longer did she care what I wrote.

"Sure, you don't want to talk about it anymore. You just want everything handed to you without working for it. You enjoy this home I've made for us, but what did you ever do to deserve it? You didn't have any problem letting my parents buy it for us. Do you expect them to continue footing the bill?"

"This conversation is over, Ally. Why don't you apply for the position? You need something to do during the summer."

"I might do that, if you could handle your wife earning more than you."

"Allison, money means nothing to me. You should know that by now."

"If it means so little, then how come you can so easily accept my daddy's money?"

I got up from the breakfast table and stomped away. I hated these arguments. Allison seemed to be changing before my eyes, and I much preferred my novel's characters to those living in my own house. Also, I knew her words of accusation held the hint of truth.

By the time school ended in June 1967, Allison and I no longer talked of finishing the hardwood floors in our house and instead argued about who would get custody of our German Shepherd. My toast at Gary's wedding, just two months before, echoed its falsehood in my mind.

Allison received the appointment to vice principal and was seriously being considered as principal of the new high school being planned near the Huron River on the north side of town. Even though it wouldn't open until the fall of 1969, Allison would probably leave PHS in 1968 to begin working on the plans and design and hiring of an entirely new faculty. She would be making more money than the two of us combined if the job materialized.

During the summer of love everywhere else in the country, Allison and I decided to separate. Allison would keep the house, while I would be forced back into an apartment just like my college days. However, instead of minding, I found myself eager to be on my own again. I managed to find a small place in an old house on Main Street across from the University of Michigan's stadium and close to PHS.

However, before moving, I began the first of what would become an annual summer adventure of travel. Allison graciously allowed me the use of the spare bedroom to store my meager belongings, which consisted of everything I owned before the marriage, until I returned in August.

With my little savings, I bought a used Volkswagen van and set out for the West for two months. I had little money but lots of notebooks and film for my camera. I didn't know what I would write, but I hoped it would be something that captured the changing mood of the country.

I visited my parents one warm evening in late June. We sat in the living room of their small house in Ypsilanti.

"Mom, Dad, I need to tell you something. Allison and I are getting a divorce."

My mother looked at me sharply while my father continued watching Walter Cronkite relate the day's events on the small TV set in the corner.

"What will I tell Claire and Philip? You'll be the first one in the family to ever divorce. Somehow Claire will manage to blame me," my mother said.

My mother, Marjorie Townsend, was ashamed of everything in her life except for me. I was her one proud success, and now I disappointed her beyond measure.

I ran my fingers through my hair as I stared at my mother who turned gray and old before my eyes. My dad said little from his recliner in front of the TV. He grunted and told my mother it was my life.

"Stanley, say something to him."

"He never listens to anything I say, why would he start now," my father said as he lifted the beer can to his mouth.

I decided to make Gary's and Pamela's house the first stop on my trip west at the beginning of July. They had moved to Evanston, an upscale suburb of Chicago, and lived in a comfortable old two-story home that seemed ready-made for many children.

"Eddie, I'm so glad you came to visit," Pam gushed as she greeted me in the driveway before I could even open the door of my van.

"Pam, good to see you. Where's that cousin of mine?" I reached to hug her and could smell the gin of her late afternoon cocktail.

"Oh, he'll be here shortly, I imagine. Some nights he's really late, but not tonight, not with you here." She hugged me and pressed her perfect figure against me. She would have continued to hold me close if I hadn't pulled away from her.

"Eddie, you're so handsome." She tried leaning toward me again.

"Come on, Pam, stop it," I said.

"Come on inside, then." She grabbed my hand and pulled me across the front lawn and into the house.

"How about a drink, Ed?"

"Sure, a beer would be fine."

When she came back into the living room, she handed me the beer managing to let her hand linger a long moment over mine. I grabbed the drink and turned away to open it.

"I scare you, don't I, Eddie?" she asked.

"No, of course not, Pam."

"Yes, I do. It's all right. Gary will be home soon so I won't attack you again. Besides I think I'd rather have you as a friend more than anything else." She walked over to the bar and poured herself a healthy shot of gin.

"Where's that hippie cousin of mine," Gary boomed as he came in the back door through the garage.

"Right here, and what do you mean, hippie?" I pretended to be offended.

" I hear that's what Uncle Stanley's been calling you since you bought the van. Except I think he uses a couple of expletives along with hippie," Gary said as he hugged me. "Besides, your hair is too short to be a hippie."

"Actually, I do feel like something of a vagabond this summer. When I pass this way in late August, my hair may be a little longer, especially on my face. I don't plan on shaving for two months. Now, that's real freedom."

"Pam, you didn't tell him?" Gary asked his wife.

"No, he just got here. Besides it's your wonderful news, now isn't it, *dear*," Pam said. She finished her drink in one long gulp before getting up and going for another one.

"What news?" I asked.

"I've been transferred. We won't be here in August unless we can't find a place to live on Long Island. Even at that, Pam would stay here, but I'll be gone."

"Long Island?"

"Actually, I'll be working in the Manhattan headquarters of Weston Advertising, but Long Island is the best place to live. I'll commute, like here. It's a good promotion, Ed."

"Yes, a good promotion, Ed, with me and the other wives stuck out in the boondocks while the hubbys get to play with the big boys and girls," Pam said from behind the bar. "Need a drink, Gar?"

"Sure thing, Hon. Pam's not that excited about the move, but I think she'll adjust. Imagine, New York City." Gary grinned like a little boy.

"Congratulations, Gary. Next summer maybe I'll get a cheap place in the Village. I almost did this year, except I've always wanted to see the West." I didn't know what to say to Pam who abruptly left the two of us alone as she made her way very carefully into the kitchen.

"What happened with you and Allison?" Gary asked when we were alone.

"It's hard to say. I thought we would be together forever. We dated for six years and barely stayed married a year." I shook my head at the absurdity of it all.

"Marriage changes things, I guess," Gary said.

"I don't think I'm meant for marriage. Even though I'm sad about the divorce, I like the freedom that's suddenly come my way. Besides, now I'm the black sheep of the family, while you've become the paragon of middle-class life. Your parents are probably thrilled, and mine, at least my mom, are in mourning."

"Thanks, Cuz. I've finally got Philip off my back. And if Pam isn't too happy right now, I think that will change in New York."

I stayed the weekend in Evanston. The undercurrents between Pam and Gary seemed worse than between Allison and me for some reason. Allison and I, even during our worst moments, managed to remain civil. Pam seemed to be a hostile captive in her perfect home in the suburbs. She barely spoke to Gary, and when she did, her voice dripped with heavy sarcasm, and worse, Gary seemed to ignore her most of the time.

As I left them standing in the driveway waving me away on my adventure, I wondered if the marriage would survive the move to New York.

I ended up in San Francisco during the summer of 1967 and watched the whirlwinds of change occur within this city on the Bay. I didn't participate, but I became a great watcher of people as I traveled from Berkeley and Telegraph Avenue to the other side of the water where the lost souls of teenagedom had converged in Haight-Ashbury during the media-hyped summer of love.

I began my trek back home, wiser and sadder about the future of our country. While I knew the goals of the hippies held an attraction for me, I saw many youth jumping on the bandwagon because it was the cool thing to do as long as one had the money for the drugs and the right clothes to project the image.

By the beginning of 1968, I settled into the apartment on Main Street, just a five-minute walk to my job at Pioneer High School. I enjoyed the challenge of keeping pace with the current events swirling around us by trying to allow my students the space to express themselves in a manner acceptable for the public school system.

I learned much from the teenagers in San Francisco, many of whom had left home because they felt ignored and unappreciated. Ann Arbor's large student population was embroiled in the fight for students' rights and protest of the Vietnam War. I learned quickly that my high school students were not immune to the atmosphere of the city and quite often took to the streets themselves. I tried to advise them about using common sense while standing up for what they believed.

My parents still felt I should have done something more with my degree than become a teacher. After all, my mother often reminded me, they had slaved to put me through college and for what? To earn less than my father who worked in a factory? I didn't even coach like Uncle Philip who had made a financial success of every venture he attempted. I never bothered to remind my mother they hadn't paid one dime toward my education, except to allow me to live at home during the years I attended undergraduate school. She wouldn't have understood.

I certainly never mentioned that teaching was only a temporary stop before I became a published author. They would never have believed me. Sometimes I didn't believe me. Recently, I had become doubtful if I would ever finish a novel. I didn't seem to have a real grip on what to write even though I knew I had plenty to say.

I heard through the family grapevine that Gary and Pam settled into life on Long Island. I hadn't seen them since the summer, and I wondered how the marriage was surviving.

Claire and Philip visited them for Christmas, so I hadn't seen Gary in nearly a year when he called in March of 1968 to tell me that Pam and he were expecting a baby in September. When I heard his voice, I fully expected to hear the news of their separation, not the beginning of a family. Things must have improved since last summer, just as Gary predicted.

"Congratulations, that's great news," I said. "How's Pam?"

"Mom says she'll get over the morning sickness soon, actually any day now. It's hard for Pamela to be too excited right now when she's spending most of the day hugging the toilet," Gary said.

Pamela confessed to me a year later, during one of her late night drunken phone calls while Gary worked late, that she wanted to abort the unplanned pregnancy. Gary and she fought and screamed for weeks over the accidental conception. Gary finally won out because in New York they would either have to lie and say the pregnancy was the result of rape or incest, or they would have to seek an illegal abortion. Pam finally gave up the argument.

I went to visit them during the summer of 1968. Gary seemed worried about Pam's drinking, but she wouldn't listen to him. In those days, no one knew the serious dangers involved in drinking and smoking during a pregnancy so Gary stood alone in trying to reason with his wife. He thought she should slow down on her drinking because in her drunkenness she often became clumsy. He worried she would fall one night and miscarry. She did seem to get drunk quite often during my short visit, but she never fell.

The baby, Kristina, born in September 1968, weighed five pounds, three ounces. It didn't help matters that she was a fussy baby, crying most of the time. Aunt Claire went to stay with Pam and Gary after the birth, and she ended up staying two months. According to my mother, Pam didn't seem to notice the baby much, and Claire was afraid to leave her alone with Kristina. Claire and my mother assured all of us that Pam's depression was normal and would soon disappear.

Finally, Claire convinced Pamela to bring the baby and come home with her right after Thanksgiving. They decided Gary would drive to Ann Arbor for Christmas. By then, everyone was certain that Pam would have recovered, and the new family would go home for a new start and a new year.

The mist enveloped her small body as he continued to call her name. He could hear the tiny whimper of her crying, but he couldn't determine the exact location of the sound. The heavy mist dripped thousands of sprinkles of invisible rain making one mass of wetness against his lonely body.

CHAPTER SIX

JUST AS CLAIRE SUGGESTED, we all gave Kristina time – time to grow up and time to adjust to having a family who loved her. After our Christmas together, I didn't see Gary or Kristina for a few months, although I kept my ears open for news of her.

Claire told me sometime in 1987 that Kris had gotten a job at a restaurant in New Orleans and hoped to learn the ropes in the kitchen. She was contemplating cooking school. She moved out of Gary's apartment and into one of her own with Gary's help monetarily. After she moved, she called to give me her telephone number.

"Do you like your job?" I asked her once the pleasantries were out of the way.

"It's OK, but I don't see a future there," she said.

"But your grandmother said you hoped for a career in this area."

"That's the great thing about having a grandma; they believe what they want to believe. Honestly, I'm not sure what I want to do. I never had so many choices before, so I guess that's good. Claire and Philip would even send me to college if I showed an interest." She sounded sincere for once. "What was it like for my father growing up with Claire and Philip? It was so different from my childhood, right?"

Her question took me by surprise. Gary had more advantages than me because of our economic differences, but he had other things to deal with in his life.

"That's a difficult question, Kristina. You really want an answer?"

"I guess I'm curious, yes. Gary won't talk about his childhood."

"It wasn't always easy for Gary."

"In what way?"

I thought back over the years and remembered. I debated whether to tell Kristina one story in particular since I'd never told anyone before. Gary and I never discussed it after that day, but if it left a mark on me, Gary must have scars running deep through his soul and heart over that one Sunday dinner. But maybe the story of that day would help Kristina understand her father a little more.

"I remember one time. Gary and I must have been around ten. He did something stupid at the dinner table. Both families were there, plus Aunt Susan and her husband.

"I asked Gary to pass the ketchup bottle. He picked it up to hand it to me, but first he pretended like he was sucking on the top of it. It was just a kid thing, typical of us when we were goofing off. But the Townsends didn't goof around at the table, and I guess Gary momentarily forgot that.

"When Uncle Philip saw his son pretending to suck on the bottle, he said, 'Little baby, Gary, such a cute little baby. You like that bottle so much, sit there for the rest of the meal sucking on it.'

"Gary had to sit there and actually suck on the ketchup bottle while the rest of us sat in embarrassed silence for him. Whenever Gary tried to pull the bottle down from his mouth, his father began a tirade of verbal insults, calling him a baby, a sissy, a little girl. It was awful. Gary began to cry and choke while still attempting to keep the ketchup bottle in his mouth."

"What about the other adults at the table?" Kristina asked.

"Claire finally spoke up. Of course, Aunt Susan tried to intervene several times to no avail. My father ate his roast beef as usual. My mother would never have stood up to the great Philip Townsend. But Claire finally removed the bottle and said, 'That's enough, Philip. You've gone too far this time. Come on, Gary.'

"Claire took Gary by the shoulders and directed him back to his bedroom where she stayed with him for the rest of the meal. As soon as I could escape, I went back there, too. Claire sat on the bed holding Gary, rocking and soothing him. When Claire saw me in the doorway, she held up one arm for me, and I ran to her side. For what seemed like a lifetime, Aunt Claire held her two boys and gave us comfort. Without that, I doubt Gary could have survived."

"Philip sounds like a real bastard. But he doesn't seem capable of that kind of thing now," Kristina said.

"He's mellowed over the years, but give him a chance, and he'll manage to say something intended to humiliate Gary. He doesn't do it as often. Plus, Claire has become stronger and stops him before he can really get started on something."

"What about me? Do you remember me as a baby? I mean, did they all love me?"

Her question moved me because of the note of wistfulness and uncertainty I detected in her voice. She rarely allowed her vulnerability to show.

"Are you kidding? You were the crowned princess of the Townsend family. Until you came back last Christmas, I don't think Claire's heart ever healed."

"Tell me about that time. Pam would never, ever discuss anything about it except to tell me my father had died."

After my divorce from Allison, I struggled with my novel trying to use all of the characters from my notebook as composites within the story of change centered in 1960s' society. My main character, a troubled woman, came from my haunting images of Pam and her unnamed unhappiness.

I went over to Claire and Philip's house one evening soon after Pam and Claire's return from New York. Aunt Claire answered the door with the baby in her arms.

"Hi, Ed. Look at my beautiful granddaughter. Isn't she the most wonderfullest baby ever made?" Aunt Claire loved to make up those silly words, lisping as they escaped her lips.

"Where's Pam?" I asked. I watched as Aunt Claire's brow formed a deep furrow.

She pointed her head down the hallway toward Gary's old room. I rubbed my hand over Kristina's downy head, looking directly into her blue eyes, which seemed to reach inside of my heart and tug at its tough interior. Slowly the baby's hand reached for my face. I reluctantly left to find this beautiful baby's mother.

I knocked cautiously and heard a muffled, "Come in." Pam sat in a rocking chair by the window dressed in a pink mini-dress. Her hair had been set and combed out and her make-up looked flawless. She was reading *Cosmopolitan* and looked up after a few seconds to see who had intruded into her quiet space.

"Ed, I thought it would be one of the doting grandparents with earth-shattering news about the spittle of their new granddaughter," she said.

"Hi, Pam. You look wonderful. Are you taking a break from everyone?"

"Sure. Ed, I'm going nuts here. Why don't we go out somewhere for a drink? I haven't been out in ages. Claire and Philip don't seem to ever go out."

" I don't know, Pam. What about Kristina?"

"What about her? She's being taken care of. Please?" she pleaded in a little girl voice.

"Let me check with Aunt Claire first." I wasn't sure about this whole situation.

Claire looked at me for a long moment before answering. "I think it might do her good to get out. Go ahead, Ed."

"What about Kristina?"

"What about her? Pam doesn't pay much attention to her daughter. I take care of her most of the time."

When Pam and I settled in the lounge at the Holiday Inn, I noticed that every time I mentioned the baby, she changed the subject. She also out drank me three to one on the vodka gimlets. I don't know how she put away those sickeningly sweet and sour drinks so quickly.

"Pam, when do you plan on going back home?" I asked.

"I guess Gary's coming here over Christmas, and we'll go back after that," she said.

"It's been great to have Claire and Philip to help out, hasn't it?"

"Yes, Claire's been wonderful, but I don't think she likes me much. But, Philip?" She snorted into her drink and curled her lips.

"Philip isn't much with babies, I know, but he did allow Claire to come for two months to help," I said.

"Now isn't he the greatest, though," she said.

"What is it, Pam? What's wrong?" I really did like this troubled woman and wanted to help. If I could just understand the source of her unhappiness, I would be able to bring more textures to the main character of my novel. At times, I wondered if I cared more about the fictional characters in my stories than those sitting right in front of me agonizing over the mundane details of life.

"Nothing, Ed. You wouldn't understand." Tears formed in her big blue eyes.

"Try me."

"Philip, he's not really…" She faltered and then seemed to regain her composure. "Forget it, Ed. It's nothing."

I didn't believe her, but I couldn't imagine what Philip had to do with her marriage. Then suddenly Allison's warning about my Uncle Philip came to mind. What had she said about not leaving her alone in a room with him? I downed my drink and told Pam we'd better be getting back to the house. I didn't like the progress of my thoughts.

On the way home, she asked if we could stop by the liquor store for some supplies. She came out of the store cradling two fifths of vodka in her arms.

As we walked up the front sidewalk to the house, we could hear Kristina's cries, before we even opened the front door. I went immediately over to Aunt Claire and the baby to see what might be wrong. Pam pushed past me and went directly to her bedroom carrying the two bottles of Smirnoff's, ignoring the piercing screams of her daughter.

"She's a little cranky tonight, but she'll settle down soon," Claire said.

I reached out my arms to hold my little cousin, and Claire reluctantly turned the squalling baby over to me. I began humming a Bob Dylan tune as I walked around the living room with the baby on my shoulder. Soon the cries stopped, and I placed Kristina in the crook of my arm. She looked at me once again with her intense blue eyes. She began to coo and reached for my face with her tiny hands. I turned to kiss the inside of the soft palm and inhaled the sweet scent of babydom. I didn't understand how Pam could ignore this little creature who seemed to need very little.

Philip came in from the kitchen. "Has she gone back to the bedroom?" We both nodded. "It's time I had a talk with that girl. She needs to start taking care of this baby and go back to Gary. She needs a reason, and I've got the best one in the world," he announced over his shoulder as he made his way down the hallway to see his daughter-in-law.

I looked over at Claire, and she shrugged. I wondered if Philip was going to offer her cash to love her daughter.

I decided I had seen and heard enough for one night. I knew that Gary's marriage was in trouble, and so was the baby who had a mother without a maternal bone in her body. I said good night to Claire leaving her bouncing Kristina on her knees. My last image that night of a smiling, gurgling baby cooing at a doting grandmother remained indelibly inked on my memory.

Whatever Uncle Philip said to Pam that night worked. By the time Gary came home for the holidays, Pam seemed to be finally taking care of Kristina. But whenever she could, she eagerly turned the baby over to whoever happened into the room, usually Claire or my mother.

I edited some of what I told Kristina now on the phone, but it was probably evident in what I didn't say that Pam was a disconnected mother right from the beginning.

"At least someone loved me," Kristina said.

"We all loved you. You stole my heart the first time I held you in my arms, Kristina. I've never forgotten that."

"What about now?"

"Now let's worry about you and what you are going to do with your life." I was anxious to steer the topic of conversation away from anything intimate. I had just shared with this young woman more about my life than I had ever shared with anyone else, except Gary. I needed to steer the conversation to lighter material.

"So do you have an interest in anything?" I asked.

"Nope, not me, Eddie, boy," she said.

"Kristina, you know you're smart and attractive; you've got the whole world before you, don't blow it," I said.

"No, I'd rather blow you," she said. "I've never forgotten that kiss."

I hadn't forgotten it either or the sight of her naked as she stood in Gary's apartment. I ended the conversation shortly after that. It shocked me that she would reduce our conversation to a cheap sexual innuendo. I hung up the phone angry, frustrated, and incredibly aroused.

"That's not yours," he screamed as she picked up the watch on the table and dropped it into her purse. She looked at him with wide eyes and snapped her purse shut before walking out the door, leaving the impression that she had every right to take what was not hers. And he was powerless to stop her.

CHAPTER SEVEN

DURING MY INFREQUENT CONTACTS with Gary over the next two years, Kristina's name never popped up much except when he became worried over something she had or hadn't done. During the summer of 1988, they came to Florida for a visit.

Gary and I didn't have much time alone because of the relatives' demand on both Kristina and Gary's time. Gary looked gaunt and tired. When someone asked him about his health, he said little, if anything at all. Gary was the expert on avoiding the unpleasant. Because he still managed to do all the family things, I wrote it off to job stress or maybe even a problem with Rick who had become Gary's most serious partner so far.

Kristina seemed worried, too, although we only talked about it one time. I tried to avoid being alone with her as much as possible. I didn't trust my emotions in her presence. Just looking at her sometimes aroused such feelings of passion that I could barely keep my hands at my sides. Those were the moments when I usually escaped back to my apartment in Gainesville. I felt much safer that way.

"Do you think Gary looks all right?" she asked one afternoon as we sat on the porch at Claire and Philip's.

"He seems tired. What do you think?

"It's weird. He won't talk about it, but I know something is wrong. He coughs a lot, too. He does seem better here, but I think he's trying real hard in front of his parents."

"That's Gary. He would never admit to even having a cold when we were kids. That's probably all it is, but when you two get back to New Orleans, make a big deal about his going to a doctor. He'll listen to you, Kristina."

She promised she would watch over him and keep me posted, but

when Gary didn't come home for the holidays in 1988, I became more worried. I called him on New Year's Day. He called to wish me a Merry Christmas.

"Happy New Year, Gar," I said when he answered the phone.

"Hey, Cuz," came the weak reply.

"What's wrong?"

"Just getting over the flu. It's a rough one this year, but I'll be all right. How're you doing?"

"I had dinner with your folks tonight. Your dad is still trying to get me to move to Ocala. Now Aunt Susan's started putting on the pressure, too."

"Well?"

"I'm thinking about it. I'd like to be closer to Mom. You saw her when you were here. She's not doing so well, although I thought she'd be happier in Florida after my dad died. I'm not sure how much longer Susan can live alone with her in the apartment. I guess, temporarily, I'd move in with them. Besides I can write anywhere."

"Who could ask for more? What are you working on now?"

"I'm fooling around with a few ideas. I just sold an article to a local travel magazine, but I'm still waiting for the muse to move me on the next novel."

"You'll find something, buddy. I know Mom and Dad would enjoy having you closer to them. Sometimes I think they'd rather have you as a son. At least you don't disappoint them all the time." He sounded dejected.

"Gary, what's wrong?" I was very concerned now. He never felt sorry for himself.

"Could you manage a visit anytime soon, Cuz? Maybe before you embark on your next bestseller? I could use a few good laughs."

Now he really had me concerned. Gary never asked me for anything. He never wanted to appear weak even in his weakest moments.

"Sure, Gar, I could get away next week, OK?" I imagined all the things I needed to accomplish before then, but they paled in comparison to the plea I heard on the other end of the line. "You better keep me out of the strip clubs. I need to come back here clean and sober," I said, keeping my tone light on purpose.

"That'd be great, Ed. Listen, can you keep it to yourself that I asked you to come? Mom and Dad might think something was wrong."

We hung up the phone after making final plans for my trip. I wondered if Kristina had done something that required Gary to beg me to come for a visit.

I arrived in New Orleans on a foggy January evening just as the sun set over the Mississippi River. Now that I was accustomed to the New Orleans' climate and peculiarities, I quite enjoyed my arrivals. The weekend Kristina first arrived, the fog seemed to add a level of mystery and intrigue, which kept me on edge that whole Thanksgiving weekend. I realized that Kristina probably had more to do with my nervousness than the weather, but the density of the air that weekend indelibly marked my view of Kristina forever and left me sexually aroused whenever I thought of New Orleans or the fog. However, this winter cold and humidity cut through to the bone like a Michigan winter never had. And even though I learned to enjoy the weather of this area, I still felt wrapped in a cloud of confusion whenever I arrived, although I didn't find it unpleasant any longer.

Rick answered my knock on the door of the apartment. Several months before, Rick moved in permanently with Gary. The two formed a comfortable and hopefully lasting relationship. Gary once remarked that in Rick he had finally found someone who accepted all of his complications and insecurities and didn't try to make him into someone else. If only I could be so lucky in love.

"Ed, I'm glad you're here." Instead of opening the door wide for me to enter, Rick came out into the hallway shutting the door behind him.

"We'll go inside in a minute. You haven't seen Gary since ...?" he asked.

"August. Why?"

"Things are different now." Rick looked me straight in the eyes.

"What do you mean?" My knees begin to shake, and I felt my usual panicky reaction when confronted with the unpleasant. I wanted to run back down the stairs, get into my car, and drive back over that long bridge to 1-10. I suddenly knew that Kristina had nothing to do with Gary's request for me to come to New Orleans.

"He's sick, Ed. Real sick," he said. The stern gaze of a moment ago melted and tears formed in his eyes. He put his hands over his face to compose himself. "He's ..."

"What? For chrissakes, Rick ..." I wanted to reach over and grab the collar of Rick's shirt to make him tell me.

"AIDs," he said so softly that I had to lean toward him to hear.

"You mean he's HIV positive?" I had been reading about the disease as I researched an idea. I knew people sometimes confused the two. Unfortunately, Rick knew the difference.

"Not anymore. He's got full-blown AIDs." He hung his head while I reached out for the wall to steady myself. We stood like that for a few minutes, neither of us moving.

"I want to see him." I saw Rick hesitate. "Now," I practically shouted.

He opened the front door and led me down the familiar hallway to Gary's bedroom. He was asleep with his back to me when I opened the door. I wasn't sure it was Gary. This form before me didn't resemble the one I was so accustomed to over the years.

"Gary," I said softly, approaching the bed.

The form moved and moaned softly as if every effort brought excruciating pain. When he turned toward me, I used every bit of strength not to cry out in horror. It was Gary, a thinner Gary, an unshaved Gary, but a Gary with open sores all over his once handsome face. His jaws, sunk into his teeth, no longer carried the stone-like authority I used to depend on for strength. The strength had seeped from him, leaving behind this weakened and frail creature lying on the bed.

"It's a bitch, ain't it, Cuz," he said through his cracked lips. "Here, I finally begin living openly and honestly, and I get struck down. Great joke God played, huh?"

"Come on, Gar, this is just a temporary setback. You've fought much worse things than a silly virus," I said to try to convince myself as much as Gary.

"No, Ed, this time it's real. The demons I fought for so many years have finally become real. This is the end, and I'm tired. You've got to do one last thing for me, buddy." He paused to catch his breath and gain some strength.

"Anything, Gary, you name it. You know I'll do anything for you." I fought to control tears threatening to break through my thinly veiled façade of bravado.

"You've got to tell Mom and Dad. I want to see them before I die, and they need to be told before they arrive," he said, attempting to raise his head from the bed.

"Gary, are you sure?" I knew he had given up hope if he wanted Claire and Philip to know the truth.

"Just tell them about the virus. They can ask me about the rest. I'm ready to put all the subterfuge to rest now. And one more thing, Cuz. Take care of Kristina for me. She admires you, and she needs a strong, positive influence in her life, and I don't think she's dealing with this very well."

The first request would be easier to fulfill. I wanted to distance myself as far away from Kristina as possible. I wasn't sure I was the positive role model he might think I was, but I told him not to worry, anyway. I'd handle it all.

When I walked out of his room, I found Kristina sitting alone in the living room looking out the window. She moved her head slightly when I entered the room.

"How's he doing?" she asked.

"He's sleeping. You may want to wait awhile before you go in. He wore himself out talking to me."

"That's OK. I haven't been in to see him since he got so bad. I can't go in there, Ed." At this confession, Kristina's eyes filled with tears, and she hung her head losing a battle to fight the sobs that began to wrack her body.

I went quickly to her side on the couch and put my arms around her, rocking her back and forth like a baby until the crying stopped. Finally, she leaned quietly against my chest. I pulled her thick dark hair back from her face and wiped away her tears.

"There, there, it's OK, Kristina," I said.

Kristina looked up at me with those trusting blue eyes and reached with her hand to touch the side of my face in a familiar caress. I smiled and turned my head slightly so I could kiss the palm of her hand very tenderly. I pulled her close to me, and we sat there together on the couch as darkness settled over the city of New Orleans, and Gary lay in the next room with the life ebbing from him.

During the holidays of 1968 when Gary had come to take his family back to New York, we made plans for the summer of 1969. I decided to go and live in Greenwich Village for two months. I had postponed this visit for two years, and now I knew I needed the atmosphere of this area to complete my book about a woman unable to love during the late sixties, the decade of love. But other issues kept nagging at the back of my mind. I wanted to weave the story around the false attractions of outward appearances, too. I worried that maybe I had set up an impossible goal for my first novel.

Because of my confusion, I felt that the book had stalled. I hoped the different cultural and artistic atmospheres in the Village would inspire me as I waited for the muse to direct me.

Gary managed to find me the perfect efficiency above a used bookstore overlooking Washington Square Park. The apartment was big enough for him to stay over sometimes if he didn't want to take the long train ride out to Long Island. I didn't see it until the day I arrived, but he hadn't disappointed me. The dark woodwork would have been oppressive in the winter, but in the summer with its ceiling-to-floor windows, I could see the treetops. By midday, the sun shone brightly, lightening the atmosphere in the room considerably.

The activity in this small section of Manhattan throbbed with excitement by early evening. I wrote every morning and afternoon, but by dinnertime I ventured out to the cafes, bars, and coffee houses that made the Village famous.

That summer, many of the younger kids couldn't stop talking about the music concert to beat all music concerts in August. It would be held in upstate New York and many groups had already been booked.

I listened politely but had no interest in going because I wasn't familiar with the music. I still listened to Elvis and the early Beatles. Somehow, the new rock missed its mark with me. But I wrote about all I heard, never realizing the opportunity I would be missing by not taking the talk about the Woodstock concert seriously.

I had several notebooks filled by this time about all of the characters I met on my travels. I knew the people I met this summer would eventually become a part of the rich tapestry of my novel that I had decided would trace the history of the past decade.

One night in July, Gary and I sat and watched the tiny black and white TV in the apartment as Neil Armstrong took the first steps on the moon. I became even more convinced that this era would have an historical impact on the future like no other time in history.

I also heard rumblings about raids on a few of the neighborhood bars around my apartment. The police knew of open homosexual activity at several of these establishments and decided that it must be stopped. They began raiding the bars and forcing everyone to leave. They especially picked on an establishment called the Stonewall Inn on Christopher Street. One night soon after my arrival in June, I tried to get Gary to go with me to the Stonewall.

"The Stonewall? Why do you want to go there?" Gary asked when I suggested it.

"Because I want to see what's the big deal that the police have to go in and harass these folks."

"I don't think it's a good idea, Ed. What if the police come while we're there?"

"Then I'll see what happens. I've heard they get a little rough with the guys in there."

"I think we'd better stay out of it. I can't afford to get arrested."

"Maybe you're right. Where do you want to go then?"

I did go visit the next night on my own. The police didn't show up, but lots of other people did. For the first time in my life, I saw men openly affectionate with one another. I felt a little like a voyeur, so after one drink I left, wondering why the police would find it necessary to come in and disturb such a peaceful setting.

At two in the morning in late June, my phone rang, waking me up.

"Ed, is Gary staying in the city with you tonight?" Pam asked.

"No, I haven't seen him. He's not home yet?"

"No, and he usually at least calls if he's staying with you. Will you call me if you hear from him?"

"Sure, Pam, don't worry. I'm sure he was held up with a client after dinner. You know how it goes."

"Yes, that's one thing for sure, I know how it goes." She hung up the phone.

I had just drifted back to sleep when the phone rang again.

"Ed, you awake?" Gary asked. There was a great amount of noise in the background, and I had difficulty hearing him.

"Gary, is that you? Where are you? Pam's worried."

"Listen, can you come down to the precinct station around the corner on 10th Street? Bring your checkbook. I'll make it right when I get out."

"Have you been arrested?"

"I'll explain it all after you bail me out, Ed. Please come right away." Gary sounded scared and angry at the same time.

The Sixth Precinct house overflowed with hysteria when I arrived. There were probably two hundred men and women herded into the lobby. An officer greeted me at the door.

"You here to get someone?" he asked me as I tried to find Gary in all of this mess.

"Yes, Officer. I'm here to pick up my cousin. What happened?"

"A riot, outside the Stonewall Inn. A bunch of queers started throwing rocks and bottles at us when we were just doing our job. What's your cousin's name?"

"Gary Townsend. I see him over there."

I made my way through the crowd to Gary who sat on a bench against the wall with his head held between his hands. I noticed some blood on one fingernail, but otherwise, he seemed unharmed. He didn't fit with this crowd in his suit and tie, but here he was, right in the middle of it.

"Gary, hi," I said when I reached him.

"Ed, let's go. We have to go to the desk over there and sign some papers. They didn't put us in cells; they just want our money." He jumped up and began pulling me toward a very haggard looking woman sitting at a desk in the corner arguing with a rather ugly female dressed in a tight evening gown. When I approached the desk, I suddenly realized that the gown actually housed the body of a man.

"Please, just go sit in the corner, Sir. I can't help you right now."

"That's ma'am to you," he said as he flounced over to the benches under the windows.

"Yes, may I help you?" the officer asked.

"I want to get my cousin released. Gary Townsend."

"That'll be $250, please. Make the check out to 'New York City Police,' and I'll need one form of ID."

I handed her the check and signed all of the papers before guiding Gary outside into the fresh night air.

"I called Pam and told her you got a little drunk and would be sleeping it off at my place," I said as we headed back to my apartment.

"Thanks, Ed, thanks for everything." We walked in silence the rest of the way.

"Aren't you going to ask me?" Gary finally broke the quiet when we settled on my couch with our beers.

"Ask you what?"

"Damn it, Ed. Why are you always like this?" Gary said.

"Like what? If you have something to tell me, Gary, tell me. Otherwise, it's none of my business."

"You're not even curious about why I was at the Stonewall tonight?"

"Yes, I guess I am since you refused to go with me."

"If I'd gone with you, then you would have figured out that I'd been there before," he said.

"This wasn't your first time?"

"No, Ed, it wasn't the first time. I go down there about two or three times a week, and I meet people there."

"People?"

"Homosexuals."

"What are you saying?" My question hung in the air until Gary finally lifted his eyes to meet mine.

"I'm a queer, Ed," he said. "What do you think old Philip would make of that?"

I watched Gary for a few minutes as I tried to absorb his news. He began picking at his finger where I had noticed blood earlier. For some reason, I wanted to find a bandage for his wound rather than responding to his news.

"Gary, I don't understand. What about Pam?" I asked.

"I've told you before about how it was with girls, right? That never changed, even with Pam. It was a miracle she managed to get pregnant because I've only managed to complete the whole act with her a few times since we married. And believe me, Ed, it's always been just an act for me." Gary continued to pick at the finger.

"What happened?" I asked pointing at his hand.

"Nothing, just a hang nail."

"Quit picking at it, or it will bleed," I said. I knew without a doubt Gary would make it bleed.

We sat up until dawn as Gary explained what happened with his life during the past decade. He told me as a teenager he pushed all thoughts of homosexuality from his mind because of his father. The closest he'd ever come to discussing it with someone had been on those walks with me. However, he never could go further than those meager attempts.

He suffered immeasurable guilt all through high school and college when he developed crushes on his best buddies. He never enjoyed sex with his female partners unless he fantasized about one of his male friends. In Chicago, he met a man who finally forced him to admit the truth. They fell in love. However, Gary still couldn't face the truth publicly, so in order to hide the reality from everyone else, he married Pam who had been a friend of a friend. He confided the terror he felt whenever he imagined someone finding out. Yet he couldn't stay away from places like the Stonewall.

"Are you involved with anyone now?" I asked.

"Yes, sure, I'm *involved*, as you say, with about a hundred nameless, faceless young boys. A new one every night, Cuz." His hair usually combed back smoothly, fell over his forehead. His gaze rested on the carpet in front of him.

"Does Pam know?" I asked.

"No, but she doesn't understand why I don't find her attractive. She tries to get me into bed and when she fails, she drinks. She drinks a lot. And she's a lousy mother. And I blame myself for it all."

"Gary, quit being so hard on yourself. You've been caught in an intolerable situation." I said. "Are you sure staying married is the right thing?"

"You know when I moved here, I thought it would all work itself out. There were actually places for me to go where I could meet others like me. Then the raids began, and even though I got scared, I still kept going back because for once in my life, I felt like I could manage both areas of my life."

"What happened to the man in Chicago?"

"He didn't think I should marry Pam. He also didn't like the fact that I found it impossible to be faithful to him. Once I admitted I was gay, I couldn't get enough. So he decided to leave when I got married."

"What now, Gary?"

"I think now I'd like to try again with Pam and the baby. I don't have anyone special in my life, and I can't go back to the Stonewall. Maybe I can succeed at being a better father than Philip."

"Are you sure? You can shut off the other just like that?"

"I can damn well try, Ed. I certainly can't let anyone else know that I'm a homosexual. I know I don't have to ask you to not tell my big bad secret."

"Of course not. If you do give it one more try with Pam, promise me one thing. The minute you know it's not going to work, leave. Don't hurt Pam anymore."

"But if I leave, what happens to Kristina?"

I didn't have an answer to that question. What would happen to Kristina if she was left with a mother who didn't love her, at least not the way a mother should love a daughter.

As light began to edge its way into the windows, Gary and I prepared for sleep. I looked over at my cousin lying on the couch. I suddenly realized I what was wrong with my novel. The story belonged to Gary, not to Pam.

He sits at the bar alone with his thoughts when he notices him sitting at a table, also alone. Their eyes meet for a split second, and they know. He picks up his drink and moves closer. As he sits down at the table to introduce himself, the front door of the bar slams open and several blue-suited policemen enter. He pushes his chair back and tries to sneak out the back way, but he is caught with no escape.

CHAPTER EIGHT

KRISTINA AND I SAT for a long time holding one another. I broke the spell when I reached for the lamp on the table next to us and turned it on.

"Ed, you know you told me about your first marriage. But what about your second one?" Kristina asked.

I sighed. This creature before me was not going to let me forget the past. Why not tell her? After all, without her knowing it, she sparked a memory from my wedding to Kelsey that involved Kristina as a young toddler; a memory I relived when she touched the side of my face gently in an effort to comfort me.

I went back to Michigan in August of 1969 hoping everything would work out for Gary and Pam. After Gary's arrest, I saw them frequently that summer on the weekends when either I would take the train out to their house for a barbecue, or they would both come into the city for a show. Then afterwards the three of us would have a slumber party in my one room apartment. As far as I could tell, Gary never stayed in the city without Pam after Stonewall.

Pam even slowed down on her heavy drinking, although Gary seemed to have more than his usual amount when I was at his house. Kristina was an adorable and happy toddler, but Pam still didn't display the same type of mothering skills used with Gary and me as we grew up. She did everything correctly from changing diapers to feeding her on schedule. However, any special cuddling or cooing seemed fundamentally lacking in her interactions with her daughter. Gary made up for that missing ingredient. He absolutely doted on his daughter and mentioned once or twice to me during that summer that he hoped for at least one more child.

Whenever I spent time at their home, I also indulged the pretty baby. It wasn't difficult to do. Kristina seemed to thrive when given attention. She even began to recognize me when I visited. I eagerly held her and played with her on the floor as she crawled about chasing the cat.

When I got back to Ann Arbor in late August, the winds of change seemed to have permanently blown into this Midwestern college town and taken up residence. After the images of Woodstock, the concert I had heard about all summer long, hit the national consciousness, very little would remain from the leftover stagnation of the 1950s. In Ann Arbor, the first noticeable change occurred in the dress of the college students. No longer did the sorority Peter Pan collars and fraternity button-down shirts of the Eisenhower and Kennedy years exist. Instead they were replaced by brightly colored T-shirts, often tie-dyed, and jeans, the uniform of the new youth. Instead of cute dress shops on Liberty and State Streets, bead shops and head shops and small dark cafes became the fad. And everywhere I went that year, I smelled the sweet, leaf-burning odor of marijuana. I even smelled it in my classroom. My students were suddenly aware of things like Vietnam and the politics of Nixon who had been president for almost a year. No longer, did I have to prod them to write; they had plenty to say and many of their pieces made it into the school newspaper.

Teaching became a joy as well as a challenge as I attempted to keep pace with the world around me. I had never really been political before, but now I watched as those younger than me began the protests that have come to mark this period indelibly as the one in which much of American society became radicalized. Even sweet little mothers like my own became political as they took to the streets to protest the Vietnam War. Some of these women had sons, who had been drafted, but others had young sons at home, and they hoped to make a difference before they became eligible for the draft.

Women, blacks, and students took to the streets trying to make the world a better place while attempting to give corporate and governmental America a social conscience. One group, who also began organizing and politicizing after June of 1969, didn't receive the same amount of publicity as those other groups. I read with interest everything I could about the formation of the gay and lesbian rights organizations. Unfortunately, nothing much was written unless the news reports were slanted to make it seem as if the police were being harassed by a disgusting group of individuals.

Right after Gary's arrest, protesters rioted every night on Christopher Street after the bars closed. For four nights, the same ritual occurred.

My writing remained stuck because I didn't know how to express Gary's torment. I wrote about a character who wandered endlessly looking for his place in the world. At this point in my life, that character could either be Gary or myself.

My teaching seemed to be the only satisfying part of my life that year. I couldn't get published even though I tried every summer to get something in print. So far, I had only managed a letter to the editor in the *Ann Arbor News*.

I was lonely. I'd been officially divorced for more than a year, and I had met no one else. The sexual revolution swirled all around me, yet I found it difficult to participate. One of my friends from work tried several times to get me to go out on the town with him, and I tried. I even went home with a girl one night, but since I didn't know her, I found the whole experience distasteful. However, it did give me a release for a short while.

One cold and cloudy Saturday in early December, I was walking around town after breakfast at the Fleetwood, an old-fashioned diner on Ashley Street. As the rain began, I slipped into one of the new co-op stores cropping up on the west side of town. The smell of fresh baked bread assaulted my senses as soon as I opened the door.

"Hey, come on in and get dry," a friendly voice greeted me from behind the counter.

I looked up while shaking water off my jacket and found myself gazing into the biggest set of brown eyes I had ever seen. When I investigated more, I saw that the eyes were attached to a very open and welcoming face. Blonde hair cascaded down to the middle of her back. Her tight white t-shirt would leave nothing to the imagination if she should step into the rain outside. I noticed right away that she wore no bra.

"Hi, yourself. I guess I got caught in a downpour," I said.

"How about some coffee?"

"Sure," I said as I looked around the warm room. The ovens dominated the back part of the store along with long tables covered with bread pans and large bowls. The soft lighting in the retail section showed off the bread-filled glass cabinets now separating my beautiful rescuer and me. Yeast-rising bread aroused me, as I felt surrounded by female fertility and tranquility.

"I'm Kelsey," she said as she brought me a small cup of steaming warmth.

"Ed. Nice to meet you." I extended my hand.

"What brings you here on this bleak day, Ed?" She pulled up a stool next to mine. The customers weren't exactly knocking down the door to get inside.

"Just ate at the Fleetwood and decided to take a walk. How come there aren't more people in here on a Saturday morning?"

"We had a rush about two hours ago, but nothing since. Most people don't like to come out in weather like this." She grinned at me.

"But see what they're missing? The chance to sit in here with you and drink the best coffee in Ann Arbor." I grinned back.

"That's right! They don't know what they're missing, do they? What do you do when you're not walking in the rain?"

"I teach English at PHS," I said. In the past, this admission had brought unpredictable reactions from disdain to awe to fear, but when I looked at Kelsey, I saw her friendly smile widen.

"Great! I loved English in high school. I had the biggest crush on my teacher, too. When he read Wordsworth, I would swoon."

"Lucky guy," I said. "Kelsey, are you married?"

"Married? Me? No way. What about you?"

"Divorced last year. Would you, I mean, do you ... Let me start again, it's been awhile," I said.

"Ed, let me help. I'd love to." She put her hand on my arm, which helped to settle my nervousness.

"That's good; that's fine. When?"

"I'm not busy tonight. We could catch the new movie at the Michigan."

"Great. Where do you live?" Girls sure had changed since I had been a part of the dating scene. I found it exciting.

"Here," she wrote her address and phone number. "Call me later, OK? I'll be home after four."

"Adams Street? That's right around the corner from me. I live in one of those big rambling houses on Main Street across from the stadium."

"No kidding? Aren't you glad football season is over for another year? What a crazy mess! I have a feeling we were destined to meet."

I grinned foolishly at her and then bought a loaf of bread before heading out into the darkened streets covered with the rain of a few moments ago. As much as I wanted to stay near the warmth of Kelsey's personality, I decided that now would be a good time to make a break for it.

We began seeing one another exclusively from our first date that ended at my place. And our second date began there the next morning over the *Detroit Free Press* and *Ann Arbor News* and bagels with cream cheese.

Kelsey reminded me nothing of Allison for which I was grateful. It probably intensified my attraction to Kelsey. I still felt the failure of my divorce and I was determined not to repeat my past mistakes.

She came from Fowlerville, a rural community thirty miles from Ann Arbor. Her parents barely made it on their century-old farm growing corn and raising dairy cows. Kelsey, the oldest of seven, received a scholarship to attend Washtenaw Community College and then because of her excellent grades, received a full tuition scholarship for her last two years at U of M where I met her in her first year. She worked at a west side bookstore in the evenings and on the weekends, and she volunteered at the two food co-ops in exchange for food.

Her major in business belied her interests in causes swirling around us at the time. Often at night, while I hacked away at my typewriter or sat at my desk grading papers, Kelsey would sit on the floor lettering signs for one of Ann Arbor's latest causes. Sometimes a cause might be serious, like a protest of the Vietnam War; other times frivolous, like promoting the Ozone Parade, the hippies' response to U of M's homecoming parade.

We grew content with each other and even enjoyed one another's families. My father and mother had never been comfortable around Allison, although Allison and Aunt Claire hit it off the first time they met. Claire even mentioned that she and Allison had played golf a couple of times since the divorce. She wanted me to know, she said, instead of hearing it from someone else. She wondered if I was upset, and I assured her that she could play golf with whomever she pleased without upsetting me.

Kelsey and I decided to make it legal in the summer of 1970. We wanted a small wedding and party with little fuss. Even though it was Kelsey's first marriage, she didn't like the formality of large weddings. Besides her parents couldn't afford it and neither could Kelsey. She wanted to do the whole thing herself from baking the cake to sewing her dress. Again, Claire and Philip offered to host a wedding in their back yard, and we accepted.

Gary, Pam, and Kristina all came for the wedding. I couldn't be married without Gary standing up with me.

"Are you sure you want me to do that again? Maybe I jinxed you and Allison," he told me quite seriously, when I asked him over the phone.

"Allison and I jinxed us. Come on, Gar, I can't do it without you," I said.

The day of the wedding held the promise of a lasting relationship with bright sunshine giving its blessing on our nuptials. We kissed under a flower-strewn gazebo brought in by the florist and greeted our guests with large flutes of champagne provided by my aunt and uncle.

"Ed, I hope you two will be very happy," Pam said as she kissed me. "Kelsey's a doll."

"She is kind of cute, isn't she?" I grinned foolishly.

Pam jabbed me with her elbow at my understatement. We both turned to watch an almost two-year-old Kristina waddle toward us. Kristina's black curls framed her small face and were only upstaged by her bright blue eyes.

"Now there's the real doll," I said as I held out my arms for Kristina. I picked her up, and she reached up to touch my face. With her hands on either side, she brought my face close to hers and gave me a big smack on the lips. "That's my girl," I said as I gave her a big hug.

Kelsey pulled me into the kitchen for a private plea. "Ed, keep your uncle away from me, please."

"Why?"

"He keeps coming up behind me and touching me or pressing his body against me when he thinks no one sees," she said.

"Philip? Come on, Kelsey, he's just had too much to drink." I tried to make light of the situation, but I also remembered nearly the same request at my first wedding.

When I walked back outside, I looked around for Uncle Philip and vowed to keep an eye on him for the rest of the day. I found him in the closed garage when I went to get more beer out of the spare refrigerator. Or rather, I heard him.

"Pam, please, you know you want it. My son can't do for you what I can." I paused at the door when I realized who was speaking.

"Philip, no, not here. I do want you, I do. But Gary's been better, so please, stop," she said, and then I heard her sigh. I couldn't see them yet because my eyes hadn't adjusted to the dark of the garage.

I stood still as I heard Philip moan and then heard the release of a long zipper. At that precise moment, I flicked on the lights.

"What the hell ..." Philip pulled himself away from Pam whose dress was down around her waist.

"Pam, you might want to pull up your dress. Philip, Aunt Claire needs your assistance uncorking some more champagne." I kept my voice neutral as I watched the two traitors pull themselves together. They didn't look at one another or at me as they took different exits out of the garage. I pulled a twelve pack of beer from the refrigerator.

"There you are," Kelsey said when I came back outside.

"Just getting some more beer. Hey, don't you think it's about time we thought about the honeymoon." I reached for her as I spoke. I needed something concrete to hold onto as I watched Philip go across the lawn to his wife.

"Yes, let's go. Hey, Ed? What's with your cousin, Gary?"

"What do you mean?"

"He's married to Pam, right?"

"Yes, and that little beauty right there is his. Why?"

"I don't know. There's just something different about him. If I didn't know better, I'd say he was gay." Then she reached up and kissed me on the cheek.

I gave Kristina an edited version of our meeting and wedding, hoping that would satisfy her, but I was wrong.

"What happened then?" she asked. "How long were you married?"

"A few years. It gets kind of complicated."

"I've got all night. My parents were still married then, right?"

"Yes, at the beginning of my marriage to Kelsey, they were still married."

Kelsey and I didn't talk to anyone again for four weeks. We spent our honeymoon camping in Vermont and Maine, a location neither one of us had visited before. I gave up my summer traveling so Kelsey could come back to work at the bookstore the week of the Ann Arbor Street Art Fair when thousands attempted to crowd into the small city. I usually stayed away from the event, but this year, I looked forward to the circus-like atmosphere, which surrounded the area for four days at the end of July.

Kelsey and I had never camped together before and sometimes that takes a special adjustment. However, we adapted well to the rhythms of tenting it. We relocated whenever the spirit or the rain moved us.

I spent hours writing as the sunshine glimmered through the treetops of the tall pines and oak trees surrounding us. We hiked through mountainous terrain and made love while the rain softly slapped our tent that stayed amazingly waterproof. We started our married life in a positive and natural way.

Frequently, I pondered the mess of my cousin's life as I sat in the mountains. I kept replaying the scene I witnessed in the garage and wondered where it would all end. As the vacation worked its magic on me, I began to write about a character who was trapped by his longing to be accepted and chained to his desires. Once I removed myself from the situation and wrote as an observer, the words came to me easily. My writer's block ended just as quickly as it started.

Soon after we returned home, Pam began phoning me late at night usually very drunk, and I found myself right back in the middle of Gary's troubled life, no longer just observing.

"Eddie, howshit going." I heard Pam's late night slur when I answered the phone.

"Pam, what's up?" I always began. "Where's Gary?"

"Your guess is as good as mine. He's not home yet. Sometimes he doesn't even bother to come home at all, that bastard."

"Pam, try to get some sleep. He probably just had to work late again."

"Yes, that 'work late again' crap. I wonder which secretary it is this week."

It sometimes surprised me that Pam never suspected the real reason for Gary's absence. As it stood now, she actually thought she was competing against another woman. If she knew the truth, she'd know there really was no competition at all. It was hard to tell which situation would be harder for her to accept.

I tried calling Gary several times at home unsuccessfully, even on the weekends. I wasn't even sure if he still lived there except that Pam never mentioned anything about his moving out. Finally, I decided I would try him at work one day when I managed to get home from school early.

"Gary, it's Ed. How are you? Have you gotten any of my messages?" I asked.

"I've been busy. Sorry I haven't returned your calls." He didn't really sound sorry at all, or even friendly.

"How are you? Pam tells me you're not home much."

"I told you, I'm busy," he said.

"What's going on, Gar? Remember it's me."

"Can't really talk about it. But don't worry. Ed, I've got a client here." That was the end of the conversation.

Any further attempts to get Gary to talk to me were futile. He kept me at a distance, and I knew that meant only one thing.

One night in late January of 1971, Pam called again, crying uncontrollably. When I finally got her quieted down, I strained to understand.

"I just had a miscarriage," she said after the crying stopped.

"You were pregnant?" I asked.

"Gary didn't tell you, huh? He never told Claire and Philip either."

"Where is he right now?"

"He stayed in the city. He's had enough of my crying and carrying on, I guess. He's a real gem, you know. He can't even stand by me when there's trouble."

I had finally written the first line of the new novel, and the rest came pouring out of me. I worked at night and on the weekends. Kelsey had to practically tie me up and carry me out of the house if she wanted to do anything with me. But she was busy herself. In her final year of college, she was doing an internship at the newly franchised Domino's Pizza chain. The corporate offices were small but with plans to expand on acreage owned by the founder, Tom Monahan. Kelsey hoped they'd hire her when she graduated. She liked the atmosphere at the company made up mostly of young people like her.

I finally spoke to Gary several weeks after the miscarriage. He told me he hadn't told anyone about the pregnancy because of the chance of losing the baby in the early months. He mentioned that Pam's drinking was out of control again. Now that it had happened, he didn't have to go through telling his parents, he told me. He even laughingly said that his father would find some way to blame him for it.

"But how are you really doing, Gar? We never talk anymore, and I guess, as corny as it sounds, I miss you," I said.

"Busy, Ed. You know how it goes." Again, the wall began to rise between us.

"Just remember what you promised me after Stonewall. If it's time to leave, just do it and quickly."

"I don't remember promising you anything, and I can't leave Pam right now. She's in bad shape."

"Gary, she's in bad shape because you're never home," I said.

"Look, Ed, I'm handling it, OK?"

There was nothing else to say. The wall rose all the way to the ceiling, and there would be no further discussion.

I wrote and wrote trying to forget the coldness of Gary's voice and the hurt at his distance. I would try to make sense of all of this nonsense in my own way.

When I wasn't writing, Kelsey and I were enjoying the Ann Arbor scene that exploded in the early '70s. Clubs popped up all over the west side of downtown and music, from jazz to Motor City rock, pounded our senses as we marveled at living in a microcosm of Greenwich Village.

I was nearly finished with my novel, when the phone rang early one Sunday morning. I was already up and working at the typewriter. Something woke me before daylight, and I wanted to get my thoughts down on paper as soon as possible. I quickly reached for the phone, puzzled about who could possibly be calling at six on a Sunday.

"Ed, it's Pam."

"Pam. Is everything OK?" I asked.

"No, everything's not OK. It's over, it's all over." She began to cry

"What's over? Come on, Pam, pull yourself together and tell me what happened. Where's Gary?"

"Always concerned about Gary, aren't you? What about me?"

"Where's Gary, Pam?" I was becoming increasingly worried. This wasn't one of Pam's late night drunken calls. She sounded perfectly sober.

"He's asleep. He had a rough night in the park with the other perverts."

"What are you talking about?"

"Didn't you know? Your cousin Gary is queer. Or maybe you did know. Maybe you're queer, too."

"Tell me what happened from the beginning," I said.

"From the beginning, it was a normal night. One a.m. and still no Gary. Then around 1:30, there's a knock at the door. Two policemen shoved Gary in the door saying, 'M'am, we found your husband with his pants down in New Rochelle Park. We decided not to arrest him but to just bring him home and let you know what he does in the evening with other men.' Then they walked away leaving me with that wasted human being. He's a queer. And all these years, I thought it was me." I heard her bitter laugh.

I could only imagine Gary's devastation. He'd never wanted anyone to know and now he had been revealed in the most humiliating way possible. I worried something might happen to make things worse, but I couldn't have imagined him being brought home by the police and treated so inhumanely. As a result, Pam was a woman scorned and humiliated now. Things were not going to work out easily.

"Gary's still in the house?" I asked.

"Yes, he went to bed. We talked for a long time, and he told me everything. We made some decisions; or rather, we made some deals. He doesn't want his parents to know at all costs, and if I keep my mouth shut, I get what I want when I walk away."

"What is it you want, Pam?"

"I want to cut all ties with the Townsend family, and I want enough money to get started over again somewhere else. Gary's going to sign over his rights as father, and I'll get the proceeds from the sale of the house. You know Philip and Claire bought the house for us when we moved. And the final stipulation. I don't want anyone to know where I've gone or try and find me. I'm through with this family."

"Pam, I always thought we were friends. You'll still keep in touch with me, won't you?" I wanted to keep some connection to Kristina, for Gary and Claire's sake, as well as for my own. I'd fallen in love with my little cousin during her short life.

"We'll see. I've got lots to do. So, thanks, Ed, for always listening. You have been my one true friend through all of this."

"Are you sure you want sole custody of Kristina?" I asked, not knowing what other solution might work.

"You bet, Eddie. She'll be my trump card if I need one in the future. Good-bye, Ed."

"Give Kristina a big hug, please. And Pam, good luck." I hung up the phone with an uneasy feeling about the advisability of a three year old being used as a poker chip in a very dangerous card game, but I was powerless to do anything else but hope Pam would keep in touch with at least me after she left Gary.

Gary left New York in the summer of 1971 shortly after the house sold. My mother told me Pam left with Kristina and hadn't left a forwarding address. When I went to visit Claire, she was destroyed. She asked Philip to hire a private investigator to find them, but he refused. Then Gary disappeared in June. A funereal cloud hung over the house on Bydding Street. Kelsey and I spent lots of time with Claire trying to help her through her depression. Even my mother tried to help, forgetting for once her resentment of Claire.

Things brightened slightly when Gary showed up in September. He said he'd had to sort through things for himself, but now he was back and ready to start over. Claire welcomed him with open arms. Philip was openly hostile and threw blame at Gary whenever he could. After trying to live with his parents for a couple of weeks, he asked if he could stay with us until he got back on his feet.

"Of course, Gary, I'd like nothing better, if you don't mind the couch," I said. Maybe we could get back to our old ways. Gary seemed to want that, too.

"Honestly, Ed, sometimes I feel possessed. I can't help myself. I really tried with Pam, but the harder I tried, the harder the demons pressed on my brain," he said one night as we took a long walk through the darkened streets of Ann Arbor.

He went to San Francisco for the summer and found life there disturbing. Everyone was openly gay, and that almost made him more uncomfortable than hiding. He kept looking over his shoulder when he was with a man always waiting to be caught. He decided to come back to his home turf and try to live the single life.

He didn't say which lifestyle he would pursue, and I didn't press the issue. And without a wife, it didn't matter what he decided to do as long as he was happy with himself and his choices.

I did notice that he continued to rub his thumb and forefinger together. Often he had hangnails that bled. This nervous habit became even more pronounced when his father came anywhere near him. At least he was talking to me again, and I hoped his nervousness would soon disappear.

Within a few months, Gary established himself with General Motors as an advertising rep. He moved to the Detroit suburb of Dearborn in November, ready to begin a new life with only the sadness and uncertainty of his daughter's well-being standing in the way of his contentment and freedom.

"So that's what really happened," Kristina said when I finished telling her about the end of her parents' marriage.

"I thought Gary explained it."

"He gave me the sanitized version. Thanks for being so honest, Ed. I do appreciate that." She gave me a quick peck on the cheek.

"Now how did your marriage end and how did my father ever end up marrying Miss America for God's sake?" she asked.

"That story is for another time. I need to get some sleep tonight. Tomorrow will not be an easy day."

His loneliness surrounded him like a shroud protecting him from the family who tried to break into his disguise. He sat alone at the table while the others around him did not notice his dis-ease with himself and them. They didn't even notice that he was alone.

CHAPTER NINE

I LAY IN THE bed of the spare bedroom after Kristina left and wondered how I would tell Claire and Philip the news about their only child, a child who had managed to never live up to their expectations for very long. His second marriage to Elizabeth had been a temporary salve, but, of course, it hadn't lasted.

My thoughts turned to Kristina and her genuine grief over Gary's illness. She exposed her raw feelings to me that afternoon, needing confirmation that she had been loved at some point in her life. I hoped I gave her some comfort.

And it was a comfort to me to know that she suffered at the thought of losing Gary also. She left several hours before, and now I remembered her sweetness and sadness. I could have held her all night like that, just the two of us facing the unknown together. As I remembered how fragile she had been just a few hours before, I began to drift off to sleep.

As if in a dream, Kristina was beside me in the bed. I sensed her presence before I felt her hardened nipples pressing into my back as she formed a spoon with my body. For a long moment, I lay there in the state between wakefulness and sleep enjoying the pleasant sensations of another human body joining with mine.

I finally realized it wasn't a dream when I felt her hands pressing and exploring my back, then my chest. I was barely breathing, not sure how to respond, but not wanting it to stop. Then the hands lowered themselves to the waistband of my shorts. Her fingers began exploring regions of my body that became fully awakened at her touch.

"Kristina," I moaned as I rolled over to make sure this was not an apparition.

"Ed, I need you, I need to feel you inside me, please. I've wanted this for so long and so have you." She continued to speak in a soft, low voice as her hands performed their magic. "We need each other, especially now."

The sleep of only moments ago began to wear away, although I performed the task of pulling off my shorts still in a dreamlike state. I sought her out with my lips and hands that easily found their destination in the dark.

"Kristina, we have to stop," I said as I continued to press myself against her while a part of my mind attempted to disengage unsuccessfully. However, my passion for her, and my need for another human being at this point were too powerful for me to fight any longer. I was crushed by the waves of emotion that began washing over me the minute she touched me. The fog rolled over me and lost me in its thickness.

"No, we don't have to stop, Eddie. Love me, please love me," she said in her angelic voice. She reached one hand to caress my cheek.

She was so vulnerable, and she needed me. I reached for her, and I forgot everything else as I pushed myself on top of her. I forgot my promise to Gary as I gave myself over completely to the pleasure of this creature beneath me, still begging me to love her.

When I woke in the morning, she was gone, and if not for her scent still upon my pillow, I might have thought I'd been dreaming. But as I remembered the way we had clung to one another as if to an inner tube in a lonely sea, I knew it had not been a dream. I knew that I had compromised something within myself the night before and with that knowledge, the enormity of the act hit me full force. I let everyone down. I even forgot to get the condom out of my pant's pocket before I lost myself inside of her.

With a dread and sickening feeling at the pit of my stomach, I showered and prepared for the day and my long drive back to Ocala to face my aunt and uncle. I had to tell them their only child was dying, while deep inside of me, I knew I was the one who had died sometime during the night and a new, not improved Ed, stood before the bathroom mirror trying not to shake while I shaved away the night's stubble.

By the time I hit I-10, I began sorting through the events of the night before. I hadn't pursued her; she came willingly to my bed, I told myself as I drove faster and faster to put distance between myself and Kristina. I also knew in my heart that I was the older one who should have stopped what occurred in that bed in the middle of the night. It didn't matter that we both were seeking some sort of solace in the midst of an intense grief. I felt hopelessly lost as I drove east.

Ever since my move to Florida, I had been going either to the Atlantic coast or the Gulf when the time came to recharge my batteries. Whether the middle of winter or in the heat of the summer, I would throw a few things in the car and head to the place that would provide me with what I needed most.

The Atlantic made me feel alive with the large waves and coquina beaches of north Florida. Even in the rain, I would walk the beach feeling a part of nature, an insignificant part, at best, but at least a part of the forces that make up the universe. It is necessary to feel the sense of forces larger than oneself to remain humble. I would write sketches or scribble feeble attempts at poetry or fill journal pages when I came back to my rental place of choice. I felt a sense of freedom from the struggles of my life and those around me.

The Gulf, on the other hand, with its flat white beaches and cool soothing ripples of baby waves gave me a sense of calm and peacefulness, which allowed me to forget for a short while the failed marriages and relationships of my life. It always amazed me when people said they felt safe and secure to talk to me because I made them feel important. It certainly hadn't made either Allison or Kelsey feel safe. I guess most women don't like those characteristics in a husband.

So on this journey back to my newly adopted home with the currents of my family's life resting in my shaky hands, I knew I needed the solace that the Gulf of Mexico might bring me before I faced the hurricane named Philip.

I got off I-10 and headed south for my favorite winter haunt, St. George Island in Apalachicola Bay. I decided to spend two nights there before heading home. I spoke briefly to Rick at the last rest area. He told me the doctor visited that morning and given Gary some new medications that seemed to relieve some of his pain and allowed him to even eat a little. When I mentioned to Rick that I might stop for a short respite on the island, he encouraged me and assured me that my news for Gary's parents could wait an extra day.

I felt my shoulders relaxing as I drove over the four-mile bridge connecting the barrier island of St. George with the mainland of Florida. It was dark as I approached the Buccaneer Inn, but the sign assured me that there was a vacancy. After a long walk on the beach, I headed to Harry A's on the bay side for a few beers and a game of pool with one of the locals.

I spent the next day walking the beach, sitting on the balcony of my beach front room, and writing about the illness that stood poised ready to take Gary. I thought about his comments over the years about his demons. Now they had a name, and they came from hell. The self-inflicted wounds on his fingers now manifested themselves all over his body.

I walked the beach leaving deep footprints in the sand. When I turned around to head back to the Inn, the tide began its journey back into shore and my footprints disappeared as if I had never been there at all.

When the sun set that night, I remembered the sunset of two days ago when Kris and I attempted to comfort one another. I wondered if she could be watching the same sunset in New Orleans, and just as quickly as the thought had come, I shoved it from my mind forcing it back into the dark depths where it belonged. The time had come to forget about myself and concentrate on what lay ahead of me tomorrow. I couldn't face Gary's death, his parents, and my descent into hell all in one day.

Instead, I thought back to the memories that Kristina had evoked two nights before when I told her about meeting Kelsey. When I thought of my second marriage, I couldn't help but remember Gary's second marriage to Elizabeth and his temporary attempt to make his father proud of him.

Kelsey finished her degree in 1972 and then immediately began as an account executive with Domino's. She loved the camaraderie of her colleagues, and even I had to admit that some of the social gatherings were fun. Volleyball became a corporate favorite, as well as the competitive softball rivalry between the different divisions within the company.

During the summer, I finished a rough draft of a novel about the horrors of growing up homosexual in America. Gary's character, very well disguised as a star athlete during high school and college, ended up differently than its prototype. My fictional character finally comes to terms with his homosexuality and becomes openly gay by the end. In the novel, the turbulent years between 1967 and 1971 serve as a backdrop, creating a metaphor for the turmoil within the main character's life.

By 1972, Gary's life had not followed the same pattern. In fact, he did everything he could to bury his true feelings in order to be accepted. Mostly he wanted acceptance from his father, but I grew tired of telling him that Philip Townsend would never accept him no matter what he did. Gary tried to prove me wrong when he began a romantic relationship with a beauty queen.

When they met, early in 1973, Elizabeth Jackson had just won the title of Miss Michigan as Kalamazoo's entry, and Gary had been working at GM for six months. Gary's department was considering using Elizabeth for a series of ads for the Impala, and Gary met her to set up the final contract. He later told me they liked one another instantly and became friends over several long lunches. Once I met Elizabeth, I could easily understand the friendship. However, I still worried about his intentions and motives as the relationship developed.

When the partnership between Miss Michigan and GM was announced, Gary asked Elizabeth if he could escort her to the cocktail party that would launch the new campaign. Soon after, they began dating whenever Elizabeth was in town or whenever they landed in the same town together since Gary traveled quite a bit with his job, too.

Elizabeth was probably the most active Miss Michigan ever. Gary once told me, "Elizabeth has her eyes on the big prize. She's determined to be Miss America and nothing, not even me, comes before that."

I tried several times to talk with Gary seriously. I watched as he picked at his finger. The rawness of that wound showed me he was trying to shut out his innermost feelings and me. So I decided, as I always did, that I just needed to be his friend. Any attempt on my part to help him sort through the complications of his life, and he would cut all contact with me as he had done before when I tried to scratch beneath his carefully constructed veneer.

By this time, I had met Elizabeth several times and liked her. I always thought of beauty queens as being rather shallow, but I soon found that Elizabeth had substantive goals.

"Please, don't ever call me 'the beauty queen'," she told me the first time we met.

"Why not?" I asked.

"I'm preparing for the Miss America competition like it's a job. In fact, I hope it leads to many jobs for me as an actress. Do you know how much money is awarded in scholarships alone?"

"I hadn't really thought about it," I said.

"No, you wouldn't have reason to think about it would you." She laughed. "It's enough to fund my entire college education, if I want and allow me a comfortable life. With the contacts and endorsements alone, I could walk right into a career in television or modeling when the year is over. I want it all, even if it means I have to put on those stupid bathing suits and parade down the runway like a mannequin. It will all be worth it."

"Elizabeth, if determination can win this contest then you're sure to come in first," I said.

"Tell me about your wife, Ed. When do I get to meet her?" Elizabeth asked.

"Ed, that reminds me, Mom and Dad want us to all come over for dinner Friday night. Can you and Kelsey make it?" Gary asked.

"Sure, I think so. But let me ask Kelsey. So I guess, Elizabeth, if she can make it, you'll meet her Friday night at Claire and Philip's. By the way, have you met them yet?"

"Oh, yes. I just love Claire. She's so sweet. Philip's very nice, too, and just as handsome as his son." Elizabeth winked at Gary and reached over and squeezed his hand. Her hand momentarily covered his open sore. Gary picked up his drink with the other hand and took a long sip.

Of course, Aunt Claire and Uncle Philip were thrilled with Gary's new girlfriend. When he told them, they both seemed to have forgiven him for sending Pam and Kristina away. Although Claire never blamed Gary openly, he told me he sensed from his mother's questions after the divorce that she secretly thought he should have been a better husband and father.

Claire would ask, "Why didn't you hire help for Kristina so Pam wasn't so overburdened?" or "I wonder what would have happened if you had moved back to Ann Arbor before Pam left?" leaving Gary with the feeling that if he had only done something more, he could have salvaged his marriage. He knew rationally that nothing would have saved it; but children don't think rationally when parents place blame. I always sensed that his mother's insidious remarks wounded him more than his father's blatant attacks on his manhood because his mother had always supported him no matter what. In fairness to Claire, she had no idea the amount of power wrapped up in her seemingly simple questions.

I also had a feeling that Philip would behave himself around Elizabeth since she was a no-nonsense kind of girl. She wasn't a flirt and wouldn't tolerate any touching or hugging from him, and Philip probably knew it. I never heard him belittle Gary in front of Elizabeth. He must have sensed that this woman would stand up to him.

At dinner the following Friday, even Kelsey, who had laughed when she heard about Gary's new girlfriend, found herself attracted to Elizabeth's easy-going style. She put Kelsey at ease immediately by asking about Domino's and Tom Monahan. Kelsey wasted no time regaling her with stories about the growing company.

In September of 1973, Gary went to Atlantic City with Elizabeth's parents for pageant week. He wasn't allowed to be alone with Elizabeth, according to the Miss America guidelines, but he was invited to all of the events and watched her win Miss Congeniality and Best Overall Talent with her tap dance version of "If My Friends Could See Me Now."

Gary called his parents the night before the pageant telling them that the scuttlebutt around the pageant put Elizabeth at the top of the list for winning the whole thing. He said he didn't want to jinx anything, but everyone was very hopeful and excited.

Kelsey and I watched the pageant with Mom and Dad at Claire and Philip's house trying to catch a glimpse of Gary in the audience without success.

"Look at her, Claire. She's going to win; no one else can touch her now," Philip said during the talent competition. "She can't miss."

"That's the prettiest girl in the world, that's for sure," Claire said as she raised her glass of wine for a refill.

Even my father, usually quiet and disdainful of Philip's boasting, couldn't help but enter into the celebration.

"Gary got himself a real little beauty there, didn't he?" Stanley said. "Almost as beautiful as our own sweet Kelsey here."

"Thanks, Dad." Kelsey reached over and gave him a kiss on the cheek. "I think I'll leave the beauty pageanting to Elizabeth though. I'll stick to selling pizzas." Kelsey picked up a piece of pizza with pepperoni and put her head back. She stuffed a huge bite in her mouth in a very unqueen-like motion.

We rooted and cheered for Elizabeth all through the show, and when the audience stood on their feet after her performance, we knew she had the title. We hooted and booed when the other contestants came on the screen.

"Miss Kentucky might as well pack her bags and get on the train right now," Claire shouted when she appeared on stage with her batons.

"And the new Miss America for 1974 is Miss Michigan, Elizabeth Jackson." Bert Parks crowned her, and she began the walk unsteadily down the long runway. We missed most of it because we were jumping up and hugging one another as if we had won it ourselves. Philip opened the chilled bottles of champagne, and as we drank toast after toast, we had no idea what lay in store for the newly crowned Miss America.

In actuality, Gary didn't see much of her during the next year. However, he would fly to meet her in different cities, and occasionally she would come home. Those visits left them little time alone because everyone in her hometown of Kalamazoo, and even the whole state of Michigan, claimed her time. I often wondered if Elizabeth ever suspected that something might be missing in their relationship. I began to assume that because of her schedule, she might not notice anything amiss in Gary's behavior. They had so little time alone, that intimacies were probably rare if nonexistent.

I also figured that Gary had curtailed his other life during this time. He was a favorite of the media, too. In all the articles about Elizabeth, his name always slipped in as, "fiancé, Gary Townsend, an advertising executive from Dearborn, Michigan."

At one party in Kalamazoo, Elizabeth almost fainted during a receiving line. Elizabeth invited Kelsey and me to this event. I watched as Gary ran to her side when she began to swoon. The people on either side of her, including her mother, didn't even notice as they continued to shake hands and receive congratulatory words. Gary led her outside into the fresh air.

The next day when I asked Elizabeth about it, she said, "You know, Gary was the only one there who even noticed that I went down. He's so sensitive and attentive. I feel terrible that we have to put everything on hold for this year because, Ed, I really love him."

Gary never told me the same about her, and I wondered how long Gary's lack of affection for her in public and private would go undetected. I noticed that Elizabeth reached for his hand and touched him quite often, but Gary would soon disengage or pull away. She would tenderly reach over and stop his nervous habit with his fingers. Sometimes he would place his hand lightly on the small of her back to lead her through a crowd, but that was the extent of his physicality toward her.

Gary loved to dress nicely in silk imported suits and Italian shoes. He began to talk about clothes and cars and stereos and boats incessantly, unless I could steer him to a less superficial subject. This obsession became pronounced during this time in Gary's life. I often wondered if he felt safer on these topics especially with me who knew the truth of his pain.

However, the material aspects of my life rarely concerned me. Not that my life was perfect as a result. I probably lost Allison, my first wife, because of my lack of concern about my clothes and cars and houses. Gary would try to encourage me to care more about my clothes, especially whenever I appeared in public with Elizabeth and him. He remained constantly aware that a photographer might be near to shoot a picture or two. It mattered a great deal to Gary that everyone looked perfect in every photo. He would stand, hands behind his back with his head tilted to one side, with his slightly crooked smile lighting up every photograph. I never saw a bad photo in the newspapers, and I never saw one that wasn't posed very carefully.

I knew Gary loved the limelight radiating from Elizabeth. Therefore, even though I was concerned, I wasn't really surprised when he called to tell me that he and Elizabeth would be married on Valentine's Day of 1975. Elizabeth would have four months from the end of her reign until the wedding in order to make plans for what would most likely be a certain media event.

Like Gary, Philip and Claire both thrived on the outward trappings of a successful life. When Gary disappointed his parents in the past, he always found some way to make up for it. This time, he did it in a big way. His marriage to the former Miss America, Elizabeth Jackson, became the ultimate redemption to make up for the loss of Kristina.

I left St. George Island reluctantly the next day. The rolling hills of horse country greeted me as I approached Ocala. I breathed a sigh of contentment to see the bright winter sun shine through the Spanish moss hanging from the nearly bare trees. Already I could see thunderheads forming ahead of me as I drove to my destination. I decided to go directly to Claire and Philip's house upon my return. As I pulled into their driveway, the thunder clapped overhead and a limb from a live oak tree in the driveway broke away from its host and deposited itself in front of my car, missing my front bumper by a couple of feet.

He wandered the streets endlessly searching for anything that might help him understand the numbness that enveloped him. The rain beat down creating puddles at his feet. He stepped carefully around them hoping to keep his feet dry and warm on a night that provided neither dryness nor warmth.

CHAPTER TEN

"ED, WHAT ARE YOU doing out in this weather?" Claire said when she opened the door in the garage to let me in. "I thought you were at the beach," she said as I came into the kitchen.

"Ed, I was just going to have a beer. Want one?" Philip asked, as he stood with the refrigerator door open.

"Sure, Philip, that'd be great," I said as I hugged Claire.

"Can't sit on the porch, now can we," Claire said as she motioned me toward the living room.

"How come you came back early? I thought Marge said you'd be gone all this week. Was it the Gulf or Atlantic this time?" Claire asked.

"Neither, although I did stop at St. George on the way home," I said.

"Your mother is getting more and more forgetful, Ed." This remark came from Philip.

"On the way home from where?" Claire asked.

"Mom got it right this time, Philip. I mean, that's what I told her. I was in New Orleans. Gary called last week and asked me to visit him. And he asked me to come home and tell you something."

"You went to New Orleans? To see Gary?" Claire seemed surprised but not upset. "Did you see Kristina, too?"

"Yes, I saw them both. Claire, Philip." They both looked at me expectantly. "Gary's sick, very sick."

Silence met my words, except for the storm raging outside the sliding glass doors. The rain began slashing against the windows.

"Sick?" Claire echoed my words after a moment.

"He wants me to bring the both of you back to New Orleans. We need to leave first thing in the morning."

"What is it? Cancer?" Philip asked.

"AIDs," I said without emotion.

"AIDs? That's that gay disease. It's killing all those homosexuals. Is that it, Ed? Is that the one?" Claire's voice rose several octaves as she sat forward on her chair.

"There's no cure, if that's what you mean. Claire, I'm so sorry to have to tell you this, but Gary doesn't have very much longer." I said this as gently as I could.

"God damn it!" The outburst came from Philip. The storm moved inside. "He's a queer, isn't he? I always knew it. A pansy, Claire, that's what you raised. Couldn't even satisfy his wives, queer all along." Philip finished his beer in one gulp.

"Shut up, Philip, just shut up." I stood up and went over to his chair with tears streaming down my face. "Don't you do this to Claire or to Gary. I swear I'll kill you if you don't shut up."

Years of frustration with this man, who had nearly destroyed Gary's life and now in his death wanted to strip him of his last shred of dignity, came bubbling forth from deep inside me. Philip rose from his chair, and we faced each other nearly nose to nose.

"Stop, both of you," Claire said. "Ed, sit down, you too, Philip, and shut up. Now our son is dying, nothing else matters. Ed, when do we leave tomorrow?"

"I'd like to leave as early in the morning as possible, Claire," I managed once I sat back down. "I need to go over to the apartment and check on Mom and Aunt Susan. I have to tell them, too. Then I need a good night's rest, and so do the both of you." I looked over at Philip who sat with his head in his hands. "I'll come by around five to pick you up. That should get us to Gary's by five or six in the evening. OK?"

"Should I call him?" Claire asked in a wounded little voice.

"It might be better to let him get his strength back. His roommate told me that the doctor started some new meds yesterday, and he seemed to even want something to eat last night."

"His roommate." Philip made a snorting sound.

"I mean it, Philip, if you say one more word," I turned toward my uncle.

"Philip, that's it, I'm warning you, too. One more word, and I walk out that door forever," Claire said.

When I left, I was still angry with Philip. I realized I blamed Philip for Gary's situation, for the fact that Gary had AIDs and lay dying while Philip sat in his easy chair drinking beer with his white shoes and striped blue seersucker pants. He disgusted me.

I didn't blame Philip for Gary's homosexuality. I believed that kind of thing is already predestined at birth or earlier. No, I blamed Philip for giving Gary the sense that he was inadequate, the sense that Gary was always lacking in some way. It was that sense of failure, of never measuring up, that left Gary searching and wanting and seeking out lovers at any opportunity. Gary never shared the details, but he told me enough for me to know that most of his adult life he led a promiscuous gay life. Only in the last year or so with Rick had he settled down to one partner. It was those multiple partners that caused his mortality to be reached long before its time. And for all of those reasons I raged at Philip in my mind as I drove to my mother's apartment.

Gary went so far as to marry Miss America in an attempt to win his father's approval. Probably for the few moments of his lifetime while he was in the limelight with Elizabeth, he earned his father's superficial acceptance, but at what cost and for what reasons? I thought back to that time when Gary made the ultimate sacrifice for his parents as he entered into his second marriage.

"The Wedding of the Year" many of the papers announced. Elizabeth's parents certainly spared no expense. The wedding itself was held in the First United Methodist Church in downtown Kalamazoo with the reception at the country club east of town.

Most of the week prior to February 14 consisted of party after party. The wedding attendants, all fourteen of us, were invited to almost all of them. Of course, in my role of best man once again, my presence was particularly necessary. I had to take the week off work, not an easy task for a teacher, but the principal at PHS didn't seem to mind since it was for such a famous Michigan girl's wedding. He seemed honored in some way that I worked for him. Fame brings out strange and surprising reactions in some people. I would have been happier to be left out of the whole thing. I couldn't help thinking that Gary once again managed to put himself right in the middle of a vast ocean of trouble. And because of the notoriety of this marriage, he was treading in shark-infested waters.

I continued to write. I began looking for a publisher for *Looking over His Shoulder*, my first novel. I thought several times about approaching Elizabeth since it was possible that she might know someone who could help me. But I hesitated. Would she see through the disguised main character? I hadn't even discussed the subject of the book with Gary. What would he think? Would he be proud or ashamed or just angry?

So, I began a new book. This time I focused on the price we pay for maintaining youth and beauty using Elizabeth and Gary as my models. I also watched Claire and Philip carefully. They were attracted to the lights of the media like moths. They seemed to float into nearly every picture taken that week. Aunt Claire had bought a whole new wardrobe, and Uncle Philip kept telling everyone about his wonderful son. At least I didn't need to worry about Elizabeth with Philip. He wouldn't dare make a pass at someone like her, and after catching him with Pam, he knew I was now watching.

Elizabeth and I established a friendly relationship, but because of the attention always focused on her, we rarely had moments to talk. She and Gary came to Ann Arbor over Christmas, and the four of us spent some time together at our place. One night they stayed over, but with Gary sleeping on the couch and Elizabeth in our small study/spare bedroom. They made it clear they wanted separate sleeping quarters.

"We're waiting until the wedding night," Elizabeth said as the color rose in her cheeks. Kelsey seemed touched by the sentiment; I wasn't.

At one of the cocktail parties before the wedding, Elizabeth and I did have an opportunity to talk. We sat in a darkened corner with fresh drinks and took a moment away from the frenzy surrounding us.

"Do you ever get tired of it all, Elizabeth?" I asked.

"Sometimes, but I figure it comes with the territory, and it won't always be like this, you know. I've got maybe another fifteen years of looking this good so I might as well make the most of it," she said. The remark coming from her seemed honest rather than conceited.

"That's a fairly realistic way to assess it, I suppose. You know, I've never told you how glad I am that you and Gary are together. You'll be good for him."

"He's a good man. I've never understood what happened with his first marriage, though. He won't talk about it." She looked at me with a question in her eyes.

"No, Gary probably won't talk about it. When he's hurt the most, he clams up. It just didn't work out. He and Pam were very different people."

"Yes, I suppose they were. Claire and Philip have told me more about her and the child than Gary. I hope we can have Kristina come and stay with us once we're settled."

"Stay with you?" She nodded. "Elizabeth, no one knows where to find Pam and Kristina," I said.

"No one has ever tried to find them either, have they? I want to surprise Gary, so that's one of the first things I'm going to do after we're married."

"Find Kristina?" I asked.

"Yes, I really want to do something. I know it would mean so much to Gary."

"Elizabeth, I don't think that's such a great idea. It was a very bitter divorce. I think you should leave it alone." Pam would enjoy telling Elizabeth some stories, I thought.

"But that's his daughter. She needs her father," she said.

"My advice, given as someone who cares deeply for everyone involved, is to leave it alone. Please," I said.

"Honestly, sometimes I just do not understand you Townsends." She paused before continuing. "But I do trust you, Ed. Are you really sure?"

"I'm sure. You wouldn't be doing anyone any good. Someday, I hope, Kristina will want to find her family, or maybe Pam will be less bitter, but for right now, they need to be left alone. As much as he loves that little girl, he doesn't want Pam back in his life."

"I'll let it go for now, but none of it makes any sense. Just look at Gary over there. Doesn't he look gorgeous in that color of blue? Sometimes I can't believe how handsome he is. Thanks, Ed, for everything." She leaned over and gave me an air kiss, a very practiced kiss, done carefully so she wouldn't smear her lipstick. And then she was off into the crowd shaking hands making everyone feel as if she thought they were the most important person in the room. I really believed she thought they were, for those few moments.

I found my new novel easier to write, partly because of Elizabeth. She looked and acted the part of a sweet angel with one tragic flaw. She loved my cousin with all of her heart. And he loved no one, not even himself.

Finally, the big day arrived. The church, decorated in red roses and baby's breath, glowed beneath the flickering multitudes of candles as Gary and I walked out of the minister's chamber to the altar to await the show about to begin. First, the bridesmaids, escorted by the groomsmen, made their way down the long aisle. The red velvet dresses next to the black tuxedos created a startling contrast. As I stood next to Gary, waiting for the maid of honor and then the bride, the deep pink roses in the attendants' bouquets floated down the aisle toward us.

Then the moment the crowd had been anxiously anticipating arrived. The chords struck on the organ, and the former Miss America appeared on the arm of her father. Dressed in an all white, simple gown with long sleeves, Elizabeth floated toward her groom. A small crown of pearls held the veil that cascaded down her back. Her red rose bouquet looked like blood against the pure white of the dress. I watched her triumphantly march down the long aisle to the side of my cousin. I turned to see Gary's reaction to the vision of loveliness approaching him, and he looked a little green around the edges as he reached a finger inside the collar of his shirt. Then in a very practiced pose, he put his hands behind his back and waited expectantly. But he smiled when she drew near to him, and went through all of the appropriate rituals associated with a wedding of this magnitude.

The reception seemed more like a grand ball than a celebration for a wedding. I had heard that six hundred people were invited and because of who had just been married, I think all of those invited showed up. Except for the picture-taking moments, I never got close enough to Gary or Elizabeth to offer my congratulations privately. This time my congratulations to Gary and his bride were spoken into a microphone and blasted out through the loud speakers. I don't even remember what I said. When all of the proper things were done, Kelsey and I snuck out to drive the hundred miles back to Ann

Arbor that night. We were beat and wanted to sleep in our own beds for the first time that week.

The next morning while we sat at the kitchen table reading the papers that contained stories and pictures about the wedding, the phone rang.

"It's probably Mom wondering where we went last night," I said as I went into the living room to answer it.

"Ed? It's Pam."

"Pam? Where are you? How's Kristina?"

"First, don't ask where I am. Kristina's fine. She just started school last fall."

"I bet she's a real charmer. I'm glad you called. How are you?"

"Oh, the usual, you know. I've been thinking about all of you lately. It's pretty hard not to when every paper I pick up has something about the wedding of the year," she said.

"It was last night," I said.

"Yeah, I know. I'm surprised you're at home, but I thought I'd give it a try. Has Gary turned over a new leaf?"

"I'm not going to discuss Gary with you, but I'm glad you called. We worry about you."

"We?"

"Kelsey and I. Can I talk to Kristina? She's probably quite a little talker by now."

"Ed, I just wanted to touch base with a friend." Pam continued as if she hadn't heard my request. "We're doing fine, really. And I'll call again, OK?" She sounded like she wanted off the phone.

"Good, please, call again. You don't need to tell me. I won't tell anyone you called."

"Thanks, Eddie, you're the best."

I kept my promise to Pam. I didn't really have anything to tell anyway. I didn't know where she was. Next time I would again ask her to put Kristina on the phone. She would be old enough to talk now, and I could tell her things about her family.

We didn't see anyone in the family, except for my parents, for nearly two months. My father would probably retire within the next year, and they were deciding what they wanted to do. They wouldn't get much out of the house, but at least it was paid for. I knew my mother wanted to move to Florida and buy a little place, even a trailer. But my father didn't like the idea.

"What's in Florida anyway except a lot of water and a bunch of bugs," he would grouse whenever the subject came up.

"It's a paradise," my mother said.

"That's all you can say, huh?"

I agreed with my mother that the weather would be better for them in the south. But I kept quiet in front of my father. Even at this stage of my life, I avoided the venom from his mouth as much as possible.

During the summer of 1975, I decided to take a trip to Europe. I missed my annual treks and hoped that a trip abroad would be like a second honeymoon for Kelsey and me. However, when I tried to get Kelsey to come, she wouldn't even take a two-week vacation. The new corporate headquarters for Domino's were in the planning stages, and she was obsessed with the design. For the first time since our wedding, we would be separated for a month, which is all I thought I could reasonably manage without causing a rift in our marriage.

Elizabeth and Gary spent their honeymoon in London, Paris, and Rome. They managed a month away by themselves, but I hadn't seen them since their return. I wondered how everything turned out once they were out of the media glare and left on their own. They bought a new house in Grosse Pointe more in keeping with their highly visible lifestyle. Elizabeth hoped to land a job at one of the Detroit television stations as a news anchor and spent her days auditioning and making tapes. We planned to get together at Easter when they would come to Ann Arbor for the weekend.

Claire and Philip's social life had never been so active. I wondered when Philip would be retiring and made a mental note to get them to talk about something other than their wonderful daughter-in-law. I did notice the last time I visited them that the photograph of Kristina on the mantel was replaced with one of Elizabeth shaking President Nixon's hand during her reign and the final days of his presidency. I asked Claire about the missing photo.

"I don't know. It really became too painful to look at it every day. I've tucked it away in the closet. Do you want to see the wedding pictures?"

So, we pored over the proofs that she had to choose from for her enlargements. They were all gorgeous photos.

"Look at this, your mother, crying. I've never understood why anyone would cry when they're happy, do you? Crazy."

I wondered if Claire ever cried, period. I had never seen her shed a tear even in the worst moments after Pam left. She became depressed and sad, but she never cried.

Claire rambled on about Elizabeth and Gary. She told me that when they went to Europe they took ten pieces of luggage with them. This bit of news, she delivered with an air of haughtiness as if it was a badge of honor that they owned so many clothes. Another artificial watermark of success, I guess.

At Easter, Elizabeth and Gary seemed very relaxed. When Gary and I could, we slipped away for one of our walks around the neighborhood.

"So, it's working, Gar?" I asked when we were into the second block.

"I think so. You know, Elizabeth is very sweet. She doesn't expect great things from me. Since she was a virgin on our wedding night, she probably doesn't realize that something's missing. But you know, when I'm with her, it's very tender, and I almost feel something. I feel the need to protect Lizzie. I've even stopped rubbing my fingers together. See?" He held up his hand to show me his perfectly manicured nails. No hangnails, no bleeding, no raw spots. Everything had healed.

"Yeah, Cuz, I think it's going to work this time." He slapped me on the back as we continued our walk.

I remembered I wished as much as Gary that Elizabeth would help him heal, as I drove around a little bit before I pulled into the parking lot of Susan's and Mom's apartment complex. I didn't want to carry my anger with Philip when I saw my mother. She was becoming more and more disoriented, and I needed my full concentration when dealing with her. When I entered the apartment, I heard her singing loudly in the kitchen.

"Mom, it's me, Ed," I said so she wouldn't be frightened.

I found her standing on a chair with her blouse and bra off and her arms high above her head searching for something in the cupboard above the refrigerator.

"Mom, Mom, what are you doing?" I groaned as I reached for her blouse flung carelessly on the floor.

"Hi, Ed. I'm just doing some cleaning here. I can't seem to find anything anymore so I thought if I rearranged the cupboards, it would be easier," she said turning around to look at me.

I tried not to look at her exposed breasts as I handed her the blouse. "Put your blouse back on, Mom," I said as she giggled.

"Now how did that happen?" she asked almost to herself as she began dressing.

"Where's Aunt Susan?"

"You know, I can't remember what she told me, but I know she was here earlier. Now, let me think." She put her finger in her mouth and stared off into space with a scowl on her brow.

"That's OK, Mom, let's have some coffee."

Susan came home soon afterward, and I could tell by her welcoming hug that she was happy I had returned. However, her happiness was short-lived.

After I told them both about Gary, I noticed that my mother's reaction seemed vague. I almost expected her to ask who Gary was, but she didn't. She just got up to make dinner.

Susan and I sat holding hands on the couch after she left.

"Aunt Susan, I know I have to do something about Mom," I said.

"Yes, I did want to talk to you about some things, but they don't seem important now somehow." She gave my hand a gentle pat. "We'll talk when you get back. Please tell Gary how much I've always loved him. I was always in his corner. Sometimes I hated my brother for the way he treated Gary."

"I know, and he loves you, too. I'll tell him."

She reached up and touched my face before getting up to help my mother who seemed to be pulling every pot out of the cupboard in search of something she lost.

I hated leaving Mom with Susan, but for now, I had no choice. I couldn't be in two places at once, and Gary needed me more than my mother right now. Susan was more than capable of filling in for me temporarily, but it still felt like I was letting someone down.

The next morning, I pulled into Claire and Philip's driveway in near darkness, but with edges of light beginning to form on the horizon. I could see the kitchen light on through the open garage door, but the rest of the house stood dark.

As I began to get out of the car, Claire opened the kitchen door in the carport and slammed it behind her carrying a small suitcase and overnight case. I went to help her.

"Where's Philip?"

"He's not coming," she said. "He's decided that he couldn't visit without keeping his stupid mouth shut so I told him to stay here and wallow in his miserable self."

"I'm sorry, Claire," I said as I lifted her cases into the trunk of the car.

"Don't be. I'm the one who should be sorry for not divorcing him long ago when I discovered what kind of man he was. But then if I had done that, Gary never would have been born, and I wouldn't have had you as a nephew. That's my silver lining. Now, let's get going."

Claire always met life's challenges by seeking out the most positive parts of the world around her. Sometimes it meant that she dwelt on superficial things; other times it was a solace. At least Gary had one parent who could love him no matter what.

As we sailed along one of the longest and flattest stretches of highway in the Florida Panhandle, Claire and I talked about many things. I found myself sharing the details of my two failed marriages and my frustration at not being able to find someone with whom to share my life.

"Ed, you've always fallen for the wrong girl for you, that's all. At least you always understood that and didn't stay in either marriage making yourself or them miserable. Not everyone does that," she said. "Look at Philip and me."

I looked at her in surprise. "Thanks for saying that, Claire. I always saw myself as lacking in something other folks had. I never cared about the same things as either Kelsey or Allison."

"I envy you sometimes, you know? You never got caught up in the things that have made Gary unhappy and even Philip and me. It seems we're always searching for something we can hold on to, like a car or house, to make us happy. You've never been that way."

"No, and it used to frustrate Gary, especially when he was married to Elizabeth,'" I laughed now at the memory. "But Claire I've done some things I'm not very proud of lately."

"Who hasn't? That's just being a normal human being. Ed, tell me something. It doesn't matter one way or another to me now, but I'd like to know before we get there. Is Gary a homosexual?"

"Aunt Claire, that's for Gary to tell you. I just told him I would tell you about his sickness. He'll talk to you now."

"I guess that's my answer. It does make sense now that I think about it. Pam, Elizabeth, no reasons for the end of the marriages, both wives leaving with no word to us. And your book? I just realized something. That was about Gary, wasn't it?"

"I used a lot from Gary's life to write it," I admitted for the first time.

"I must not have wanted to know at the time, but it all comes together now. Poor kid, he's really suffered for years, hasn't he?"

I turned to give her a grateful look. Gary made the right decision to have her come. Philip had made an even better one by staying home.

Finally, he found the shelter he had been seeking. The walls, made of cardboard and glue, protected him from the cold. When he saw her sitting in the corner, the warmth enveloped him as he approached her. He would stay here until the weather changed.

CHAPTER ELEVEN

WE ARRIVED IN NEW Orleans, as planned, right at dinnertime. However, in Gary and Rick's apartment, there were no signs of dinner preparations. Rick let us in the front door. After the introductions, he told us that Gary was sleeping peacefully. The new medication left him free of pain, allowing him his rest.

"I want to sit by the bed; I won't wake him," Claire said after the report.

"Of course, Mrs. Townsend, whatever you want is fine," Rick said.

"Please, Rick, call me Claire."

He held out his hand to her, and they walked down the hallway to the back bedroom joined together in their mutual grief.

I tried to prepare Claire for Gary's appearance, but no amount of telling ever prepares a person to see a loved one in the last stages of life. Rick said she faced the reality with a tiny gasp and a hand brought to her mouth. Immediately, he said, she pulled the chair next to the bed and sat quietly with her hand resting on Gary's. He left them like that and came back to the living room visibly moved.

"You told her everything?" Rick asked me.

"She figured out most of it. I told her Gary would have to answer her questions since I promised to just tell them about the illness."

"Where's Philip, darling?" he asked, feigning the limp-wrist stereotype of gay men.

"Couldn't handle it, I guess. He got pretty upset yesterday. Actually, if you knew Philip, you'd know that it's better for Gary this way. He'll be hurt when he finds out his father didn't come, but believe me, if he had come, you both would be hurting more. Gary doesn't deserve to die that way." I finally said it. I verbalized the word "die" in regard to Gary. Somehow, the mention of it made it seem all the more real and terrifying.

Rick covered his face with his hands and quietly sobbed. I didn't know how to comfort him in my own grief, so we just sat there, already mourning the man who lay a few feet away, no longer fighting the demons that tortured him.

An hour later, Claire staggered out of the room and came to sit by me on the couch.

"He's still sleeping. How long will he sleep, do you know, Rick?"

"Maybe, if he's lucky, through the night. Before I go to bed, I usually check to see if the bedding needs changing, though. With his new medication, even that doesn't wake him."

"Oh, God!" Claire's agonized cry hung in the air for a long moment as Rick's words sunk in. Gary could no longer manage his bodily functions, and this man before us dealt with it.

"What about the hospital? Shouldn't he be in the hospital?" Claire asked once she'd composed herself.

"They're afraid of AIDs patients, actually. When he was first diagnosed, he was in the hospital. After the staff found out, they left Gary alone. Only after I ranted and raved would someone come in to care for him. This is better."

"Aren't you afraid? I mean isn't it highly contagious? And you're changing his sheets?"

"I use gloves, and I've read everything I can about the disease, which isn't much. It's not caring for him now that scares me. I get tested every few months, but so far all the tests have come back negative."

"Thank you, Rick, for taking care of him," Claire said, as she leaned forward to touch his knee. "If you have any of that reading material here, I'd like to read it tonight. I don't think I'll be sleeping much. If you've got more gloves, I'd like to help you tonight, too."

"Thanks, Claire. Gary always said he had the 'bestest' mom in the world. I never believed him until now." They smiled at one another coming to an understanding that bonded them in their love for Gary.

"Where's Kristina?" I asked.

"She's been in and out. She's not handling things very well. Maybe you could talk to her, Claire?"

"I can try. Where is she right now?"

"Probably at her apartment. Give her a call; she could probably use a friendly voice about now. She hasn't been able to go in the bedroom, you know. She comes over, asks about him, but says she doesn't have time to visit. It's hard to explain to Gary without upsetting him."

Claire left to call her granddaughter while Rick and I went back to our silent vigil. I had come to respect Rick more and more over the past few years. I was glad that Gary had someone to love him at the end.

Later that night, Claire and Rick went into the bedroom. Together, they rolled Gary to one side of the bed and then back to the other side replacing the soiled sheets and mats with clean ones. Gary didn't open his eyes during the process, they told me. Claire decided she would spend the night in Gary's room sitting in the chair by the bed. Rick didn't argue.

When I woke in the morning, I peeked in the bedroom, and Gary and Claire were holding hands and talking to one another very quietly. I shut the door soundlessly and left the mother and son to their private conversation. I went back to the guest bedroom and wondered at how differently things had turned out for Gary and me. Gary's slide had been more dramatic and visible than mine, especially now, but I had sunk to lows that no one knew about but me and, of course, Kristina.

I sat on the bed and wished I could pray or wished that something like a prayer could help me. Instead, I remembered a time filled with great changes in both my life and Gary's.

I went to Europe alone during the summer of 1975. Because Kelsey couldn't or wouldn't come with me, I only stayed for a month. I saw much of France, Germany, Switzerland, and Italy by rail, staying only a night or two in each place. Before I left, I completed what I thought was a final copy of *Looking over his Shoulder*. During my travels, I kept a journal, but with no particular object in mind. I decided to take an hiatus from my second novel, which had begun easily but now stalled as I began to realize that Kelsey and I were drifting apart. Her days as a college radical had changed as quickly as the country's mood at the end of Watergate. Her interests turned toward making a living and ignoring the rest of the world as much as possible.

The respite provided me with long stretches where I could think about my life and its direction. By the end of the month, I felt quite ready to head back to Ann Arbor, satisfied with my work and determined to get back on track with my wife and my writing.

However, I came home to a different Kelsey. In my absence, she traded her '67 Volkswagen Beetle for a brand new Volvo. She assured me she could afford it because she had just been promoted and given a great raise.

" I'm shocked you would buy such a big item as a car and not even discuss it with me," I said, feeling rather hurt at this seeming deception.

"I knew what you'd say, 'Why spend so much money on a vehicle? My dad could get us a good reliable Ford with his employee discount.'"

"And, he can. What's wrong with that?"

"Ed, just forget it. It's my money, and I wanted something dramatically extravagant for once in my life. Let me enjoy it," she said, making me feel like the neighborhood bully who had stolen her Halloween candy.

"I'm sorry, Kelsey. You surprised me. It seems like a big decision."

"I'm sorry, too. Next time I'll warn you before I make a big purchase," she laughed, and I wondered what other surprises would come my way.

"Pam called a couple of times in the past month," Kelsey said. "Can you tell her about the time difference? I think she's calling from out west someplace. One night I complained about the lateness of the call, and she said something about it only being nine o'clock. I know she drinks, but I think she was serious."

"Did she leave a number?" I asked.

"Nope, but the last time she called, last week, I told her to try calling tonight since you'd be home. I asked her to call at seven or eight o'clock her time, and she agreed. I guess she might have gone to California?"

"Maybe. Sorry she woke you, but I'm glad she's trying to get in touch with me. I feel kind of responsible for her and the kid."

"I know you do, although I can't say I've ever understood why, but at least you stand by people. I hope you'll always stand by me, too," she said.

"You first of all. But why do I need to stand by you? I'd like to lie by you instead," I said as I took her in my arms.

Making love with Kelsey after such a long time felt like I'd really come home. I forgot about her new shiny car in the driveway, and I hope she forgot about everything else as we discovered that there's no place like home. After several hours, we decided to make Domino's work for us for a change so we ordered pizza. At 10 p.m., the phone rang.

"What do you know. She followed directions," Kelsey said with a mouthful of pizza.

I playfully slapped her leg and reached for the phone determined this time to find out where Pam and Kristina lived.

"Hi, Eddie," came the familiar voice sounding sober for once.

"Hey, Pam, I'm glad you called."

"How was Europe? European?" We both laughed.

"You could say that. How's Kristina?"

"Fine, fine. A chatterbox and all excited about school."

"Is she still up?" I asked.

"Yeah, she's over playing at the neighbors. Why?"

"I'd like to talk to her sometime. Hear her voice."

"Won't do any good, Eddie, she doesn't know a thing about you or the rest of the crew. I told her that her daddy died. I called to tell you that I'm getting married again. Next month. His name is Oscar Timmons. He owns the club where I've worked for the past three years, and he's real nice to Kristina and me. In fact, he's going to adopt Kristina." She seemed breathless at the end of her recital.

"Why not tell me where you are, Pam? What does it matter now?" I worried with a new husband that she might stop all contact with me.

"Not ready yet. I'll keep in touch though. You never knew when I might need the Townsends' millions. I won't be working so much after we're married, but Oscar spends every night at the club, you know, protecting his investment, he says. I'll call regularly, OK?"

"OK, Pam, don't forget that I'd like to talk to Kristina next time."

"Where's she living?" Kelsey asked when I hung up the phone.

"Won't say, but she's marrying again. Some guy who owns a club where she works."

"Sounds like Vegas to me," she said before going back to the old movie on TV.

"Maybe. She says she'll still keep in touch with me though," I said.

For the rest of the summer I decided it was time to get to work again on my second novel, *When Beauty Fades*. I also tried to spend time with Elizabeth and Gary, but they were swept up into the social life of Grosse Pointe and that didn't include Kelsey and me. They did like Kelsey's new car though.

When a new publishing firm opened in Ann Arbor, I visited their offices hoping to speak to an editor. Because it was a small place, I instead spoke to the publisher himself. A New Yorker by birth, transplanted to Michigan by choice, he decided to take a small inheritance left by his father and merge two of his favorite hobbies, writing and reading. I told him about my first novel, and he seemed interested.

"Now, I'm a small firm, but what I could do is print it here and then try to sell the rights to a larger publishing house who would promote and sell it to the public. Bring it in, let me read it, and we'll see," he said, shaking my hand as if we were sealing a deal.

Even though it wasn't official, I felt like I finally had a good chance of being published. However, I had one thing keeping me from being too excited. I needed to tell Gary about the book. I pondered for a week about how I could tell him. I also had to tell Kelsey who had never shown any interest in even reading the novel.

I decided to practice on her. I told Kelsey about the publisher, Eugene Haslett, and she seemed interested.

"How much did he offer?" she asked.

"How much did he offer? That's all you have to say?"

"It's an important question, Ed. You've been working on that thing for years and not bringing in any money during the summer months, and now you have a chance to recoup your losses. It matters," she said.

"It seems that first you would ask about the subject of the book."

"Sorry. What's it about?"

"It's about a lost soul always searching for the wrong pot at the end of the rainbow," I said.

"That's why I didn't ask. I knew you'd give me a bunch of mumbo jumbo about some ethereal subject."

"Let me try again since you obviously didn't like my first description. It's about a homosexual who does everything in his power to deny his true desires just so he can please those around him." *What was happening between the two of us that she couldn't understand my first description of the book*, I wondered.

"Does Gary know you wrote a book about him?" she asked.

I had never talked with her about Gary and his troubles. She mentioned a few times that she thought there was something different about him, and once even suggested that she thought he might be gay. But I had never talked to her about Gary and his problems.

"Why do you say that?"

"It's about Gary, isn't it?"

"No, it's about a homosexual who tries his hardest to..."

"All right, Ed, if you don't want to tell me, you don't have to. It sounds interesting, but do you think mainstream America is ready for something like that?"

Thankful that she decided not to pursue the conversation about Gary, I launched into my reasons why I thought the country was ready to hear about the horrors of growing up gay in a heterosexual world.

"But more than that, it's about anyone who lives his life to please those around him instead of examining his own truth by hiding behind walls, not revealing emotions. We all do that to a certain extent, but no group more than the homosexual male." I looked at her when I had finished.

"Sounds like it could be about your own emotional state as well, although I'm pretty certain you're not gay. Good luck with it. And Ed, I know you won't talk about it with me, but you'd better tell Gary about the book before anything else happens." She reached over and gave me a kiss on the cheek.

"Thanks. I can't talk about it, even with you. I promised such a long time ago and you know me and my promises." I kissed her back.

I had kept Gary's secret for so long now that I didn't know how to break the silence even with my wife. Besides, I felt strongly that Gary should be the one to tell people. But at this stage in his life, he wasn't telling anybody anything. He had gone completely back into his protective shell and wouldn't let even me in this time.

The next week I made arrangements to meet Gary for lunch close to his office building. The invitation was casual even though I felt tremors in my hands as I clenched the phone and wrote down the address of his favorite lunchtime restaurant.

By the time we ordered lunch, we had only exchanged pleasantries and news about our wives and my trip to Europe. We spent a few moments comparing notes about our respective trips although the hostels and bed and breakfasts of my trip in no way compared to the five star hotel accommodations of Gary's and Elizabeth's honeymoon.

"Gary, you know I finished my first novel last year," I said.

"No, I didn't know that. Hey, that's great, Ed. What's it about?"

"The novel traces the life of its main character beginning in a high school in Iowa where he is a four-letter varsity athlete. He spends most of his life trying to fit into the image that everyone around him has conceived. I try to show the dangers of not dealing honestly with oneself. By the end, the pressure is so great within this person that he ends up killing himself."

Gary put his fork down and looked at me intently. "What is it that your main character should have dealt with?"

I looked at him just as intently for a long moment before answering. "His homosexuality," I said very quietly.

Gary didn't move; he didn't even blink. "I see." He paused. "Is there any resemblance to your main character and anyone we know?"

"Only on the inside, Gary. No one else will be able to see any similarities. It's an important message."

Gary let out a long sigh and shook his head as if to clear the cobwebs that had gathered there. We didn't speak for several minutes. I did notice the nervous twitch begin between his forefinger and his thumb. Suddenly he stopped and put his hands in his lap.

"What are you going to do with it?" he asked, no longer making eye contact with me but staring intently at his broiled rainbow trout.

"I'm trying to publish it," and then I told him about Ernest Haslett.

"I see. Why did you wait so long to tell me?"

"You're not the easiest person to talk to when it comes to this subject." I tried to keep my voice light.

"But why now? Everything is going so great for Elizabeth and me. Why now?" I thought for a moment he might start crying.

"I didn't write it with any intention to harm you or your marriage, Gary. But it might help someone else who could make better choices before it's too late. Gary, I know your demons are never very far from the surface no matter how hard you try to deny it. I love you like a brother and seeing your pain hurts me, too." I stared at him willing him to look at me once again.

"When I first began writing the book, I had it end with the main character facing up to the truth and living happily ever after. But the more I researched the topic, the more I discovered that rarely happens. I wanted to make a more powerful statement," I said.

Finally, he lifted up his head, and the old Gary appeared before me as his grin lit up his still-handsome face. "All right, Cuz. Let me know if I can help with contracts and all that junk. I don't want anyone taking advantage of my best friend. I want the first autographed copy, righto?!" And then as quickly as his bravado appeared, it disappeared. "You're sure my folks or Elizabeth won't know?"

"I'm sure, but how about reading it before anything happens? Then you can help me change anything that might identify you, OK?"

"Thanks, Ed, that's a deal." We shook hands before finishing our lunch and heading back to our very different lives.

When I pulled myself from thinking about the past, I left my bedroom and headed for the kitchen where I found Kristina and Rick sitting at the table drinking coffee.

"Hi, Kristina. When did you get here?" I asked.

"About an hour ago. Is Grandma still with Gary?"

"Yes, I peeked in the room, but they're talking so I left them alone. Your grandmother will be pleased that you're here."

"What about you? Are you happy I'm here?"

"Well, of course, Miss Kristina. I'm always delighted to see you." I wanted to keep it light especially with Rick sitting right there looking at the both of us.

"How about a big breakfast? I make killer omelets," Rick said.

"Sounds good to me. I just remembered that we didn't eat dinner last night. Claire could use some sustenance too, even if we have to force her. We also need to see that she gets some rest today," I said.

"Why didn't Grandpa come, really? Grandma said he had a cold, but I don't buy it," Kristina said.

"He had some trouble digesting the news. It's better this way, I think."

Kristina nodded her head as if understanding. Then she gave me a big grin, "You always know best, *Cousin* Ed."

I blushed remembering how "best" I knew her body just a couple of nights ago. I looked away not wanting to see the open desire now spreading across her face out of fear it would cause my body to defy my vows never to be seduced by her again.

"I called my mom and told her last night," she said.

"Told her what?" I asked.

"What do you think? About her ex-husband Gary."

"How did she take it?"

"You know, good ole Pam. Real sympathetic like. Glad I let her know. Asked about Gary's money. All the important stuff." Kristina had reverted back to the tough kid. "She said she wanted to talk to you sometime, though. When I asked her why, she said you two used to be real close. I never knew that."

"Your mom and I were good friends before she left with you. Then she used to call me until I left Ann Arbor. That's why you remember talking to me on the phone. She wouldn't let me know where she was so I couldn't call and tell her I was moving."

"Give her a call sometime. I don't want her pestering me," she said before she flounced out of the room.

Rick turned away from the stove where he had been preparing the eggs. "I wish sometimes, she'd just stay away," he said. "I'd never say that to either Gary or Claire."

"Why do you wish she'd stay away?"

"She's usually trouble. I know she's all choked up about her father, but then at times she seems pretty heartless. This morning she came over to ask about her father's will," he said.

"His will? Good God, he's not dead," I said as I slammed my hand on the table.

"Tell me about it. I refused to answer her questions. Then you blessedly walked in. Probably just as well she won't go in and visit Gary."

"That's probably what Pam put in her head. You heard her say that her mother was asking about Gary's money."

"I don't know, Ed, maybe. But I think Kris is capable of thinking of those things on her own." Rick turned back around to pour the beaten eggs into the hot pan.

Late in the day while Claire finally rested in the spare bedroom, and I dozed on the couch, Gary asked Rick to bring Claire, Kristina, and me to his bedside.

"Kristina left a few hours ago, Rick," I said him as I uncurled myself from the couch. "Should I call her?"

"Let's not. I don't quite trust her with him right now. Besides she probably wouldn't come. I'll tell him I can't reach her. I can be forgiven for one small white lie, I think." He smiled sadly.

"What's he want?"

"He seems to be feeling better. He asked me to sit him up and shave him, brush his teeth. He even wanted me to put on one of his silk shirts. You know, Gary." We both shook our heads and laughed.

"Good sign, don't you think?" I asked.

"Sure, Ed, sure."

Claire and I entered the darkened bedroom. Gary was very sensitive to light, and the blinds were kept closed all of the time now. The only glow came from a small lamp on the other side of the room. Gary did look slightly better with his freshly shaven face and clean shirt. He smiled when we came in.

"Two of my favorite people! The most beautiful mother in the world and the handsomest cousin around," he said in his old voice. Except when he finished he began coughing uncontrollably and motioned for us to hand him the spittoon kept under the bed.

"'Gary, don't get so excited. We don't look all *that* good," Claire said as she held the large container for him.

"You're probably wondering why I've called you both here," he said when he was calmer. This time he kept his voice low.

"You wanta bust out of this joint?" Claire asked.

"Soon enough, Ma, soon enough. Seriously now, I want to tell you two a few things. I'll leave you both to tell Kristina. It's probably better this way, " he said.

"What is it, Gar?" I asked. I could see he had something important to tell us.

"First, I love you two probably the most in the world along with Kristina. You've stood by me when I didn't always deserve it, and you both have made my life easier at times without even knowing it."

"Gary, you don't have to tell us things we already know," Claire said.

"Yes, I do. It's important to me. Mom, you always made me feel loved. I admit that most of the time I just wanted Dad to love me, but you kept me grounded. There were times when I was in high school that I felt like killing myself because I knew I was different, and I wanted so desperately to be like everyone else. But, Mom, you always brought me back from the brink. Either through humor, the way you did just now, or just by being my mom and holding me when the pain was too much. And you never even knew the source of my greatest pain, but I believe if you had, even twenty years ago, you would have accepted it and loved me anyway." He looked at her with great affection. Claire blinked back the tears.

"You know I would have. You're my bestest son," she said as she squeezed his hands resting on his stomach.

"And now, Ed, ole buddy, my favorite cousin." Gary grinned at me.

"I'm your only cousin, Gar," I said as we both chuckled at this old joke.

"So you are. But you were the one who knew everything early on and never judged me. Even when I couldn't name it, you knew and accepted me even when I pushed you away. I love you like a brother, Cuz. Even when I turned away from you because you wanted me to face my demons, I loved you. I always knew you were right. And then, your book. I could never tell you what that meant to me. When I read it, I knew for sure you understood me intuitively. We never talked about most of the stuff you wrote, yet you knew."

"I always thought you were mad about it. And I always felt guilty because I sensed it's what broke up you and Elizabeth."

"I never should have married her although I did love her in a way. It wasn't worth it. But you understood. Thank you. You gave me more than I ever gave you."

"That's not true, Gary. You were and are my best friend. That's a lot, and I thank you," I said desperately trying not to cry.

"Now, that's out of the way. I wanted to tell you both some other things. First, let me say, that I also have loved Rick. We started out by me pushing him away like every other relationship, but with him, it didn't work. He's like you that way, Ed. He's stuck by me through this horrible illness that's robbed me of every bit of dignity I ever had. I wondered if he would leave me when I first found out. Because you know, I'd heard the stories about partners leaving the minute they heard. I honestly believe that he never thought about leaving. He's been a saint."

"I will always love him for that, Gary," Claire said.

"Do that, Mom. Keep him in your heart. His mother won't have anything to do with him, and I think he could use a good mother in the next few months." Gary paused to catch his breath for a moment.

"Almost everything that I have saved in my lifetime has gone to my care. No one will insure an AIDs patient. I have put aside a small amount for my funeral, and Rick has directions on how I want that handled. All of my debts will be paid. Anything left, I'm leaving to Rick for his undying devotion to me during the past year. He hasn't worked and will probably have some difficulty finding something right away. How does a grown man explain a year away from work on his resume?"

"I haven't left anything to Kristina," he said. He looked for a long time at Claire who met his gaze. "Mom, you must not let her take advantage of you or Dad," he said.

"What do you mean?" Claire asked.

"When I'm gone, she will try her tricks on you two instead of me. I've mostly given in to her demands until recently. Since she won't come in here and see me, Rick is under strict orders not to give her any money when she asks."

"Kris needs money?" Claire asked.

"Always. I've felt guilty since she showed up here, and believe me, she knows how to play that card, and I've given her what she's asked for. In fact, if I hadn't been so generous, I would be leaving more money behind that could have been split easily between her and Rick." He paused to cough once again. We waited patiently.

"But Kristina is greedy. So be a good grandmother to her, but don't fall for her stories. Make her stand on her own, Mom. Remember, you have nothing to feel guilty about so don't let her use that against you. Trust me on this one point. If she finds your Achilles' heel, she will use it." Gary's voice started to rise, and his coughing began again.

"Gary, please don't get upset. Of course, I'll watch over Kristina. Don't worry about that. I think things will improve the longer she's away from that mother of hers."

"Promise me, both of you, try to love her, but give her more than that. Give her the strength to stand on her own without either of you propping her up."

"We promise, Gary," I said. I could tell these last few words were said with all the strength he could muster. "We'll help give Kristina what she needs."

With that, Gary fell back against the pillow and closed his eyes. We quietly left the room, both Claire and I wrapped in our own private thoughts. For Claire, hearing the truth about her granddaughter probably came as a shock, but she would digest it and deal with it. To me, it seemed the guilt that Gary had carried for the last two decades left his body and floated away from him. Then it landed and perched itself right on my shoulder. I could taste the bile rising in my mouth as I realized that Kristina had already found my Achilles' heel.

He calmly contemplated the amber bottle of pills on the table before him. He picked up the container and caressed it with his right hand before carefully flipping off the lid revealing the small round pills that promised him a final release if he chose to take it.

CHAPTER TWELVE

NEAR MIDNIGHT, RICK CAME to wake me. He and Claire had been sitting with Gary who had not wakened since we talked to him earlier. Rick called the doctor when he couldn't rouse Gary for his evening meds. He also hadn't had to change his sheets all day nor had Gary used the bedpan. The doctor informed Rick that most likely Gary had slipped into a coma. He doubted that he would ever regain consciousness. He told Rick that Gary's body was beginning to shut down. He also told Rick what we could expect to occur in the next few days or hours, however long it took Gary to let go.

After Rick explained everything to me, my mind went back over our life together and as always, I wondered if I could have helped Gary more. But then, I had my own troubles. Although I never faced my own feelings as well as I tried to help Gary face his.

I wanted to be published so badly that I didn't think about the consequences of getting that first book out in the market. I went ahead only slightly aware of the currents flowing and pulsating all around me, first with Kelsey, and then with Elizabeth.

Ernest Haslett liked the book but wanted to find a larger publishing house to handle it. He decided to represent me, for a small fee, and I was flattered that he thought that much of the book.

After Gary read the book, he handed it back to me.

"Do you think I need to change anything?" I asked him as he tried to avoid my eyes.

"No changes needed," he said. He didn't say anything more.

By late 1975, Kelsey had begun working even longer hours at Domino's. I didn't mind because when she was home, she harped about buying a house that would be closer to the new corporate headquarters now under construction. I liked the old house on Main Street just fine. She hated paying rent. I liked the lack of responsibility for maintenance. She hated not being able to take out walls and paint at whim. Some days when she talked about changing the interior of our apartment, I felt I was back in high school dating Sally, my first girlfriend, or remodeling the house with Allison.

Then one night Kelsey met Allison, my first wife, for the first time. Domino's had just announced its intention to help Huron High School fund business classes in the coming school year, and we were invited to attend the reception where the formal partnership was announced.

Kelsey and I stood near the food table talking to several of her colleagues when I looked up and saw Allison enter. Since becoming principal, she wore tailored suits and silk blouses, and every time I had seen her in the last six years, a string of pearls adorned her neck. Very classic, very professional, and very elegant. Allison's cuteness and perkiness had been groomed into what her parents wanted her to be. She was a very handsome woman with an important job. However, I'm sure her parents wished she'd remarried after our divorce, if for no other reason than to change her last name from Townsend.

"Allison, hello. You look lovely as usual tonight," I said as I leaned down to kiss her cheek. We managed to remain cordial and warm with one another after the bitterness left.

"Ed, good to see you," she said as she looked over my shoulder at Kelsey.

"You've never met my wife, have you? Allison, this is Kelsey. Kelsey, Allison Townsend."

They shook hands and appraised one another.

"It is very nice to finally meet you, Kelsey."

"Same here. I thought you might be at this shindig since you're the big shot at HHS," Kelsey said as she popped a crab puff in her mouth.

"Yes, and you are an up-and-coming executive at Domino's, correct? I can't tell you how much your support will mean to our school. If you had anything to do with it, I thank you."

"It was really Tom Monahan's idea. You know, wanting to help young kids get a chance for job training. However, I sat in on the meetings and know how important it is. I especially want to encourage the girls to become involved so they can see that they really do have choices now in the work world. Just look at me," she said with a wide grin as she beat her fists on her chest.

Allison gave her a small smile, the Mona Lisa smile. No one can tell what she is thinking, but it can't be good. "We encourage all of our students to become the very best that they can be at Huron High. You will have to excuse me, I see some of my PTA parents over there, and I must greet them. It was a pleasure to have finally met Ed's new wife. And Ed, it is always a pleasure," she said squeezing my hand and reaching up to give me a quick brush with her lips. None of it escaped the glare of Kelsey's eyes.

"Sure thing, Allison. See ya around," Kelsey said.

That night Kelsey badgered me endlessly about Allison. She had never seemed too interested in my first marriage before this meeting. Somehow lying in bed with my second wife who wanted to talk about the woman I had divorced did not appeal to me or make me want to make love.

"What's wrong, Ed? Did seeing Allison make you less horny for me?" she asked when I couldn't seem to get aroused after all of her questions.

"No, but you talking about her endlessly has dampened my desires somewhat."

"I didn't expect her to be so, I don't know, so sophisticated, so suave, so polished."

"Someone like that would never marry me, right?"

"No, well, yes, I guess so. You are pretty unconcerned with those things. But you always manage to remain cool and calm in public so that no one would ever guess how miserable you are in a suit and tie."

"Please, can we go to sleep now? I've got a big day tomorrow." I pulled the covers up over my head so the discussion and the attempt at lovemaking would end for the night.

"What kind of car did you two have when you were married?" Kelsey began as soon as I sat down to breakfast the next morning.

"Who?"

"Who? How many times have you been married? You and Allison, of course. What kind of car did you have?"

"For god's sake, Kelsey, let it go. It's not important."

"It's important to me. What kind?"

"A Mercedes, an old one. A hand-me-down from her parents," I said not wanting to look directly at her.

"I see. What about the house? I know you lived somewhere on the old west side. Where?"

"Near Huron and Seventh. Behind those large Victorians."

"What kind of house?"

"It was an old colonial. There aren't very many over there, and her parents wanted to give us the house for a wedding present. It needed a lot of work, and we spent most of our short marriage redoing it. Allison still lives there." I decided to give her what she wanted so maybe she would stop. "How come you never asked these questions before?"

"Because your first marriage never seemed real to me until I met Allison. So if my parents were rich, would you let them buy us a house?"

"Never. I've told you, I don't want the responsibility of a house. And I'd never want you to hold it over my head that I couldn't afford to buy the house."

"But if you sell your book, you'll get a big advance, right?" She hadn't asked about the book in months.

"Not necessarily. I might get a small advance, but it's doubtful. The book won't make me rich."

"Or rather you don't want it to," she said thoughtfully.

"Possibly," I said.

Thankfully, the questions stopped there as I watched Kelsey slowly stir her coffee. I hoped she would forget all about Allison and a house. She worried me lately as I watched her changing before my eyes from the young college girl who cared about causes into the successful executive who cared about the outward trappings of a seemingly prosperous life.

Allison and I had had very little contact with each other since our divorce even though we lived in the same town and worked in the same profession. However, our orbits circled around different planets. Allison cultivated and fertilized her relationships with the business community with the help of her father. Probably the connection with Domino's came from one such cultivation with Tom Monahan. Kelsey and I, on the other hand, socialized with the art community and our friends from work, hardly the same social path as my ex-wife.

However, Allison and I did keep in touch. One of us would call the other once or twice a year just to check on one another. For some reason, I never told Kelsey about these calls. It never seemed very important to our marriage.

The day after the awkward meeting, Allison called me at school and asked me to stop by the house on my way home from work, even though it was slightly out of the way. She wanted to show me something.

When I arrived, she had already changed from the business suit attire of her workday into jeans and a sweater. She looked young and perky once again, like the Allison of fifteen years before.

"Would you like a drink, Ed? I just opened this bottle of wine," she said.

"Sure, Ally, that sounds fine."

We sat on the couch that we had purchased together in our only year of marriage, probably the first major purchase we had made. We sipped our wine quietly slipping back into an old comfortable feeling.

"Thanks for coming over. When I saw you last night, I realized how much I've missed you and these quiet moments," Allison said.

"I've missed them, too," and when I said it, I realized that it was true. We had been together for a long time. I looked at her shiny hair and gave it a slight pat.

"What happened to us, Eddie?" She looked at me with tears forming in her large brown eyes.

"Oh, Ally, who knows?" I said pulling her close to my chest.

She began tentatively kissing my neck, and I was astounded by the intense pleasure of her lips against my skin. I lifted her face to mine, and we kissed for one long languorous moment. I forgot about everything, except wondering about how far away the bedroom was or whether Allison would agree to making love on the couch unlike during our marriage. I definitely forgot about our divorce and about Kelsey in this moment of intense rediscovery of my lost lover.

"Ed, oh, Ed," she whispered over and over again in my ear when our lips finally stopped their journey down memory lane.

I pulled the sweater over her head and looked at her small yet firm breasts still encased in their white bra that I managed to remove quicker than I'd ever done anything in my life.

"Ally, is this all right? I've missed you so much." I was overwhelmed at the sight and smell of her and wanted to possess her completely now.

"Hurry, please hurry," she said in answer as she began unbuttoning and unzipping the clothes still covering me.

When we finished, we lay back down together on the couch and tried to regain our breath. I pulled the afghan that rested on the back of the couch over our bodies so we could lie there peacefully reveling in the beauty and calm afterglow of spontaneous sex.

"What about Kelsey?" Allison asked.

"What about her?" The first stab of guilt hit me.

"What will you tell her? How will you tell her?"

"Tell her? Tell her what?" I didn't understand what she meant.

"Tell her about us. You two don't belong together. That was painfully obvious last night. You can't go on living with her now that we've rediscovered each other." She faltered when she looked at my face that must have registered disbelief.

"Ally, this was wonderful, but it doesn't change anything," I said.

Immediately, Allison got up and began pulling on her jeans and sweater. She became the steel trap of yesterday, cool and reserved.

"You better go, Ed," she said as she threw my clothes on top of me.

"Come on, Ally, you couldn't have believed that I'd leave Kelsey and move back here?" I asked.

"Just go, please," she said as she walked up the stairs. "Just tell me one thing, Ed. Did you ever cheat on me like you just did on Kelsey?" Then she started up the stairs again not waiting for my reply.

She wouldn't have believed me if I had told her the truth. I had never even contemplated adultery. Today had been the first time, and it was totally unexpected and unplanned on my part. I didn't feel particularly bad about it except for hurting Allison and the potential of hurting Kelsey if she ever found out. What Allison and I had done seemed quite natural. I saw it as a spiritual meeting of two people who had once loved each other very much. I couldn't understand why Allison didn't view it in the same way.

I headed home grateful for the several hours I had to recover before Kelsey came home. She usually worked until seven or eight at the office. We rarely even ate dinner together anymore.

When I pulled in the driveway, I saw Elizabeth's car parked out front. When I got out of my car, she opened her driver's door and yelled over to me.

"Ed, can we talk?"

"Sure, come on in, Elizabeth. Good to see you," I said as we hugged in the front yard.

"How's Gary?" I asked.

"Fine. Can we just go inside, please?" She seemed on edge, and I quickly unlocked the front door and led her into the living room.

"Would you like some coffee or tea?" I asked.

"Yes, if it's not too much trouble, a cup of tea, perhaps?"

"Sure, come on into the kitchen, and we can talk there, OK?"

I began measuring water and placing cups on the counter. I looked around for some cookies or something in the cupboards to put out. I realized that Kelsey and I rarely ate at home and so our cupboards were nearly bare. Luckily, I found some tea bags.

"What's up, Elizabeth?" I asked as I put two steaming cups on the table.

"I was hoping you would know," she said, and then the tears began. She took a long time to control herself, and I felt a certain sense of dread and déjà vu at what I might hear next.

"It's Gary," she said. "He's changed in the last few months," and she began crying all over again.

"It's OK, Elizabeth, take your time." I patted her hand sympathetically, and she looked at me gratefully as she tried to regain her composure.

"Thanks, Ed, I knew you'd understand. You always seem to know just what to do and say."

I only knew what to do because I had done it before. I had known Gary all my life, and now I was comforting his second wife and hoping against all odds that Gary hadn't done something stupid.

"Has something happened?" I asked.

"No, that's the problem. Nothing happens, especially in our bedroom."

Once she began, there was no stopping her. I had heard it all before but this time from a completely different type of woman, but the scenes were the same. No sex, no communication, late night business meetings, and a general uneasiness in Gary's demeanor.

"I think he's having an affair," she said when she finished relating the litany of his distant behavior. The tears began once again.

When Elizabeth had finally spent herself with the saga of Gary, I sent her home with a half-hearted promise that I would speak to her husband.

"You're the only one he ever listens to," she said before she headed off into the night.

Then he must not listen to anyone at all, I thought. I knew that talking to Gary would be futile, but I also knew because of my strong bond with him, I would make the attempt. However, right now, the day had taken its toll, and it wasn't even 9 p.m. The icing on the cake would be a call from Pam.

I poured myself a scotch and went into the dark living room to sit and contemplate the events of the last five hours. I also wondered where Kelsey could be. She was much later than usual. She hadn't called, at least not since I had been home, and she almost always let me know when she would be working late.

I poured another scotch and thought of Allison and how she looked when I had removed her sweater. Soon another one obliterated that picture. I saw her icy glare as she stood on the stairs and asked me about cheating on her. Then I thought of Elizabeth and her suspicions about her husband. She was probably right; Gary probably had started having an affair or at least gone back to his old ways to try and ease his pain. Elizabeth never thought of any other possibility than Gary spending time with other women on his evenings away from her.

I heard the front door open and the sound of someone tripping as Kelsey banged into the narrow walls of the hallway of our apartment. When she appeared in the doorway of the living room, I could tell she'd been drinking.

"Hi, honey, sorry I didn't call. Last minute happy hour, you know, all the guys from work. How come you're sitting here in the dark?" she asked as she proceeded to turn on the lights, disrupting my solitude.

"Rough day, I guess." I saluted her with my empty glass. "I better catch up with you," I said as I went to refill it.

"We went to the Holiday Inn, and you know they just put in a new disco there. The DJ's great. Lots of fun. Maybe next time you'll go?"

"Maybe. Who was there?"

"You know, the usual, Greg, Sue, and some other folks you don't know," she said. Then she sobered up and looked at me seriously. "Ed, I need to ask you something. Would you at least come with me to look at those houses on the north side of town?"

"Sure, Kelsey, sure," I said.

"Really, you will? You'll love them; just wait and see."

I looked at her skeptically and noticed that her blouse wasn't buttoned correctly, and her hair looked messy. From an emotional distance caused by the day's events, I realized I didn't even care enough to question her story. Now she looked at me with a wide grin, and I wondered what happened to the young woman who gave me coffee during a rainstorm while bread rose and baked in the co-op bakery three years ago. Where had she gone?

Pam didn't call that night, thankfully. I woke up the next morning with a hangover barely in time to make it for my first period class. The dull ache behind my eyes throughout the day prevented me from thinking about all that had happened in the last twenty-four hours.

Even though I didn't want to go back to Allison, the encounter with her had opened my eyes about something. I no longer felt the same way about Kelsey. At some point, I think I stopped loving her. I didn't share her vision for our future. I couldn't even see us together in any future life. I didn't know what to do about it.

Not only did I know that my marriage was headed for the brink of disaster, but I was certain after my talk with Elizabeth that her marriage was about to catapult over the edge much sooner than my own. I decided to wait until the weekend before contacting Gary.

I called him Saturday morning and suggested that we go out for lunch sometime soon. He wanted to go to a favorite bar in downtown Ann Arbor that he liked for its low lights and mellow jazz on Sunday afternoons. He said he needed to go over and visit his parents anyway, and he might as well do both on Sunday. I felt a pang of guilt because I hadn't visited my parents in a while either. When I told him, he suggested that we get them all together at his folks' house for Sunday dinner. Then he and I could go down to the

Del Rio later in the day. He said he would make all of the arrangements.

Neither one of us mentioned bringing our wives. I didn't even mention my plans for the day to Kelsey until I started to get ready.

"What's up today?" she asked when she saw that I was changing into my khakis and blue shirt, my Sunday best.

"Gary and I are having dinner with our folks and then going out to the Del Rio later. We haven't seen each other in a while."

"How come you didn't tell me? I made other plans for the day."

"I didn't think you'd want to come, I guess. Sorry, Kelsey, I didn't think of it."

"You've been doing a lot of that lately," she said as she turned away from me.

The first thing I noticed when I arrived at Claire's and Philip's house was my father's condition. He had never looked very well or strong since my childhood, but now he was hunched over more than ever and coughed uncontrollably at times. His color resembled that of a jellyfish left out in the sun for too long.

"What's going on with Dad?" I asked my mother when we had a moment alone.

"I don't know. He won't go to the doctor. He says they'll just tell him to stop smoking and drinking, and he says no quack is going to make him do that. You know how he is."

"He needs to do something. Aren't you worried?"

"I've resigned myself. He's supposed to retire next year, and I'm hoping I can convince him to move to Florida. Maybe if he's away from some of his cronies, he'll stop those habits that are killing him."

I watched my father as he sat in the living room with his brother Philip who looked twenty years younger instead of two. Even Aunt Susan, their older sister, looked years younger than my father. Maybe I should talk to him, I thought, but immediately I knew it would be futile. My father never listened to me, and worse, I suspected he didn't even like me very much. He didn't like anyone. His future looked bleaker than mine, and I couldn't imagine him living in Florida.

Aunt Susan came and sat next to me on the couch. I patted her hand and smiled at her with genuine affection. Of all the siblings, Aunt Susan had the sweetest and most sensitive personality.

"He doesn't look good does he, Ed?" she asked quietly inclining her head toward my father.

"No, but Mom says he won't go to the doctor. Can you say something to him? You seem to have the most influence."

"Neither of my brothers ever listen to me! But that's never stopped me before. I'll talk to him," she said.

When Gary and I finally extracted ourselves from the clutches of our mothers and Aunt Susan, we headed downtown. We had to wait a short while for a table at the Washington Street club. Once seated at a small table with a window, I glanced across the street and saw one or two long-time establishments and noticed a new jazz club and restaurant.

"The Flame Bar is still there, I see," I said without thinking about its clientele.

"Yes, indeed, and it's still the same," Gary said.

"You go there much?" I asked.

"I have, but there are better ones in Detroit. I've pretty much stopped going to the gay bars though. I'm afraid I might get recognized."

"So it's started again, Gar?" I asked.

"Yep, Cuz, it's started again. Your book helped me realize some things, but I just didn't know how to tell you."

"And you and Elizabeth?"

"Now that's a problem. You know, I really love her in a way. It's not like with Pam who I learned to despise. Elizabeth's sweet and kind."

"And you are destroying her," I added.

"What? Did you talk to her?"

"She came to visit the other night. She thinks you're having an affair. I tried to calm her down, but she's really hurt and confused. What are you going to do?"

"I need to end it. She's not so far off base. I am having an affair. A love affair," he said like a teenager confessing a crush.

"I don't know whether to say congratulations or not under the circumstances. First, talk to Elizabeth. Tell her whatever you need to tell her, but don't let her suffer anymore."

Gary promised me that he would deal with his marriage. Then he would introduce me to his new friend. We even managed to relax and enjoy ourselves, even though my marriage woes still hung over my head. I didn't want to burden Gary with anything more on this afternoon when we seemed to have connected once again.

My parents never made it to Florida together. Soon after Thanksgiving, my mother called to tell me that my father collapsed at work and was in the hospital. They were running tests. She warned me that it didn't look good because he was spitting up blood.

It wasn't good news. My father had inoperable lung cancer. By the time the doctors found it, it had spread to all areas of the lungs. They gave him three months at the most to live. I spent long hours at the hospital with my mother and Aunt Susan who was a rock during those weeks. Gary came occasionally and so did Philip and Claire, but mostly it was my mother, Susan, and I. Kelsey came whenever it was convenient.

My father died on New Year's Day 1976 without his family by his side. We had all spent the night with him because the doctors advised us that the end was near. When he had made it through to the new year, we went home for showers and a nap, planning to come back mid-day. I took my mother back to the house in Ypsilanti where we both had just laid down for a quick nap when the hospital called to tell us he had died shortly after we'd left.

The funeral was held on a bleak January day. Kelsey, Aunt Susan, and I rode with my mother in the limousine behind the hearse on the way to the cemetery. My mother looked out the window, and I kept my arm around her shoulders.

"I guess I'll go to Florida now," she said.

"I think that's a good idea, Mom. Claire and Philip are thinking about moving there this year, too."

"Yes, I think I'll go with them," she said.

"Live with them?"

"No, but they're going to buy a house in this new community. Claire tells me there are apartments there, too. I'd at least have family nearby."

"And as soon as the school year ends, I'm going to move there, too." Aunt Susan interjected lightly. "Forty years of teaching music to fifth graders is enough for anyone, don't you think?"

"I guess I know where I'll be taking my vacations from now on," I said, but Kelsey looked at me sharply noticing that I hadn't said "we."

Kelsey and I walked side-by-side to the gravesite not touching or talking. When it was all over, she touched my sleeve.

"Ed, we need to talk."

"I know. When we get back to the house, let's take a walk."

And so on the day that my father was buried, Kelsey and I made plans for the future.

"Ed, there's someone else," she said as we walked through the neighborhood.

She looked at me. I stared back waiting for her to say it. I didn't want to make it easy for her.

"Greg, at work. We're in love," she said.

"Greg," I repeated. "I guess I should have known."

"I'm sorry, Ed. I really did love you at one time. And I still think of you as a good friend."

"You know, it's strange, Kelsey, but that's exactly how I feel about you. I'm not sure when it happened, but at some point I stopped loving you, too. But it's OK, isn't it?"

"Yes, Eddie, it's OK."

As our marriage took its final gasps, we sadly hugged one another on this day of endings and beginnings.

In another place, at the same time, on the same day, Elizabeth and Gary also decided to part ways. Even though my father's life had held disappointment for himself and those around him, in his death others found the strength to change their lives for the better. I took comfort in the fact that at least some meaning might come from his death, even though in his life he never sought to understand those closest to him.

I slowly rose from my bed to get dressed. I would not let Gary die alone like my father. He would have those who loved him the most near him as we tried to make his passage from this world a safe one. After a lifetime of suffering, it was the least he deserved.

"Where's Claire?" I asked Rick when I passed him in the hallway on my way to Gary's room.

"Sitting by his bed. She won't leave him now. His breathing has already started to change. There's a rattle," he said.

"Let's go. From now on, we should always stay there with Claire, I think."

"I agree," Rick said.

We remained with Gary for the rest of the night. It was excruciating to sit in that room. We waited after each loud breath for the next one, dreading it, yet hoping it would come. As the night wore on, the breathing became more irregular.

Finally, around dawn with the new day emerging outside the shaded window of the bedroom, Gary took one last gasp of air, but he never let it out. He had gone from us, just as the night had slipped away, with little fanfare.

The first cry came from Rick who began rocking back and forth in his chair next to the bed. Claire had positioned herself on the other side standing near the head of the bed resting her cheek on Gary's forehead as he breathed for the last time. The tears slid down her face as I went to stand next to her, trying not to let the sob escape from my throat. We stood motionless for an eternity each thinking our private thoughts of the man who could finally rest in peace in a place where demons no longer tortured young men, where fathers cared, and where acceptance came as naturally as living on this earth.

Falling, falling, falling. Calm and peace surround the body as the soul escapes its prison. The living are left with the suffering. He watched wordlessly as the cloud lifted, growing lighter and lighter and finally leaving his soul.

CHAPTER THIRTEEN

AFTER GARY TOOK HIS last breath, Claire, Rick, and I sat for a long time in the room mourning the passage of this man we all loved. Claire was the first to break the silence.

"I need to call Kristina," Claire said as she pulled herself away from the lifeless form. She leaned down to kiss him on the forehead one last time. "What do we do now, Rick?" she asked.

"I've got all the numbers in the kitchen. Go call Kris. I'd like a few minutes alone with Gary to say good-bye."

We left him with his memories and the body that once held such a tormented soul. We went into the kitchen to distance ourselves from the very private ritual taking place in the bedroom.

"I suppose I should call Philip, too," Claire said. "I hope at least he'll come for the funeral.

Philip never did come to New Orleans. He didn't say much when Claire called, and he never asked about arrangements. Claire never told him. She said we'd be back in a few days. However, some surprising guests did attend. Both of Gary's ex-wives flew in for the funeral.

Elizabeth's presence I could understand. Gary and she parted amicably and still kept in touch during the holidays. Claire and she exchanged Christmas cards, and the whole family followed her career that had taken off since the divorce. She now hosted a daily talk show with a variety format.

I was concerned about Pam's decision to attend the funeral and hoped there wouldn't be any vicious scenes. Kristina seemed unconcerned, both about her father's death and her mother's arrival. On the morning of the funeral, Pam called me from her hotel.

"Ed, I'm here," she said.

"Hi, Pam," I said.

"Kris says the funeral is at two o'clock, right? I really just want to give Kris support. This isn't easy for her, you know. By the way, how were Gary's finances?"

"What do you want to know that for?"

"Just wondering. I suppose Kris inherits everything now. Gary did have a will, didn't he?"

"Pam, I don't want to talk about this right now. I'll see you at the funeral." Now I knew why she had come all the way from Las Vegas for the funeral of a man she despised and for a daughter she'd never really loved.

In addition to Gary's family and ex-wives, just a small cadre of friends who hadn't abandoned Gary when they found out he had AIDs, attended the funeral service. Pam looked old and worn. It was hard to believe that Gary, with his penchant for all things beautiful, had once been married to this woman. Elizabeth, as beautiful as ever, probably wondered the same thing when they were introduced. When she met Kristina, she attempted genuine affection, but Kristina would have none of it.

"So, you're the Miss America Gary married?" Kristina asked when Elizabeth attempted to hug her as she offered condolences.

"Yes, and you're the daughter he always loved," she said.

"This must be a shocker for you. I bet you didn't announce his death on your TV show, did you?"

"That would hardly be appropriate, now would it? It was nice to meet you finally, Kristina. And Pam, too, of course." She walked over to Claire leaving both mother and daughter in her dust as they made fun of her walk.

"Come on, you two. Stop it, she's a nice person, and she loved Gary," I said.

"Sorry, Ed. I forgot we were in the midst of a saint." Kristina knew she would hit me hard with that one.

"I'm not a saint, but I do have some respect for people, living and dead," I said before I walked away from them, too.

However, I couldn't avoid them for very long. They pounced on me as I finished thanking everyone for coming. I was also inviting all the guests back to the apartment for a drink. Gary was being cremated so there would be no cemetery scene.

"Ed, now that the funeral is over, when do we find out about the will so Kris can come home?" Pam said as I headed for my car. Kristina followed her.

"All right, I guess it would be better coming from me than from Rick since you're both so interested. Most of Gary's estate has been eaten up with his medical expenses. Anything left over will go to Rick."

"You're kidding, right?" Pam asked.

"No, Gary told Claire and me the day before he died. He said that Rick had stopped working to care for him. And besides he felt he had already given Kristina enough."

"That son of a bitch," was Pam's only response.

"That's rich, really rich. He gave it all away to that wimp," Kristina announced to the wind.

"He also asked Claire and me to help you understand." I gently touched Kristina's arm, hoping she would know that we really wanted to help her.

"Did he also tell you to keep your filthy paws off me?" With that, she flounced away, leaving Pam and I alone.

"What did she mean by that, Ed?" Pam asked.

"Not sure. Why don't you ask her? It was good to see you again after all these years, Pam, but I really think it would be better if you didn't come back to the apartment."

"Don't worry, Eddie, I wouldn't want to dirty the proceedings. Besides I've got some things to tell Kris." She walked away after her daughter, leaving me to wonder what things she would tell her. I also wondered whether Kristina would tell her about our encounter. With a heavy heart, I got in my car and drove back to the French Quarter.

As I pulled out of the funeral home parking lot, I thought about why Pam had come for Gary's funeral. She really thought that Gary would leave something for Kristina. She probably also hoped that Kristina would share with her. I examined my feelings carefully and found that I didn't really care anymore if Kristina told Pam about our one-time encounter. Nothing much mattered to me now that Gary was gone.

Elizabeth came back to the apartment, as did a few other close friends. We spent the rest of the afternoon swapping Gary stories and putting him to rest with dignity and respect. I saw the last of the guests out the door just as the sun set over the balcony.

"Are you ready to go back tomorrow, Claire?" I asked when the apartment was finally empty except for the three of us. "Will you be all right, Rick?"

"Sure, sure, you two go back. It's time we all got our lives back to normal."

When the phone rang, I picked up the nearest extension on the armoire in the living room.

"Ed, I wanted to apologize," Kristina said.

"For what?"

"I was ugly today, and I'm sorry. I don't want you to be mad at me. But I was pretty devastated. Here my dad dies only a few short years after I've found him, and then I find out he doesn't love me enough to leave me anything." She began to cry softly.

"Come on, Kristina, he loved you more than anyone, you know that. Leaving you money doesn't have anything to do with love. Kristina, your father loved you." I couldn't stand to hear her muffled sobs as she made a weak attempt at controlling herself. "Where are you?" I asked.

"At my apartment. I just took Pam to the airport after watching her get soused in the lounge," she said. "She was pretty angry about the will stuff. It just made things harder."

"Do you want to come over here? Your grandmother and I were just making plans to leave tomorrow."

"I'm too upset for Claire right now. Could you come over here for a little while?" she asked with a little girl plea in her voice. Without thinking, I told her that I would be right there.

"I'm going over to see Kristina. She's pretty upset. If I can get her calmed down, I'll bring her back with me," I told Rick and Claire as I headed for the door.

When I headed out into the New Orleans twilight, I noticed the thick pea soup fog had rolled in once again. I drove slowly through the quiet streets to Kristina.

When she let me in her apartment, I took in the red eyes and smeared mascara along with the big T-shirt. She wore nothing else. She hugged me as I walked through the door. She continued to cling to my neck as we walked to the couch.

"Oh, Eddie, I'm so miserable. Please just hold me," she whispered.

And so I held her and held her until she stopped crying. Then without much thought, I leaned down and kissed her. Before long, she was kissing me back and climbing into my lap and rubbing herself against me until I couldn't stand it any longer.

"Stop, Kristina, stop." I tried to pull her off me, but now she was pulling the T-shirt over her head, revealing her two perfectly rounded breasts waiting for my attention. "Kristina, put that back on," I said.

"Now, Ed, you really don't want me to do that, do you?" she asked as she licked her lips very slowly. "You don't really want to stop, now do you?" She raised herself up high enough to press one of her breasts against my lips.

As I eagerly reached for her, she continued softly encouraging me. "We need each other, Eddie. It's supposed to be this way. Don't stop now. I need to be loved tonight."

I couldn't argue; I couldn't even speak. How could I refuse to give her what she needed? She could actually make me believe that I was her savior. Only I could help save her from herself, I told myself when I most needed to justify my actions in my own mind.

I roughly shoved her off my lap onto the floor, and I buried myself in the sanctuary of her waiting body. I remembered to pull the condom out of my pocket this time, but I forgot everything else except finding a release for the both of us as we moved together.

I forgot my promise to Gary; I forgot my grief over his death; I forgot my familial

ties to this creature begging me to love her and fill the void deep within her soul. I forgot everything, except my need to fulfill her every desire, which, of course, perfectly coincided with mine. I forgot for a few bittersweet moments that I was only fooling myself if I thought I could ever satisfy the needs of this young woman in my arms. After Kristina and I finished making love, or whatever it's called when two people create a tornado of movement and feeling and cling to one another as if the passing storm would tear them apart at the limbs, I dozed on her couch.

Totally spent after the events of the past week, I fell into an immediate deep sleep. The release offered in the arms of Kristina left me even more exhausted. When I opened my eyes, Kristina walked into the living room with her suitcase.

"Where are you going?' I asked.

"With you, back to Florida," she said.

"Since when?"

"Since I called Claire when you were on your way over here. I told her I was having difficulty dealing with Gary's death, and I felt I needed to be with family. She invited me to come and stay with them for a few weeks."

"Kristina, I'm not sure that's such a good idea..."

"Why? Afraid you won't be able to keep your hands off me?" She smiled seductively. "Don't worry I wouldn't seduce you with my grandparents so near. I need them more than I need you." She flipped her long hair to her back and walked to the door.

"Ed, are you coming?"

Gary's demons may have been put to rest, but mine were just waking up, I thought to myself as the three of us drove down the flat and boring highway back to Ocala. Kristina chatted cheerfully with Claire through the entire trip.

"Ed, you're awfully quiet," Claire said several hours into our journey.

"I'm tired, Claire. And you two don't need my help talking," I turned to smile at her sitting in the passenger seat.

"Kris, what would you like to do in the next few weeks? We have lots of options, you know, like Disney World or Busch Gardens or Sea World?"

"I guess I'd like to go to the beach for one thing."

"Maybe Ed would take you to Daytona one day. Your grandfather and I don't get over there much, but Ed knows his way around. Couldn't you manage one day next week to take Kris to Daytona?" Claire asked me.

"I'll see, Claire. I'm going to be pretty busy. I planned on starting the new book, and then I've got to make some decisions about Mom."

"That's all right, Grandma. Busch Gardens would be fun. I don't want to intrude on Ed's life or be in the way," Kristina said.

"I'll try to find an afternoon, Kristina, I really will. But I'm pretty worried about Mom. Aunt Susan can't be expected to take care of her much longer," I said.

"I'm sure Philip looked in on her while you were gone," Claire said. "Have you thought about what you're going to do?"

"About Mom?" I asked. Claire nodded her head. "I'm not sure. I'm almost certain that I'll move to Ocala very soon. The doctor says it's probably Alzheimer's, and there's no telling when she might have a major setback. Right now, she can function, but her mind isn't totally there at times, as I'm sure you've noticed."

Then I told them both about finding her naked from the waist up on a chair in the kitchen. Claire sadly shook her head. Kristina sat quietly.

"I haven't wanted to overly alarm you, Ed, but she's been doing strange things like that for a while," Claire said. "One day we took her and Susan to the country club for lunch. They have the buffet set up in the center of the room, you know. We had made it back to our seats and no Marge. We looked up and saw her standing in the middle of the room with her filled plate looking so forlorn and lost. Philip went to her and she said, 'I forgot where I was.'"

"According to the doctor, it's going to be like that all the time at some point," I said. "I'm going to have to face the fact that I can't take care of her in that condition. But I don't think I'm ready to move her to a nursing home."

"No, but you might want to get her on a waiting list. There are only a few really good places, and then only a couple of those take Alzheimer's patients. Friends have told me that the waiting time can be up to a year."

"Ed, I'll go with you to look at those places next week, if you'd like," Kristina said.

"Thanks, both of you. That's probably a good idea."

When we arrived back in Ocala, Philip came out to greet us in the driveway. He acted as if we had all been away on a vacation instead of caring for Gary during his final days. I left the three of them with the luggage in the kitchen, then I headed over to Mom's and Susan's to check on them.

True to her word, Kristina only stayed two weeks. Her grandparents enjoyed her visit, and so did I. We spent one day at Daytona Beach, and then decided to take one of the ocean front suites for the night. When we weren't making love, it was almost like having Gary back with me. I managed to keep the guilt at bay as we learned more about one another. We never talked about the future except where it concerned my mother. By not examining our experience together in light of where our relationship might go, I could easily accept it for what it was. I felt the healing powers of the ocean and Kristina's need for me sooth the ache I had whenever I thought of Gary.

Kristina helped me enjoy some lighter moments when we went to Daytona. It felt good to laugh again especially when we had our picture taken in one of the small booths that line Daytona's boardwalk.

After long talks with Claire, Susan, and Kristina, I made some decisions about my mother. First, Claire and Philip invited Susan to move into their guest room. She gratefully accepted. Worry about her sister-in-law had been quietly eating away at my sensitive aunt. I decided for the time being to move into Susan's bedroom at the apartment. That way I could watch over Mom while I decided what would be the best thing for her. I hoped that my writing wouldn't suffer, but I also knew at this point that I really had no other options. Mom needed someone with her, and my schedule allowed me to be that person. I knew that either Claire or Susan would help when I needed them.

Kristina and I visited some of the Alzheimer's facilities in the area during her visit. Only one seemed to fit my concept of a place for my mother to live out her final days. I put her name on the waiting list.

Just one small occurrence during Kristina's visit toward the end of the stay haunted me. All of us, Philip, Claire, Mom, Kristina, Susan and I, sat in Claire's and Philip's living room one evening. Philip took great pride in his stock portfolio that he had set up with Merrill Lynch after his retirement. He kept the monthly statements in a three-ring binder next to his chair. Quite often sitting with them in the evenings, he would open up the notebook and look over the reports and then show me what had happened to particular stocks over the previous month. He had established a nice nest egg that he and Claire didn't really need at the present time. Philip's pension provided quite nicely for them since they had paid cash for the house. On this one particular night, Philip again pulled out the notebook and began explaining its contents to Kristina who sat at his feet listening intently.

"Wow, Grandpa, it's worth more than $200,000! What are you going to do with that?" she asked.

"I'm going to leave it for now and let it continue to grow. The potential for growth is greater if you just keep reinvesting, you know," he told her.

"That's a lot of money." Kristina's eyes moved up and down the page in front of her.

"You know, now that Gary is gone, this will all be yours one day. All yours," he told her with pride.

"Really? All mine? "

"After your grandmother and I are gone, you'll be the only one left," he said.

Kristina sat back against the chair and smiled between half-closed eyes, savoring the news that her grandfather had just given her.

Later in the kitchen, Claire handed me a beer.

"You know that's the first time he's mentioned Gary's death," she said. "And all because of money."

I took Kristina to the airport in Orlando for her flight back to New Orleans. At the departure gate, she turned to give me a long kiss.

"Ed, I love you. You know where I am if you want me."

"Kristina..."

"Wait, don't say it. I know. I'm too young, we're cousins, this is wrong. I don't believe that. I don't know how I would have survived the last few weeks without you, and I wouldn't care what anyone thought if you decided to come after me. None of those things matter. We could always go to Mexico and live."

"And you'd be happy with me for about two seconds." I kissed the top of her forehead and gave her one last hug. I wasn't sure what I had started by sleeping with Kristina, but I felt lighter as she walked toward her gate.

After Kristina went back to New Orleans, Claire told me that they had sent her off with a hefty check so she could begin taking classes at the community college.

I didn't hear from Kristina or anything about her until Claire and Philip told me just before Christmas that she had called and asked to come visit for the holidays. She asked Philip hesitantly, he said, because she didn't have any money for a ticket. She told Philip that Pam had been badgering her about money and coming to Las Vegas for the holidays. She just wanted to get away. He made plane reservations for her.

By Christmas 1989, I had moved to Ocala and into my mother's apartment. For the past year, her Alzheimer's seemed to level off, and she only had momentary spells of forgetfulness. However, I felt like my life was in limbo, waiting for something to happen.

When Kristina came to Ocala for that first Christmas after Gary's death, I decided to stay away from her as much as possible during her visit. I recently started dating a woman who I had met at a writer's conference in Daytona over the summer.

Cassie, a writing teacher at the local community college, was sweet and newly divorced and almost fifteen years younger than me. But she had been able to provide a balance of sorts for me. My mother was always calm when Cassie visited, and I found myself enjoying her quiet presence more and more. I didn't want Kristina disrupting anything I had established since my move to Ocala.

I worried what Kristina might say or do in her presence.

The last time Kristina and I had been together in Daytona we had grown close, and I wasn't sure if Kristina would be able to share me with someone else. As long as she had been back in the family, I remained single, until this visit.

However, I would not be able to avoid her completely. On Christmas Day, we all came together at Claire's and Philip's house, although Cassie went to visit her family in Deland. It didn't take the aunts long to tell Kristina about my new girlfriend.

"Isn't that nice. Tell me about her," Kristina said sweetly after Susan announced the news.

"Not much to tell. You'll meet her this week, I'm sure," I said.

"I can't wait."

Later when we had a moment alone in the kitchen, Kristina let her real feelings show.

"So, Cassie, huh? Is she as good as me? Can she do for you what I can do?" She stood very close to me as I reached into the refrigerator for a beer.

"Kristina, I refuse to answer that." I twisted the cap off the bottle and took a long swig.

"Have you forgotten me?" she asked as she reached for my face.

"I'd like to." I pushed her hand away.

"Ed, why are you being so mean to me? I just wondered why you started up with someone else when you know you love me?"

"Kristina, drop it. We can't be together. We only helped each other out when Gary died. That's it." I turned away from her and walked into the living room.

I managed to avoid seeing her for the next week. However, on New Year's Eve, Philip and Claire's club was holding a dance, and I had long ago purchased tickets from Claire. Cassie and I made plans to attend before Kristina mentioned her intentions to visit.

Claire told me that she was introducing Kristina to many of her friends and their single sons who also had come home for the holidays. I think the three of them attended every cocktail party and holiday happening since Kristina's arrival.

When Cassie and I entered the club, I saw Kristina immediately. She was hard to miss with her strapless black gown and shining diamond necklace and earrings that I recognized from Claire's collection. She would be difficult to ignore tonight.

"You look lovely, Kristina," I said as I bent to give her a cursory hug. "This is my friend, Cassie. Cassie, my cousin's kid, Kristina."

"She's hardly a kid, Ed, or haven't you looked at her lately? Nice to meet you, Kristina. Your grandparents speak of you often," Cassie said as she held out her hand in greeting.

"What? Cousin Ed hasn't been telling you all about me?" she asked teasingly with a twinkle in her eye reserved just for me.

"If you'll excuse us, Kris, I see Philip and Claire." I nodded formally to her as I placed my hand on Cassie's back to guide her away.

We spent the rest of the evening dancing and drinking, waiting for the magic moment of midnight to ring in the 1990s, the last decade of the century. I tried not to watch the spectacle Kristina was making of herself at the next table. Howard Mickle, Philip and Claire's neighbor, seemed quite taken with the young woman sitting next to him. Kris poured all of her attention on him. Howard, recently widowed, was the president of a large manufactured home company in Ocala. He was more than thirty years older than Kristina and hardly her type, but he lapped up the attention.

I saw Claire by the buffet table and decided to go and talk to her about Kristina's outrageous behavior.

"Hi, Ed, isn't this the most fantasticist party ever," she said.

"Sure is, Aunt Claire. Kristina looks lovely tonight. Did you lend her some jewelry?"

"I gave those to her. She stood to get them anyway, and I have so much. Besides they look a whole lot better on her at this stage of the game."

"She seems to be spending an awful lot of time with Howard," I said.

"Isn't she the sweetest thing! Howard has been so lonely since Helen died. Kris has been lovely to all of our friends. I think everyone, including Howard, is just a little bit in love with her."

So much for getting Claire to notice what was happening at the table next to us. When I returned to my seat, I glanced at Kris and noticed one of her hands under the table. Howard was leaning back in his chair looking enthralled with whatever she said or was doing underneath the tablecloth. As much as I detested what was happening, I also found myself quite jealous of Howard's position.

The next day Cassie and I ran into Kristina and Howard at the club's morning-after brunch. They sat very close to one another, and I even saw Kristina lean over and kiss his ear at one point.

I ran into Kristina at the buffet bar.

"Good morning, Ed."

"Kristina. Looks like you've made quite a friend there with old Howard.

"Howard's a sweetheart. And he's not afraid to be seen with me in public. Are you jealous yet?"

"Don't bother, Kristina. I'm quite content with Cassie." I walked back to the table as it dawned on me that Kristina's displays with Howard were for my benefit.

The following day Claire called to tell me that Kristina had abruptly left town. She said she needed to get back for school even though she had originally planned on staying for another week. Claire also mentioned in passing that Howard had just called her asking for Kris.

"You know when I told him that she had left to go home, he almost seemed angry. I guess he developed quite a crush on Kris. She was so sweet to him," she said.

Later in the day, I decided to pay a visit to Howard out of curiosity.

"Howard, can I come in for a second?" I asked when he opened the door.

"What is it, Ed? Do you have some information about Kris?" he asked.

"Only that she went back to New Orleans abruptly. Claire mentioned that you seemed upset about that," I said.

"I guess I foolishly thought that we had something going. I know she's too young, but she seemed to really need me." He stopped and looked at me. "It sounds crazy, but I thought she cared about me."

"What made you think that?" I asked, dreading his answer.

"She told me over and over again how much she needed me, for one thing. She practically begged me to take care of her."

"And did you?" I asked, fully aware of what his answer would be.

"You don't need the gory details. I feel like such a fool," he said.

"Because you let a beautiful young woman into your bed?" I asked as he looked at me sharply.

"Not just that."

"What else, Howard?"

He shook his head reluctant to say anything more.

"I know what Kristina is like. What else happened, Howard?"

"She kept talking about wanting to move here. She hinted at us living together. Now, of course, I would have married her. I couldn't just live with her. She seemed interested in starting a catering business. Told me that she had called around since she'd been here and felt there was a real market for something like that."

"And..." I prodded him to complete the story although I now had an inkling about where this was headed.

"This morning I wrote her a check for $5,000, the amount she said she would need to get started."

"And then she left town," I finished for him. I could have written the story. "Did you try stopping payment?"

"As soon as I talked to Claire. She'd already been to my bank and cashed it."

"Press charges, Howard. She stole that money."

"Never, Ed. I don't want anyone else to know about this. It's too humiliating. Promise me, you won't tell anyone," he said.

"I hate to see her use people like this. And I don't know how to stop her."

"Watch over Claire and Philip. That's the best you can do. Besides I doubt she'll be back here any time soon."

"OK, Howard, I'm awfully sorry. I wanted to warn you on New Year's Eve."

"It's all right, Ed. I wouldn't have listened. By then she had me under her spell. Besides she told me that you hated her, probably to ward off the possibility you might say something to me."

"She's persuasive, that's for sure. And maybe we've seen the last of her. I bet Claire and Philip sent her off with a nice check, too. Again, I'm sorry, Howard."

I went back to the apartment dejected. I felt Howard's pain because I had been in his shoes. I even broke a sacred promise to Gary because she said she needed me. I even believed, like Howard, that she required only me in this world to survive. Apparently, she needed a whole lot more than that.

Drowning, drowning, drowning. Keep awake. Don't give up the fight. Keep awake. Drowning, drowning, drowning...

CHAPTER FOURTEEN

THE ROCK AROUND MY neck carved with Kristina's name remained heavy for the next seven years. I could never break away from her. Each encounter with Kristina took me to the heights of passion and then dropped me right back down into a hell beyond imagining. The fog continued to envelop me.

No one suspected, of course. I was the anchor in the family. As soon as Gary died, everyone, including Philip, looked to me and sought my advice and help in all the decisions that make up the later years of someone's life. Taking care of Kristina also came with the territory, but no one had ever guessed at the depth of our duplicity over the years. All of them, even my wife, saw our relationship as a father and daughter who often fought and made up. There was nothing filial in Kristina's feelings or actions toward me. I very rarely felt paternal toward her. In the years after Gary's death, many changes occurred in my life although I never forgot about him. As time passed, I missed him more than ever.

Howard Mickle turned out to be right about us not hearing from Kristina for a

very long time. Claire and Philip both told me they had tried calling her at the apartment in New Orleans, but the phone had been disconnected. Claire called Rick who hadn't heard from Kris since the funeral. Neither Claire nor Philip wanted to call Pam. The task fell to me. I wanted to help ease their fears about Kristina. When I reached her, Pam told me Kristina moved back to Las Vegas and was enrolled at the community college. She wouldn't give me Kristina's number.

"She doesn't really want any contact with any of you," Pam said.

"Even with Philip and Claire?"

"That's right. Musta been one hell of a Christmas. She won't talk about it much, but she did have plenty of money when she got back, so they must have bankrolled her for a while," she said. "The Townsends love Kris, hate me."

"Pam, you made it difficult for them to like you, especially Claire. When Gary brought you home that first time you flirted openly with Claire's husband." I decided for once to tell Pam the truth. "And if I was able to catch you and Philip together in the garage, why not Claire? You obviously weren't that discreet."

"Eddie boy's showing some emotion! What did happen over Christmas? I can't get Kris to talk about it."

"All I'm going to say is that you've taught Kristina some pretty creative ways to get money out of people. Not all the money she returned with came from Claire and Philip."

"That's my kid. So you're paying her for it now? Funny, I never would have taken you for a fool."

"It wasn't me who gave her the money. She found someone else to fool."

"Ed, this is the best advice I can give you because you know out of all the Townsends you were the one who always treated me fairly. Don't let Kristina seduce you. She's got a bad habit of hurting those closest to her."

"And where did she learn that, Pam?"

"Good bye, Ed. I'll tell Kris that her grandparents want to hear from her, although I doubt it will do any good."

By early 1991, a room became available for my mother in the nursing home. It was a difficult thing to do, but fortunately, by the time her name came up on the waiting list, she no longer knew where she was. She did know me on some days, but mostly she lived in her own little world. At this point in her illness, the days when she didn't know me were the easiest. On the days of lucidity, her clarity of the situation made things much more difficult.

One day she looked me straight in the eyes and grabbed both of my wrists. "Ed, you must find a way to kill me."

"Mom, don't talk like that," I said, but I understood exactly what she meant, and I also knew that I would want the same thing to happen if I were in her shoes. It took every bit of strength I had to encourage her to live for my sake.

I know Mom always wanted a grandchild and envied Claire for having Kristina back in her life. I contemplated marrying Cassie on several occasions. I was forty-nine and Cassie was thirty-five. I knew she wanted to have children because she often talked about that old biological clock ticking away.

And so while my mother deteriorated further into her dementia, Cassie and I decided to get married. I knew we could have a happy and contented life with one another. My love for Cassie took me by surprise. I wasn't expecting it, and for a long time, I didn't realize that I did love her. However, her steady belief in me, and our mutual respect for one another lent itself to a much deeper passion than I'd ever had before. As long as I didn't think about Kristina, I could believe that I had found the one person I could live with for the rest of my life and remain satisfied. And she would remain satisfied with me.

Cassie never pushed me to be something I couldn't. In fact, she seemed content with her life and happy to move into an apartment as we started our marriage. Although we could afford to buy a house, I fought against the responsibility of owning a home. Scars run deep after a major incision, and mine had never totally healed after my divorce from Allison.

However, Cassie exuded a confidence of self that had been lacking in both of my previous wives whose quest for outward trappings kept me at a distance emotionally. And I began to trust her.

In June of 1991, I married for the third time, vowing to make it my last marriage. Again, Claire and Philip hosted the wedding in their backyard. I spent the day missing Gary more than I ever had. He wasn't there to do his job as my best man. Both Claire and I moped around before the ceremony. When Cassie realized why we both seemed so sad, she asked us questions about Gary, allowing us to miss him openly. Once we did that, we were able to smile at some of the memories and go forward with the day's events. Cassie seemed to know intuitively what both Claire and I were feeling on that day and did just the right thing to help us survive it.

We spent the summer in Europe, traveling around England and France. We both wrote, satisfied with our adventure and ourselves. By the time we came home in the fall, Cassie was pregnant.

Unfortunately, the person who I had wanted to present with a grandchild, no longer understood who I was. Mom's days of lucidity disappeared forever while we honeymooned and created. The new Marjorie Townsend little resembled my mother, which made it easier to accept that my mother died when the disease won.

Cassie and I were able to share our good news with the only family left on my side, Claire, Philip, and Susan. All of them now treated me like their son and acted as if we had given them a million bucks when we told them our news.

"That baby will be the bestest baby ever with you two for parents," Claire said.

"Your mother would be so pleased. I guess we'll just have to spoil that little baby twice as much," Susan said.

"That's right, old man, and I for one say it's about time you settled down. You sure didn't waste any time once you settled." Philip winked at me as he kissed Cassie on the cheek.

Claire and Philip, both in their eighties, remained active and healthy. Philip couldn't play eighteen holes any longer, but if he rented a cart, he could do nine holes with me. The club didn't invite him to play in tournaments anymore, but he still got out. However, Claire was unstoppable both at bridge and golf, although she also had to slow down some. They talked of selling the house but could afford to hire maintenance for the lawn and a maid for the inside. They really needed the house because of all of their visitors from the North. Philip's former students and athletes, now retired, still visited as well as their friends from Ann Arbor.

Kristina surfaced again near the holidays. She called Claire who invited her to fly to Florida for Christmas. Howard had since moved away to be nearer one of his children, and I imagine Kristina managed to wrangle that news somehow from Claire. I decided that Cassie and I would spend as much time as possible with Claire and Philip during her visit because I assumed she came for money.

Her first evening at her grandparents I called and asked if I could to come over to say hello, but Claire informed me that Kristina had requested a talk alone with them that evening. Claire invited us over the next day for drinks and then dinner at the club.

The following evening, Kristina, even more beautiful and voluptuous, kissed me in a sisterly manner.

"Cassie, you must be carrying twins. I can't believe how much weight you've gained. Are you due this month?" Kristina asked.

"I'm due in March, Kris, but thanks for your concern," Cassie said. "Ed tells me I'm beautiful with the glow of pregnancy, but I guess to someone who's never been pregnant, I just look fat. You look quite beautiful tonight, Kristina."

That's one of the reasons I loved Cassie. She never got flustered and could sweetly deflate a comment aimed at the heart by not allowing it to hit her. And just like her mother, Kristina knew how to make an enemy of a woman.

For my part, I tried to keep my eyes away from the front of Kristina's dress where her cleavage threatened to swallow me as she turned and bent in my direction. I desperately tried to keep my mind on my wife and the table's conversation.

When I went to the cloakroom at the club to retrieve our coats at the end of the evening, Kristina followed. When I turned around, she was standing so close to me that her breasts pressed into my suit.

"Kristina, I didn't see you there," I said.

"I think you've seen me all night, Eddie." She began rubbing up against me. "I've missed you so much. Can't we get together, just the two of us while I'm here?" Her voice had taken on the tone of the hurt little girl once again.

"I don't think that's a good idea, Kristina." I felt her hands grab me from behind as she pulled me towards her.

"Oh, come on, I can feel that you want to," she whispered. And she was right, my body had once again betrayed me.

"Please, Kristina. Stop," I said, but I made no movement to pull away from her clench. "I've got to go."

"Eddie, I need you. I've been so lonely. Please can't we see each other just once? Tomorrow?" She reached up and touched the side of my face.

I breathed in the smell of her and melted under her touch that always seemed to comfort me as well as arouse my sense of duty to protect this woman/child.

"Tomorrow," I said to appease her and get her to stop. I pulled away, trying to compose myself so I could go back to my wife.

I slept poorly that night. Cassie tossed and turned next to me getting up several times to use the bathroom. Once when she came back to bed, she noticed that my eyes were open.

"Can't sleep?" she asked.

"I guess I had too much to eat tonight," I said.

"Or you just got too much of an eyeful of Kris. I swear that girl flaunts herself so in front of whatever man is available."

"Kris? I didn't notice."

"Right, Ed. And I'm blind as well as pregnant. Good night."

My last thought before going to sleep was my vow not to be alone with Kristina ever again. I wouldn't call her the next day, I promised myself. However, when I woke up, I was aroused like I used to be in the mornings. I realized once I fell asleep, I dreamed of standing in the cloakroom and removing her dress and taking her right there. I went into the shower before Cassie woke.

After breakfast, Cassie left for a day of Christmas shopping with her sister. I had the place to myself, but the air felt close and stagnant around me. I found it difficult to breath and worse, I couldn't settle down to write, even though my current novel was coming together nicely.

Instead, I paced and kept thinking of making love with Kristina. Except with Kristina, it wasn't making love; it was an earthy almost primal act. I yearned to feel her pressed against me once again.

"Claire, it's Ed. I wondered if Kristina needed to do some Christmas shopping without her doting grandparents," I said when I finally gave in and called her.

"Just a minute, I'll get her," Claire said.

"Hi, Ed!" Kristina said when she came on the line.

"Be waiting in the driveway in ten minutes," I said.

We drove to a motel off the interstate near Wildwood. We had barely shut the door when we attacked one another. This had nothing to do with love, but a whole lot to do with sex.

Kris reached over and unzipped my pants before I could even shut the door. She put her mouth around me. I pushed her head down further, and for the first time I didn't try to stop her but encouraged her to do whatever she wanted with me.

"Why do you always make things so difficult, Ed?" she asked when she came up for air.

"Shut up," I said as I lifted the small T-shirt over her head and saw that she wore no bra. She pulled my hand to her thigh under the short skirt, and I could feel that she wore no underwear either. I pushed up the skirt and backed her up to the bed. She pulled a condom out of her skirt pocket and put it over me. Maybe she was learning something, but I didn't have time to think about that right now. I wasted no time in taking advantage of our protection.

Not many seconds later, I finished. Disgusted with myself, I zipped up my pants and told her to pull her shirt down. We hadn't even managed to undress all the way.

"You're not very nice today, Eddie,'" she said.

"I'm married. My wife's seven months pregnant. And you're almost thirty years younger than me. I wish you'd just go away," I said.

"We can't help this. It's out of our control. No one will ever know," she began whispering over and over again in my ear until she had lulled me back into a state of desire.

"It's OK, baby, it's OK. It's bigger than us, don't fight it." Her words and body and hands calmed me as I found myself aroused once again.

This time we went slower and undressed. She continued to lull me with her litany of reasons why what we were doing was all right.

When it was over, Kristina still clung to me and caressed me.

"Please, don't feel guilty, Ed. It's all right. It's just like with my mom and Philip," she said.

"What do you mean?" I asked.

"I know about them," she told me.

"So? What are you going to do about it?"

"Nothing. No sense in getting Claire upset. Although I've hinted to Philip about my mom before. He doesn't say much, but he always gives me what I want."

"So you just use him, don't you?"

"Sometimes. I think I deserve it, don't you? This family abandoned me when they allowed Pam to take me away. Do you have any idea what kind of mother she was?"

"She wasn't very nurturing, I'll admit. But she took care of you, and Gary really hurt her."

"She sure took care of me, all right. And I provided a good income for her and Oscar whenever a client blew into town who favored little girls," she said as she withdrew physically from me.

"You mean they prostituted you?"

"Is that what it's called? I thought it was child abuse. But yeah, when I was about ten, it happened for the first time. Then when I was around fourteen I got smarter and realized those men were paying Oscar, and I thought, *why shouldn't they pay me directly?* That's when I hit the streets. I've been hustling one way or another ever since."

"Kristina, I'm sorry, I had no idea. But why did you move back to Las Vegas?"

"It's all I really know. When Gary died, I didn't have anything in New Orleans. I'm trying to go straight though, but it hasn't been easy. Right after Gary died, Pam told me about Philip and mentioned how I could use their little affair to seal the inheritance deal. She thinks I'm going to share with her so she can leave Oscar."

"Will you help her?"

"It depends on how much she offers to help me."

"Sometimes I'd like to kill Oscar Timmons. He should be in jail."

"Probably, but Pam isn't much better. She's a whore herself."

"Kristina, I know it's not your fault; it's just what you were taught. I wish you could stop always working an angle. What's the hustle with me? What do you want from me?"

"No hustle. You're the only one who's decent."

"How can you say that? Look at me right now and tell my wife that I'm a decent guy. I don't feel so decent right now. Get dressed, Kristina, or we won't get to the mall for those Christmas presents."

"Ed, don't feel bad about this, really. You make me feel better, honest."

We held each other for a little longer before getting dressed and heading out to face the Christmas crowds at the mall.

But as I drove back to my apartment later that day, I couldn't help remember what she said about my decency. I always thought I was a decent, loyal person. But it seemed that Kristina always managed to find my weakness and bring me to a place where decency becomes the standard for derision.

My daughter, Tessa Marie Townsend, was born in March of 1992. Cassie had a long labor but never wavered in her determination to give birth to Tessa naturally. Claire and Philip were our first visitors, along with Aunt Susan, at the birthing center, even beating Cassie's parents. They brought a frilly little dress and a savings bond and good cheer. I was grateful to have some family to share my absolute joy at the miracle of tiny Tessa.

In fact, Claire and Philip became doting surrogate grandparents to our daughter. We even thought up nicknames for them for when Tessa began to talk. They would become Nomie and Boppa. Silly, but Claire loved them.

When I looked at Tessa sleeping or nursing, her main activities when we first brought her home, the turmoil within me since Christmas would subside, and I thought that everything would turn out all right after all. How could the world be anything but perfect when this delicate creature could be created? For the first time in my writing career, I wrote beautiful poetry to and about my daughter who quieted my demons and left me breathless. Once or twice, I wondered how Gary could have so easily allowed Pam to leave with Kristina.

When I finished my fourth novel, I decided to take some time off to cherish the joys of fatherhood. I was taken quite by surprise at my feelings for little Tessa. My love for Cassie deepened into something different, too. We now had a connection between us that made us related. I also wanted some time to digest the idea for my next novel. Everything I wrote seemed to have some basis in the reality of my life, and I didn't feel ready to write about my latest concept.

Claire and Philip heard from Kristina sporadically now. I listened attentively when they told me of her calls, and I worried more and more about her motives. I knew Philip had begun worrying, too. One day after I took him golfing at the club, we sat in the lounge enjoying our beers when Philip broached the subject.

"You know, Ed, I think I made a big mistake with Kristina," he said.

"What do you mean?"

"I never should have told her about the portfolio."

"Why?"

"You remember the night I showed it to her and told her it would all be hers one day?" I nodded. "Ever since then we've given quite a bit of that portfolio away to her. She seems to need an inordinate amount of money." He shook his head sadly.

"Could you say no?" I asked.

"I can't do that for my own private reasons. Neither can Claire for hers. It's that damn woman who Gary married that's caused this mess."

"Pam? How's it Pam's fault?"

"She always wanted something for nothing and was always asking for more. She calls me sometimes and reminds me about our affair. I'm certain she's coaching Kristina now to get this money out of us before we die. Claire and I may need this money if one of us ever has to go to a nursing home. Look at your mother, for instance."

It was true. My parents hadn't had a nest egg the size of Claire's and Philip's, but my father had plenty of life insurance through Ford Motor Company, and I invested it wisely after his death. However, the nursing home bills for my mother were eating through it too quickly. Her current nursing home required patients to be able to pay their own bills for at least two years before they became Medicaid patients. I hoped her money held out that long.

"Then I think you and Claire have to put your foot down with Kristina. Maybe put her on some sort of allowance that you think you can afford at this time."

"Maybe that would work. I don't know. I know I'm sorry I ever told her that it would one day be hers. That showed me, huh? I've always tried to impress everyone with what I owned, now I'm getting paid back." He drank the rest of his beer in one gulp.

This surprised me. Philip had never been one for soul searching or even honesty, especially when it came to himself, but it seemed he had come to some clear realizations about his life. Maybe there was hope for Kristina if even Philip could come to an understanding of himself.

Kristina called her grandparents in February and told them that she couldn't make it in college. She explained that she had decided too late to get a refund on the semester's tuition. And she was broke again looking for a job. Pam and Oscar refused to help. Her grandparents sent her $500 to pay for a month's expenses.

In March, she called to tell them about this great opportunity. She had just met a pilot who was starting his own pilot's school and would give her a break on the cost of lessons if she also did some PR work for him. She called Claire and Philip to tell him that she needed $3,000 to enroll, but at the end of the year, she would be a certified pilot able to fly small charter planes. They believed her and sent the money before telling me.

"That sounds almost too good to be true," I said after I had heard the whole story.

"Yes, isn't it wonderful? I knew Kristina just needed to find her niche and then everything would turn out all right," Claire said.

"I hope it works out for her, but I'm not certain you can become a pilot like that though. Must be quite a guy," I said trying desperately to keep the sarcasm at a non-detectable level.

Cassie heard it my sarcasm and looked at me sharply. "Is the money refundable if she decides this isn't for her?" she asked.

"I didn't ask, but I'm sure it will work out," Claire said.

Soon after this conversation, Philip told me at the country club about his fears concerning Kristina and Pam. They didn't hear from her again until the summer when once again she was out of a job. In addition to working for the pilot, she had been working at an upscale restaurant as hostess.

In July, Pam called Philip and told him that Kristina had broken her arm and needed money for her emergency room treatment, which cost $500. Oscar refused to pay for any more of Kristina's bills, and Pam didn't know where else to turn, she told Philip.

"How did she break her arm?" I asked when they told me they had just wired the money.

"She was walking to work and fell on the sidewalk," Claire said. Philip remained quiet at her side.

"She was walking down a street in Las Vegas in the summer and just fell and broke her arm," I repeated in an attempt to get Claire to realize that perfectly healthy young women in a sunny climate did not usually have these types of accidents.

"Yes, Ed, that's what I said. Don't you believe it?" Claire asked. "Why would Pam lie about it?"

"I don't know, Claire. Honestly, I find it a little hard to believe," I said.

"But of course, that doesn't mean it didn't happen," Cassie interjected when Claire seemed hurt at my response.

"I'm sorry, Claire, I don't mean to upset you. But don't you think Kris asks you for an awful lot of money?" I asked, watching her face as she turned to Philip who remained passive at her side.

"I guess, but when she says she's in trouble I can't not help her," she said.

"No, you can't, I know. But just be careful. Maybe putting her on an allowance might help so you don't have to hear the constant pleas for money," I suggested. Philip evidently had never mentioned this possibility to her.

"Maybe, but then maybe we won't hear from her at all. We'll just wait and see," Claire said, and Philip shrugged his shoulders.

"By the way, how are the flying lessons coming along?" I asked. Cassie jabbed me with her elbow as we walked behind Claire and Philip into the living room.

"The man left town after a few weeks, and she's never heard from him again," Claire said.

"Claire, I hate to beat a dead horse, but don't you think the allowance thing might keep you from using up all of your money?" I asked as I sat on the ottoman at her feet. "I worry about you and Philip having enough if anything should ever happen."

"I know, Ed, and we'll think about it, OK? Now bring me the mostest beauteous baby in the world." She held out her arms for Tessa.

Later Philip thanked me for trying when I went outside to take a look at his riding lawn mower in the garage.

"She doesn't want to think that Kristina might be lying to us. It's difficult for her to accept," he said.

"I know, but you and I both know that little girl is not telling the truth most of the time when she's asking for money," I said. I decided to pull no punches with Philip.

"I know, and I think deep down Claire knows it, too. But Kristina is all she has left now that Gary's gone."

He had never mentioned Gary's name to me once since his death. I looked over at him and saw a very old man with regrets standing before me.

"We all miss Gary," I said.

"Yes, but no one else regrets their life with him like I do." He pulled the cover off the mower to show me his new machine.

The next time Kristina called her grandparents Claire answered the phone. This time she wanted to start school again and needed tuition money by the next week in order to enroll for the fall classes. Claire must have told her what I suggested because I received a call from Kristina right after their conversation.

"How dare you interfere with Claire and Philip," came the indictment as soon as I came on the line.

"Who is this?" But I knew the voice instantly because it filled me with dread.

"You know damn well who this is! What the hell do you mean telling them to *put me on an allowance*!" she said.

"I think it's a good idea, Kris. Your demands are eating up their money. And your stories are getting harder and harder to believe."

"It's my fucking money, you bastard!"

"No, not yet. That money is their nest egg. Do you know what that means? It means that if they need it for some reason in the future, they'll have enough money to take care of themselves. Nursing homes aren't cheap."

"What do you get out of this, choir boy?"

"Nothing. But I do know that they need the comfort of having that money. And I don't think an allowance is a bad idea."

"They want to give me $100 per month! I can't live on that!"

"Kris, they don't expect you to live on it. Have you ever held a job or are all your stories fabricated? They will provide you with a cushion so you'll have the cash ready for all of your little emergencies. You're supposed to save the allowance."

"All I have to say to you is this: If you think I can be bought off with a piddly $100 a month you're sadly mistaken." She breathed heavily into the phone for a moment. "Oh, Eddie, baby, how's that wife of yours? And that darling baby, Tecca, is it?"

"I won't be threatened by you, Kris. And my beautiful baby's name is Tessa, not that you care much."

" I care, believe me I care. But I am warning you, leave Claire and Philip alone. They told me that money would be all mine one day; don't you forget it. Or were you too busy chewing on my tits to remember? Gosh, maybe Claire and Philip would like to hear that story about how we got in the mood to buy their lovely Christmas presents."

"You're vulgar, Kris. And I've told you, I won't be threatened. You've invaded my life enough as it is. Having a child made me realize how wonderful and sacred certain things are in this life, and I intend to concentrate on those things and not be taken down by you."

"Back to sainthood, I see. Well, let me tell you one thing, Mr. Perfect. You can say that now with me 2,000 miles away. But if I was standing in front of you, rubbing up against you, you'd let me bring you down to your knees, guaranteed."

I slammed down the phone with her jeering laughter echoing in my ears. I hoped I wouldn't have the opportunity to find out what I would do if I was faced with Kris once again. I had a sneaking suspicion that my resolve would be violently ripped from my soul as the demons hovered above my shoulders.

I also heard from Pam a day or two later.

"I wouldn't expect this from you, Ed. How could you talk Claire and Philip into this stupid idea? An allowance?" Pam asked.

"Kristina is eating away at their money. Philip got scared."

"Philip should be scared, that bastard. You need to watch yourself, Ed, because when you least expect it, your little escapades with my daughter may come back to haunt you."

She hung up the phone without giving me a chance to reply.

He pulled away from her grasp and flung her to the ground. As he turned to walk away, she grabbed his ankles tripping him and forcing him down on the ground next to her supine form. She curled her leg around his waist and held him there.

CHAPTER FIFTEEN

UNCLE PHILIP DIED ON the Fourth of July 1993 after playing a game of bridge at the country club. He won the bridge game that night and died just the way he wanted, peacefully in his sleep. When Aunt Claire woke the next morning, she tried to rouse him. When she couldn't, she called 911 and then me.

"I think he's gone, Ed," Claire said when I answered the phone.

"Who's gone?"

"Philip. I can't wake him."

"Have you called 911?"

"They're at the door now. Could you come over?"

I quickly dressed after telling Cassie what happened. I drove the short distance from my apartment to their house. The ambulance was slowly pulling away with no sirens or lights flashing.

Claire stood in the kitchen with her neighbor, Judy, and Aunt Susan.

"He's gone," she said.

"Claire, I'm sorry." I reached to embrace her, but she held out her arms to stop me. Rather than take her refusal as a rebuff, I knew she was just fighting to remain in control of her emotions.

"Don't, Ed. I'm fine. I know you're sorry."

"Will there be a service?" Judy asked.

"A small one at the church. He didn't want anything else. And quickly. We need to have it quickly."

"OK, Claire. I'll take care of everything. Which funeral home?" I asked.

"Carlton's. There's a card in the drawer. We just prepaid," she said.

"How about Kris? Have you called Kristina?" I asked.

"No. That poor kid. This will be a blow so close after Gary." She closed her eyes. I could tell she was fighting the tears pushing their way to the surface.

"Would you like me to call her?"

"Could you? I'm not sure what to say."

I hadn't seen or heard from Kristina since our last phone conversation, which ended so badly. We both had been angry that day, and I wondered if she would hang up on me now.

"I'd be happy to call her, Aunt Claire," I said as I gave her a small pat on the back, the only form of comfort she would allow.

I didn't bother checking the time or I might have waited before calling her at 4 a.m., Las Vegas time.

"Hullo," a groggy voice slurred.

"Is this Kris?"

"Yeah, who's this?"

"Kristina, this Ed, your cousin."

"What do you want?" She did not sound thrilled to hear from me.

"Philip died last night in his sleep. I told Claire I would call and give you the news."

"What's the will say?"

"The will? His body's not even at the funeral home yet. Why would we be worrying about the will?"

"OK, then, what about a service?"

"We haven't figured it all out yet. Claire mentioned just a small one at the church to be held as soon as possible."

"Is Grandma there? I'd like to talk to her."

I put the receiver down and went into the kitchen and motioned Claire to the phone in the study. I closed the door behind her and went back to the kitchen. In just a few minutes, Claire returned.

"I need to make plane reservations for Kris. Would you be able to pick her up in Orlando late this afternoon?"

"Kristina is coming?"

"Yes, she felt so bad, the poor kid. She wanted to be with me, but she couldn't afford the plane ticket, she told me. So, I said, 'Is that the only reason you can't get here?' When she said 'yes,' I told her I'd take care of everything. Can you pick her up?"

"Sure, Aunt Claire. I'm sure she'll be a great comfort to you."

I had my doubts about her reasons for coming, but I did know that Claire would appreciate her presence. Kristina knew how to pull not only wool but also the whole sheep over her grandmother's eyes. Luckily, I lived close enough to prevent Claire from going totally blind. I wondered who would protect me.

I tried to convince Cassie to come with me, but she didn't think it would be a good idea with Tessa who would be very restless on the two-hour drive. Plus, Cassie and I had just found out that she was pregnant again, and she felt a little queasy most days.

Reluctantly, I drove to Orlando that afternoon by myself to pick up a surly Kris. We didn't touch as we greeted one another when she walked off the plane. In fact, we never really even said hello. I did mention that the funeral would be the next day while we waited for her luggage to arrive on the carousel.

"What's she going to do with the house?" Kristina asked as we continued our vigil beside the slowly moving conveyor belt.

"She hasn't gotten that far, and don't bring it up yet. She needs a little time. Remember she's just lost someone she lived with for more than fifty years. Don't push her about decisions."

"How much is that house worth?"

"The Shores is one of the fastest growing country club communities in this area, so it's probably increased in value since they bought it. But I'm not sure she'll want to move."

"She may have to. How can she maintain a house all by herself?"

"Your grandmother will manage just fine. Philip left her in good shape financially."

Kristina looked at me sharply, but her luggage arrived at that precise moment. Our conversation would have to be delayed until the drive home.

Once we maneuvered out of the airport and settled on the highway heading back to Ocala, I attempted conversation with her once more.

"Why did you come, Kristina? Really?" I asked.

"Don't you think I should be here for my grandfather's funeral? After all, I'm entitled to inherit something. Don't you think I should get some of it now? That's what Pam thinks anyway. Gary never left me a dime, and Philip said it would be all mine some day."

I let my eyes leave the road for a second to look at the too-beautiful young woman who seemed to think the world owed her a living.

"You know most of Gary's money went to his care during those final months. It could have been worse. He could have left you with the medical bills. Besides Philip would never leave Claire unattended financially, even though he might have been a bit of a bastard during their marriage. Right now, we should be concentrating on helping Claire get through the next few difficult days."

"Whatever, Ed. You always know what's best, don't you?"

"Let's just get through these next few days, Kristina," I repeated. "I loved my uncle even if you just see his death as a way to make a little money. I'll forgive you that, if you'll just be kind to Claire this week. Don't let her see your greed."

"What about your greed, you asshole?"

"What do you mean?" I turned to look at her again. Suddenly her bad mood had jumped by degrees into anger.

"Your greed for me. Don't you remember, Eddie? You always want me. You probably want me right now. Shall we take the next exit and have a little go at it before we greet the family? I'll be especially happy to see your little wife. Claire tells me you've put another seed in that soil."

"You disgust me," I said. Her beauty seemed to curl up right before my eyes. If I'd had a pot of boiling water, I think I could have poured it on her at this point and watched her shrivel up.

"Maybe, but I bet you I could turn you around, just like that." She snapped her fingers.

"Kristina, can we call a truce for the next few days? I'm concerned about Claire, and I need my full concentration to take care of everyone. Let's not fight, OK?"

I turned to her, and once again, she changed. Her eyes filled with tears as she reached for my arm.

"I'm sorry, Ed. I don't know what gets into me. It's like I keep hearing Pam's voice in my head, telling me that the Townsends need to show me that they care. I think I care about you more than I even know. Forgive me, please," she said.

"It's OK. I care about you, too. Probably too much," I said.

"Can we stop for a burger or something? I haven't eaten since early this morning," she asked as we neared a turnpike station.

"Sure thing. I should have thought of that," I turned to smile at her, and she looked at me seductively between half-closed lids. My stomach turned.

When I pulled into the parking space next to the restaurant entrance, she came close to me, pressing against my arm.

"Eddie, I feel bad about Philip, too, you know. I just don't show it like you do. I'm not a nice person. I guess I don't know how to be one, not like you. Sometimes I think that maybe you'll rub off on me." She laughed as she began rubbing my neck.

"You haven't had very good teachers. I always feel guilty whenever I think of how you were raised, but you need to try harder. Quit trying to equate money with love for one thing. Enjoy Claire; she's the best grandmother around. She's always loved you from the moment she first saw you." I turned toward her and put my arm around her shoulders.

She turned her face upward to give me a kiss. At first, I started to protest, but then she began rubbing against me, and as usually happened, the sensation made me forget everything else. I began to return the kiss as I reached for one of her breasts and began working on the nipple until it hardened under my fingertips. Kris pulled back and began breathing between her teeth.

"You could call and say the plane was late," she said.

"Kristina, we can't, really," I said.

"You want me, don't you? You can tell I want you." She reached for the front of my pants and found the answer to her question as she touched me.

I went to a pay phone and called Claire. I told her the plane was delayed by two hours. Then we drove to the nearest motel and completed what we began in the car.

Slowly, I removed her clothes and picked her up and placed her carefully on the bed. She reached up and caressed by cheek.

"I love you, Eddie. Please love me," she said as I quickly removed my shirt and pants.

"Please take care of me; we're meant to be together like this, Eddie, don't feel guilty," she said as I buried my head in her breasts and cried for the pain and joy, overwhelming me. I cried for Gary and for the guilt consuming me. Kristina held me close and murmured soothingly in my ear.

I made sweet and slow love to Kristina on that afternoon as I forgot the rest of the world. She did whatever I wanted as she told me repeatedly how much she loved me.

"You love me, too, don't you, Eddie?"

"Yes, for chrissakes, I love you. What more do you want from me," I finally screamed. I had given my all to this woman who had etched herself into my very soul.

Kristina never did get her burger, but we both came away from the session satiated and satisfied as if we'd just gotten up from a Thanksgiving feast. We smiled at one another slowly as we got back in the car. Before I started the engine, I reached over and gave her a deep and loving kiss, and then I held her face between my hands and looked intently into the blue eyes that I knew so well.

"Kristina, it can't happen again, you know," I said.

"OK, Ed, whatever you say," she said. "Just remember that I love you no matter what happens. And I know just as well that you love me, no matter how you act in front of the others." She kissed me one last time before I pulled out of the motel parking lot.

Only when I began the familiar drive north on I-75 toward Ocala and the grieving Claire and my pregnant wife, did the feeling of fullness turn to nausea at what had happened on the afternoon of Philip's death.

Somehow, I managed to get through the rest of the day and the funeral without incident. I concentrated on Claire who had just lost her husband, and Cassie who wasn't feeling very well throughout most of the ordeal. I also watched Kristina who seemed to enjoy the attention from all of the neighbors. They saw her as a sweet young girl who was comforting her grandmother. The two made a sad picture, the daughter and granddaughter and the wife and mother who had both lost the important men in their lives.

As a result, nearly everyone at the funeral said something to me about the burdens I would now face in helping both Claire and Kristina. Little did they know that those burdens had been dumped there even before Gary's death.

Late in the afternoon the phone rang. Since I was the closest, I ended up answering it.

"Hello, I would like to speak to Kris Timmons, please," the voice on the other end said.

"Pam, is that you?"

"Ed? How's sainthood these days? Talking Claire out of giving Kris any more of what is rightly hers?" Pam and I had not talked since Kristina was put on an allowance.

"I'm fine, thanks for asking. Philip's death came as a great shock to all of us. Let me get Kris."

Kristina grimaced when I told her who wanted to speak to her on the phone. I gave her a comforting pat on the shoulder, and she looked at me gratefully. After a moment's hesitation, she headed to the hallway extension. I never found out exactly what Pam wanted, but from Kristina's unhappy face after her return, I surmised that she didn't give her any comfort.

That night after all of the guests left, Claire asked if Cassie and I could stay for a few minutes more. After a quick call to Tessa's babysitter, we sat in the living room, just the four of us, alone for the first time during the visit. Aunt Susan, exhausted by the day's events had gone to bed already.

"How are you, Claire?" Cassie asked, always solicitous of Claire's well-being. The two women had become close over the course of our marriage, and I knew Claire could confide in Cassie the things she couldn't with me.

"I'm tired. And I'm wondering what happens next," she said. She sounded like a lost and confused child, not a condition I'd ever seen her in before.

"Do you want to move from this house?" I asked.

"No, but I don't know what else to do. I certainly can't handle all of the upkeep and worry that comes with a home. Judy, from next door, told me today about some new apartments a few miles from here. But an apartment? I just don't know." She looked at me for help.

"What about Susan? Have you discussed this with her?" Cassie asked.

"I think you should just sell this thing," Kristina said, not giving Claire a chance to respond to Cassie's question.

"It's not as easy as all that," Claire said, as she patted Kristina's hand.

"Sure, it is. I bet you'd get a mint out of this house. Look at how this area has grown," Kristina said. "My mom thinks that you could get a good price on this house and then invest the money. The rent on an apartment would be covered by pension and social security."

"I'm sure your mother is very concerned, but the money is the least of my concerns right now," Claire said.

"I know, but you should care about it. That money could be added to the portfolio."

"Kristina, I don't think Claire cares about that right now," I said. "Claire, do you have any ideas?"

"I did think of one thing." She hesitated.

"And?" I asked.

"Have you and Cassie ever thought about giving up the apartment and moving into a house?" she asked.

Actually, this subject was a sore spot for Cassie and me. We'd been fighting about it ever since we found out about the new baby. She wanted to move into a bigger place, preferably a house with a yard. I was dragging my feet out of a reluctance to make any changes with our life. Although in the last few days, the idea had begun to hold some appeal, especially when I wondered how we could add a nursery to the already crowded apartment.

"Funny you should mention it. We've been talking about it. But we haven't made any decisions. Why?" I asked.

"You know this house is big enough for all of us. There's three bedrooms, plus the study. I could move out of the master bedroom, and we could easily take that porch that's off the master bedroom and turn it into another room, maybe a nursery. That would still leave a room for Tessa and a study for you, Ed." She paused to take a breath and to look at us. She obviously had been thinking about this since Philip's death.

"Claire, we couldn't do that," Cassie said. "You wouldn't want a toddler and a new baby cluttering up your space."

"That's right, Grandma. That would be an even bigger burden than just worrying about this house. I'm sure Ed and Cassie wouldn't even consider it," Kristina said.

"I would love having Tessa and the new baby right here under my nose to spoil. It would give me a reason to live. I discussed it with Susan, of course. She feels the same way that I do."

"You know, it's not such a bad idea," I finally said warming to the idea. I loved their house with its open rooms and large sliders in each room leading to a porch that extended for the length of the house. It could easily be expanded. "Of course, we'd pay rent."

"With an option to buy, at a very good price?" Claire asked.

"With an option to buy, and we'd pay for the addition. You know we could even expand one of the bedrooms so you'd have a little sitting room, Claire."

"Ed, are you saying you like the idea?" Cassie asked.

"Yes, I think I am. This could solve everyone's problems."

"Right, it'll be just like *Little House on the Prairie*," Kristina said as she skulked away into the kitchen.

I followed her and watched as she pulled a beer out of the refrigerator.

"What's the matter, Kristina?"

"Nothing, Eddie, nothing at all. I just thought things would be different after the other day." She looked at me sadly.

"Nothing changed, Kristina. I know how you feel, and you know how I feel, but I still have a wife and family. Anything else is impossible."

"I know, Ed, but a girl can hope, can't she?" Then she lifted the beer bottle to her lips and guzzled the amber liquid until it was all gone.

After I went back to the living room, we spent the rest of the evening making plans. We decided we wouldn't move in until the addition of a nursery was complete, which would hopefully occur before the birth of our second child.

The next day when I drove her to the airport, Kristina made sure she let me know what she thought of the idea.

"You're moving in on my territory, aren't you, Eddie, boy," she said as we sped along I-75. "Pam's been warning me for years, but I always defended you and said that you wanted the best for me."

"What territory am I moving in on?"

"Don't play so innocent with me. You know that you'll be able to control Claire's finances living so close to her. And I bet the first thing you do is cut my allowance."

"I wouldn't think of it. Claire is perfectly capable of handling her finances without my help. Kristina, this is a good thing for Claire. I'm sure she'll put our rent check back into the portfolio so you'll actually be coming out ahead."

"I'll be watching you very carefully. It's almost like you had this planned." She feigned sleep the rest of the way to the Orlando airport.

When we arrived, she told me not to bother seeing her off, so I dropped her off at the terminal. Before she got out of the car, she turned to me. "Claire will never leave you anything. She would never go against Philip's wishes."

"Kristina, please understand one thing. I don't want anything from Claire except for her to live long enough for my children to have a memory of a grandmother figure in their lives. I don't need the money, nor do I want it. It's yours when the time comes, but not before."

"You know you claim you're not greedy, and I guess you're not for money. But let's not forget what you are greedy for, shall we." With that, Kristina leaned over and grabbed me and gave me a long and lingering kiss, which left me stunned. I grabbed the back of her head and kissed her back with all of the pent-up passion I'd been feeling since the day at the motel.

"Don't forget how I feel about you, but remember it won't matter if you start messing around with what is rightfully mine," she said when we'd finally managed to pull apart.

She gave me her mother's sardonic grin and then left the car, slamming the door behind her. I breathed a sigh of sadness and of relief as I watched her walk into the terminal to the plane that would remove her from my life for now.

When I got back to Ocala, I decided to stop by the house to check on Claire. She greeted me with an angry look on her face.

"Claire, what's wrong?" I asked as I came into the house.

"That woman just called," she said.

"What woman?"

"Pamela, Gary's first wife. She wanted to tell me how sorry she was about Philip. I hate that woman."

I had never seen Claire express hatred toward anyone. She could be sarcastic and cynical, but she liked everyone and treated people with respect.

"I imagine you blame her for causing this family lots of pain," I said.

"I didn't let on my feelings while I was on the phone, but my stomach was in a knot. I kept remembering how I took care of Kristina when Pam couldn't or wouldn't when Kris was a baby. I remember the anguish I felt all those years that Kristina was away. She caused damage to this family, especially to Kristina."

"What makes you say that now after all these years?"

"Not often, but occasionally Kris gets a tone in her voice, a look in her eye. Then I remember the times you and Gary warned us about her not always being what she seemed. So I know about her pain and scars, and I blame Pam for that."

"I'm glad you can see that, as unpleasant as it is. I see it too sometimes. But Kristina does realize that you've been the one constant in her life."

"I hope so. I decided to be cordial to Pam on the phone to get the conversation over. I kept thinking if I let her do this phony bit, then I won't have to talk to her again. She even had the nerve to bring up selling the house. It was enough that she put Kristina up to asking me about it, but she had to go ahead and mention it to me.

"I know Gary probably didn't treat her very well. I know that now, but I never liked the way she was with Philip. I couldn't ever put my finger on it, but it wasn't quite normal."

"It's over now," I said. "Shall we call around to some contractors tomorrow? My book seems to be dragging right now so a break might do it some good."

"Yes, let's do that. This will be so much fun, Ed. I can't tell you what this means to me. Are you sure that you and Cassie can put up with a mean old woman like me?"

"You bet, and the meaner the better, I always say. Tessa is going to love it here with the yard and two aunts to spoil her rotten."

We moved into the house by the beginning of 1994. Claire had an expanded room off one of the spare bedrooms, and we built another bedroom at the end of the house for Aunt Susan so she could have a little more privacy. Claire's addition was not quite completed when we moved, but since the baby was due any day, we decided to settle in even with the dust.

Our son, Gared was born in February. Claire and Cassie dreamed up the name as a combination of Gary's and my names. At first, I thought it was rather silly, but it began to grow on me as I looked down into the sleeping face of the new little Townsend.

I hoped for him a happier life than that of his partial namesake, and I prayed he wouldn't fall heir to my weaknesses and faults. Even though we hadn't heard much from Kristina in the past few months, she constantly nagged at the back of my consciousness as I fought to block visions of our encounters from my mind. I replayed the scene over and over in my mind when I finally screamed I loved her. She had reached down into the depths of me and pulled out my guts.

Gared helped ease some of my pain and helped me concentrate on important things like keeping Tessa from tossing him out of his crib while she adjusted to having a sibling.

He floated on top of the water for a long moment while he watched her tread water next to him. She began to sink under the surface, and he left his peaceful pose to swim frantically to where he last saw her go under. She grabbed at him in panic, nearly pulling them both underwater.

CHAPTER SIXTEEN

IT DIDN'T TAKE TESSA very long to realize that her brother would be here to stay. With Claire's help, we gave her plenty of attention while still bonding with Gared. Soon Tessa became just as protective as the rest of us of the new addition to the family.

At eighty-seven, Claire thrived while her peers began to fail. First, my mother succumbed to a decade of weariness brought on by her Alzheimer's. When she died, I could finally cry for her death. I had been in mourning for years but never felt I could really show my sadness. For me, Marjorie Townsend died five years before.

The relief I felt when my mother finally died, was short-lived. One day we received a call from the police. Aunt Susan had been found wandering around the streets of downtown Ocala that afternoon. Luckily, her purse contained identification, and the police officer called the house so I could come and pick her up. Her car was found later abandoned on a side street. Aunt Susan had no idea how she'd gotten there and still seemed disoriented when I arrived to take her home. I had to convince her to get into the car. As I wearily drove back to our tree-lined subdivision, I realized that Aunt Susan would now require more care.

After a visit to the doctor later that same day, Claire, Cassie, and I sat and discussed the next steps. The doctor suggested that maybe Susan was in the early stages of Alzheimer's, but the only way to tell for sure would be through an autopsy, after death. He was certain she hadn't had a stroke. We began remembering the little things that

Susan was forgetting lately and realized that the doctor probably made an accurate diagnosis.

While Susan rested in her bedroom, the three of us decided that we had some time before making any major changes. However, I cautioned both Cassie and Claire not to leave the children alone with her anymore even for just very short moments. If the disease progressed anything at all, as my mother's had, she could come and go for years before losing all of her faculties completely.

According to Claire, Kristina had managed to get a job as a hostess at a casino making a small wage plus tips. I imagined the kind of place where Kristina worked, and I imagined that with a skimpy hostess outfit she would probably manage a nice amount in tips from generous gamblers. Even though the images of Kristina in Las Vegas bothered me, I knew I could do nothing about it. Instead, I concentrated on the other females in my life.

One afternoon in the summer, while Cassie took Claire and Susan shopping and the children napped in their rooms, I worked on my new book at the computer. The phone rang disturbing my concentration.

"Ed! Long time, huh?" came Kristina's distinctive deep throaty voice.

"Hi, Kristina. What's up?"

"Try to sound a little happy to hear from me at least. How's the family?"

"Everyone's fine. I'm happy to hear from you. How are you?"

I was working on a particularly difficult chapter of my book and resented her interruption. Her voice startled me because the main character of the new novel took its life form from the personality of Kristina. I had actually been visualizing her provocative way of tossing her head back and looking at me through half-closed lids when the phone rang. Her voice came over the phone lines as strongly stimulating as an aphrodisiac to my waning libido. I fought to remain in control.

"What's wrong, Eddie? You used to love hearing my voice," she said.

"I still love hearing your voice, Kristina. Is that what you want to hear? I'm just trying to be a little wiser in my old age."

"Bet I could still get you excited if I half tried," she said in her most seductive voice.

"Did you want to talk to Claire?" I needed to get her off the phone as soon as possible. I had been attempting for the past year to keep all my passions and desires under wraps. Right now, they were dangerously close to unraveling.

"Sure, let me talk to Claire. She at least will be happy to hear from me."

"She's out shopping with Cassie and Susan. I'll have her call you." I abruptly hung up the phone in order not to hear the voice that haunted my worst nightmares.

Claire told me later in the day that when she called Kristina back, Kristina was upset with me.

"What did you two talk about, Ed?" she asked when she came back from her room after the telephone conversation.

"Nothing much. She wanted to talk to you."

"She said you were rude to her. That doesn't sound like you."

"I guess I was just caught up in my work. I usually let the answering machine pick up, but today I automatically reached for the phone when it rang. Tell her I'm sorry, the next time you speak to her."

"She lost her job," Claire said.

"Again?"

"Yes, again. That kid sure has a run of bad luck, doesn't she?" Claire said.

"I guess you could call it that, Claire. What happened this time?"

"She said that the owner had a niece who needed a job after a divorce. I guess Kris had the least seniority. Anyway, I wanted you to know that I told her I would send her an extra month's allowance to help cover expenses until she can find something else."

"Claire, you don't have to explain to me, you know," I said, but Claire put up her hand.

"I know how you feel about her, Ed, don't try and hide it. I also know that you are looking out for me, and for that, I will always be eternally grateful. However, Kristina is my only living blood relative, and I need to help her when I can. I just want you to know when I do help her."

"Claire, be careful. You know that she's not all that she seems," I said before she went back to her room probably to write out the check and compose a short note to her granddaughter.

When Kris didn't call to thank Claire, her feelings must have been hurt because Kris' name didn't come up for several months in my presence. Claire confided in Cassie that she thought the least Kris could have done was to call to say thanks.

By the beginning of 1995, Aunt Susan's Alzheimer's reached the stage where she had to be cared for around the clock, and once again, I made arrangements for one of my relatives to go into a nursing home. It didn't get any easier the second time around. Susan could no longer take care of her own financial affairs either. When I visited my lawyer, I found out that I should have done something much earlier about Susan's situation.

She had named Philip as her power of attorney and health care surrogate. Since Philip was deceased and Susan could no longer make competent decisions regarding her affairs, a state-appointed guardian needed to be assigned. I got the job without applying.

Meanwhile Kristina called to tell Claire that she had been given a great opportunity with a man who had homes in both Las Vegas and San Diego. She and a friend would be traveling to California with him monthly to serve his guests at house parties there.

"All she has to do is look pretty and serve drinks. Evidently, he's going to pay her quite well," Claire said one night as she told Cassie and me about Kristina's new job.

"How well does she know this man?" Cassie asked.

I decided to keep my mouth shut. At least Kristina wasn't asking for money this time, but I knew that this deal probably entailed more than the simple serving of drinks, and I didn't feel in a position to pass judgments. However, the thought of Kristina servicing these businessmen for money left me sickened.

"He owns one of the casinos. I think Pam might have introduced them," Claire said.

"I hope she's careful," was all Cassie offered.

"Maybe you could find out something more, Ed?" Claire asked.

"About what?"

"About the situation. It may not be all that wonderful, now that I think of it. Could you call Kristina and ask her some questions? She'll expect it from you."

"I'm sure Kristina will be fine, Claire. She's almost thirty now and can make her own decisions. You don't honestly believe that a call from me would make any difference, do you? If anything, it might make her do something rash." The last thing I wanted to do was call Kristina.

Once again, months passed before Claire heard anything from her. One afternoon, when I came out of the study, I found Cassie and Claire sitting at the kitchen table. Claire held her head with both hands. Cassie looked up in relief when I entered.

"What's going on?"

"Claire just got a call from Kris," Cassie said.

"What about?"

"You tell him, please, Cassie. I can't," Claire said.

"Evidently Kris told Claire that she had lost the San Diego job and was greatly depressed. Pam and Oscar won't help her out and refuse to let her stay with them. Then she asked Claire to send her $20,000 immediately so she could get her life back in order. She promised not to call again, if Claire would just send the money."

"What did you tell her, Claire?" I asked.

"I tried explaining that taking that much money from the principle would be a great drain on the portfolio, and I didn't think I could do that."

"Good, good. What did Kristina say then?"

Cassie looked at Claire who nodded. "Kris told her that she had a gun sitting right next to her, and if Claire didn't send the money, she would kill herself."

"It's a trick, Claire. What did you say to her?"

"I told her I was sorry. I also told her that she was a grown woman now, and she needed to stand on her own two feet. And then I told her that the money wouldn't make her life better. I begged her to get help and have the bills sent to me. But I refused to send her any money." Claire took a deep gulp of air, but she did not lose her composure.

"What happened then?"

"She hung up the phone. I've been trying to call her back for the last hour, but the line is busy. I hope I did the right thing."

"You did, Claire. Don't doubt that. She just pulled emotional blackmail on you, and you refused to let her. I'm proud of you. I doubt she pulled that trigger. She probably didn't even have a gun. Besides Kristina isn't the type to kill herself."

I slept little that night because of my anger. I never thought for a moment that Kristina had killed herself after hanging up on Claire.

However, I felt like killing her myself for doing what she had done to her grandmother. Claire seemed to age before my eyes as we sat at that kitchen table talking. Finally, around three in the morning I got up and went to the kitchen phone and placed a call to Las Vegas. I knew the phone would be back on the hook by this time, and it was.

"Kris, Ed here. Claire tells me you're having some problems."

"Yeah, well, it's been tough, Ed. I owe a bunch of money. No one really cares about me. Oscar got real mean when I asked him for help. I didn't know where else to turn today."

"I want you to look in the yellow pages for a crisis center in Las Vegas. They don't charge anything. Call them the next time you feel like committing suicide, OK?" I paused.

"Yeah, sure thing, Eddie, boy," came the expected and sarcastic reply. "Can't I just call you? Or don't you care about me anymore?"

"Kris, we've already discussed this. Listen to me very carefully now. I want you to call a crisis center when you have your next bout of trouble, but under no circumstances are you to call Claire ever again and use emotional blackmail to get money out of her. If you ever pull a stunt like this again, I will see to it that you will never be able to reach her again, and believe me, I can do that. Do I make myself clear?"

"Is that all?"

"That's about it," I said.

"Good-bye, asshole," I heard before the phone banged in my ear.

I didn't have much time in the next few months to think about Kris or her problems because Aunt Susan took a sudden turn for the worse in her fight with Alzheimer's. She became increasingly disoriented and violent, causing many problems at the nursing home.

I spent many long hours in meetings with the director and social worker and nurses while we attempted to solve the problem of Aunt Susan. If she wasn't trying to get into bed with the male patients, she was walking naked through the lobby of the home causing the families of other patients' extreme embarrassment. She constantly walked, even during the night hours when her body would be nearly dropping with exhaustion.

She began to take on the look of a concentration camp victim while still moving constantly even in her weakened state. Claire, who had been a regular visitor at first, soon decided to stop her visits because she was startled whenever Susan asked about Philip. She also seemed embarrassed by Susan's behavior. I finally suggested that it would be all right with me if she stopped visiting her sister-in-law. I assured her that I would handle everything. Even though she hesitated, I could tell she was relieved that she would no longer have to sit in the visitor's lounge with Susan as she undressed herself.

Soon Aunt Susan's promiscuity and nakedness took a back seat as she became increasingly violent and difficult for the aides to handle. One day I had to kneel in her lap to keep her legs still. I held her arms with every ounce of strength I had while the facility's hair stylist trimmed Susan's bangs so she could see. When she finished cutting, I loosened my hold and climbed out of her lap. Susan looked me directly in the eye and slapped me full across the face.

Even though her physical being looked small and frail, her strength remained stronger than most grown men. In a highly agitated state, it often took three or four aides to restrain her.

When she began attacking the other patients, either by hitting or biting them, the nursing home became increasingly alarmed about the possibility of a lawsuit from one of the other patient's families. They began mentioning sending her to a facility for observation for thirty days. They warned me that during those thirty days her bed would probably be filled from the long waiting list. The unspoken implication led me to begin looking for another nursing home for Aunt Susan.

After a quick check with my lawyer, I found that indeed the nursing home was quite within their rights as long as they gave me thirty days' notice.

"What happens if I can't find a place for her after thirty days?" I asked Tim Pierce, my lawyer.

"She would have to be placed in the state mental facility," he said.

I told Claire over dinner that night about the possibility.

"You can't let that happen, Ed," Claire said as her face reddened.

"I know, I know. I need to check around for a good place first. Maybe I'll be able to find something even better."

"Claire, what's the matter?" Cassie asked when she noticed how agitated Claire had become at the mention of a state hospital.

"Ed's grandmother, Helen Townsend. She was ill, something like Susan although we didn't call it Alzheimer's. It was scarier then because we thought she had simply lost her mind, you know, gone crazy." She made small circles with her forefinger. "The doctors eventually diagnosed it as insanity or senility brought on by her diabetes."

"What happened?"

I realized when Cassie asked that question that I had never confided in her. It was something the family kept hidden because of the embarrassment it caused at the time. No one wanted to admit that Grandma had been sent away to the loony bin. Gary and I were taught by the masters at keeping those little unpleasant secrets to ourselves.

"Aunt Susan and Grandpa cared for Grandma in their home," I said. "Susan hadn't married yet. Grandma started acting very strange. First came the accusations. Weird stuff. Gary and I would go and visit Grandma, and she would tell us that Susan and Grandpa were having an affair. Of course, Gary and I were too young to realize what was going on, but we would tell our parents about these things because Grandma seemed so agitated," I said.

Claire reached over and touched Cassie's hand before she took over and continued the story. "When the boys came home with these wild stories, we began to suspect that something more was wrong than just the diabetes. Susan didn't tell us much, but we could tell that Mother Townsend was becoming an increasing burden on her. We talked her into hiring a nurse's aide to live with them. Philip and I took care of the cost."

"One night just before Christmas of 1955, we received a call from the police in the middle of the night," Claire said. "That night Mother Townsend had taken a meat cleaver from the kitchen, and when the aide came to administer the night's shot, Mother pulled out the knife and swung it wildly. She sliced off the end of the aide's little finger."

Cassie looked from me to Claire in disbelief. "She tried to kill her?"

"We don't know that. By the time we got to the house, she was sedated and mumbling incoherently, something like Susan does now. She never really spoke to us again," Claire said.

"What happened then? Did they arrest her?"

"We tried to keep it as quiet as possible. The aide fortunately was very understanding and knew that Mother's illness, or insanity, as the police called it, caused the violence. She decided not to press charges. However, the doctor told us that if we didn't want this repeated, we'd better put her in a facility that could deal with an illness like hers."

"And you put her where?"

"Unfortunately, at the time there were no facilities except at Ypsilanti State Mental Hospital. Philip and Stanley fought bitterly about this. Stanley could never admit that something was seriously wrong with his mother. Finally, Philip and Susan made the decision to commit her."

"What about her husband, Ed's grandfather?" Cassie asked.

"He was fairly broken up himself at the time and really had nothing to say about any of it. He would begin crying whenever the subject came up around him. So, as I said, the decision was left to Philip and Susan. Stanley would have no part of it. So on December 23, 1955, Philip and Susan signed the papers to commit her. Grandpa Townsend signed, too, as required by law. Although I don't think he ever knew what he was signing." Claire gave me a guilty look.

"What about Stanley?" Cassie turned to me for an answer.

"Dad never really got over the fact that his mother was insane. He and Uncle Philip would argue about it whenever they'd had too much to drink, but other than that, the subject was taboo around the family. I was always grateful that Dad died before Mom's illness began. I'm not sure he would have survived it. I've never thought about it much, Claire, but since you've mentioned it, I wonder. Do you think Grandma really had Alzheimer's?" I asked.

"When I saw Susan constantly in motion even when she was sitting, I sure thought back to visiting your grandmother."

"Exactly. I knew it was all familiar, but not because of my mom. She never had the same characteristics, even at her worst moments. But Susan reminds me of Grandma. I never put the two together before."

"We have to do something. We can't let Susan die the way her mother did," Claire interrupted my revelation by bringing me back to the present.

"No, I know. And I won't let it happen. We'll work something out." Even though I tried to sound reassuring, I wasn't sure what I would do next.

I began a several month struggle with the nursing home as I persuaded them to keep her. Finally, after adjustments of her treatment and medications, Aunt Susan's violent attacks disappeared almost entirely. The nursing home decided she would be able to stay as long as I wanted her to remain with them. Ironically, soon after they made their decision, Susan's body began to wear out.

She died all alone one Saturday in June 1995 as I sat at my computer writing about the destructiveness of a life without love.

Her death came as a relief after the months of watching her suffer, but I couldn't help but wonder why someone with such a loving spirit died in such a miserable state. *Did any of us ever truly understand the vagaries of this life*, I thought. When it became too much for me to comprehend, I wrote to escape the pessimistic edge creeping into my consciousness.

Even though I thought I was writing fiction, Kristina would soon bring a reality all her own to my writing and escape would be all but impossible.

Things became complicated when my lawyer, Tim, began to process Susan's will. As he began unraveling the pieces, we realized it wouldn't be a simple case of filing with probate.

"I found the lawyer in Grosse Pointe who held your aunt's will. It looks a little complicated," Tim told me during a phone conversation several weeks after Aunt Susan's death.

"How so?" I asked.

"Everyone she mentions as beneficiaries in her will is deceased, I think. Maybe you can help clarify. Who is Marjorie Elizabeth Townsend?"

"My mother. She died in 1994. She was Susan's sister-in-law," I said.

"Philip Paul Townsend is the other beneficiary."

"Uncle Philip, her brother. He died in 1993."

"Evidently Susan never went back and changed her will after they died."

"No, probably not. She was becoming a little disoriented around the time of my mother's death. But wouldn't Claire inherit Philip's share and me, my mom's?" I asked warily.

"No, not the way she worded the will. Your part should be fairly clear-cut, but Philip's must be inherited through direct family line, not a spouse. Did Philip have children?"

"One son, Gary. He died in 1990."

"Gary have any children?"

"One daughter, still living."

"OK, it may not be so complicated after all, except we'll have to pull death certificates and then file a special request with the court. Could take up to twenty-four months."

"Sure, no problem. I guess the money will just grow in that time, right?" I knew Susan's money needed a little rest period to build itself back after the drain of her last few years.

"Do you have Gary's daughter's address? We'll need to send her notification."

"Sure, hang on a minute," I told Tim. We hadn't heard from Kristina in over a year, but I was certain this news would make her happy.

True to form, when Kristina received her letter from Tim, she called Claire immediately. Claire told me later that she spent little time on the formalities, but wanted to know when the money would be dispersed.

"I told her it might be several months. Was that OK?" Claire asked me later at dinner.

"It might be longer, more like several years. You know how the courts are. Next time she calls, tell her you don't know anything, and she'll have to talk to me."

"She also wondered about you handling the estate. She said something about you having far too much power over her life now," Claire said.

"Too bad, isn't it? I don't see it as control. She's got her own life. Now, more importantly do you want to go to Tessa's dance recital with us on Saturday?" I asked Claire more to change the subject than any real curiosity about her answer. Where my children were concerned, Claire showed exceptional partiality.

"You think I would miss the bestest, most gracefullest dancer in the whole company? You bet, I'm going!"

Sometimes Claire had difficulty attending these events because she had become increasingly frail even though her mind remained sharp as a tack. It was difficult to remember sometimes that she was actually eighty-eight years old.

I continued signing documents for Aunt Susan's estate, but there was no end in sight to the settlement. Tim began to get harassing phone calls from Kristina who was demanding to know when she would get her money.

"I told her I would talk to her once, but after that, since I was working for you, she would have to get her own attorney. I sent her a listing from the Las Vegas yellow pages. That should keep her quiet for now. What's the deal with her?" Tim asked during one of our many phone conversations regarding the estate.

"Don't ask," I said. "She feels the world owes her a living, I guess."

Soon after this conversation, Claire received another call from Kristina. After she hung up the phone, Claire came into the study where I was diligently writing.

"What do you hear from the lawyer about Susan's money?" she asked.

I knew that Kristina must have called because Claire would never ask questions about someone else's money on her own.

"Kristina called?"

"Yes, she really wants me to see if the lawyer or I can lend her the amount she's entitled to until everything is settled."

"That's ludicrous, Claire. I hope you told her to be patient."

"I tried, but she was very agitated. She made some accusations against you, Ed. I was thinking it might be better for everyone if I just lent her the money."

"I don't think that's a very good idea."

"I called Tim Pierce after my talk with Kristina and asked him about it. I hope you don't mind."

"What did he say?"

"First he said the same thing you did. But then he said it could be arranged, but he would advise that I get a regular loan drawn up with a payment plan and interest. That sounds a little too impersonal."

"I think Tim makes sense. If you think, you should do this, then make her really pay back the money, just like anyone else. But I still think you'd just be asking for trouble."

"Ed, there's more. Kris asked that you send her a copy of every check you have ever written on the account including while Susan was still alive. She also wants all the financial statements and all of the legal documents sent to her from the time you became Susan's guardian. I told her she was asking an awful lot, but that I would give you the message."

I stared at Claire for a long time before I could respond. "Why would she want all of that?"

"She thinks you might be trying to cheat her out of her fair share," Claire said.

I let out a long breath of air. "You know I would have appreciated all of this attention while I was trying to keep Aunt Susan safe and protected. Where was our little Kristina then? Did she ever call one time to ask how her aunt was? Did she ever offer to help me with all of the decisions?" I couldn't keep my mouth shut any longer

"Ed, please don't be upset. I'm only passing on her request. You know Kris as well as me, if not better. You at least always saw through her. And I'm certain that Pam is somewhere behind all of this, pushing and prodding Kris at every chance."

"Claire, hold off on the loan. If I do send Kristina any paperwork, I will take my sweet time about it. I'm not required to send her anything, you know. And the next time she wants to talk about Susan's estate, please tell her you don't know anything, OK?" I tried to keep my voice soft so Claire wouldn't hear the anger bubbling just beneath the surface.

That night I went for a long walk and thought about the past. I thought about Gary for the first time in months and was glad he wasn't here to witness Kristina's greed. I shuddered when I remembered my passion for her and felt revulsion that I had ever touched her body. However, I couldn't take it back. Kristina's contribution to the family seemed to lie in her ability to suck up all the vile underbelly of our desires and bring them to the surface as we watched them pus and curdle and stink.

Good old Ed. Everyone trusted me and counted on me during times of crisis and times of strife. Me, who with one soft word from a child twenty-seven years younger than me, crumbled at her feet and gave over myself to the demons rising to the surface as I struggled to get into Kristina's pants.

Just when I thought I had conquered those demons lurking within my soul, Kristina would come back to haunt me as I tried to make sense of my life. As I thought of her, I became filled with disgust. I also fought against the images of her naked breasts pressing against my mouth and her mouth forming around my rising betrayer. How could I ever be free of her when those pictures could so easily float to the surface of my consciousness causing me once again to be aroused and agitated?

I walked faster and tried to push those pictures from my mind. Suddenly, I thought of Pam and her late night phone calls during my marriage to Kelsey.

"Ed," she said during one of her last calls before I left Ann Arbor, "I'm getting married. And he wants to adopt Kristina."

I remembered the words exactly, "And he wants to adopt Kristina." If Timmons adopted Kris, as I assumed he had, was she still considered the daughter of Gary? Did the law recognize bloodlines or legal documents?

The next morning, I called my lawyer to find out the answers. "Tim, if Kristina was adopted by her stepfather, would she still be able to inherit Susan's estate?"

"Was it a legal adoption? We'd need to see the birth certificate. If it was a legal adoption, it means Gary signed away his rights as the birth father and the birth certificate is changed accordingly."

"I don't know. How can I find out?"

"Do you know where Kristina was born and the approximate date?"

"I know exactly."

"Then send for the birth certificate from that state's department of records."

Four weeks later, the birth certificate arrived in the mail. On the line next to name of father, it read, "Oscar Timmons," with no mention of a Townsend anywhere on the form. I immediately called Tim.

"I'll compose the letter. Send over the birth certificate so I can send a copy of that, too. It looks like you'll be getting the whole thing. It could make life easier," Tim said when I called with the news of the birth certificate.

I put off telling Claire anything until after my phone call with the lawyer. But I decided to tell her before Kristina received her letter. There would be fireworks all aimed at me.

"So, because Gary's name appears nowhere on her birth certificate, she isn't seen as his child, legally." I tried to sum up the news as neatly as possible.

"I'll be. Serves Pam right. She's probably been putting Kristina up to all this nonsense." Claire said.

"Now, Claire, Kristina and Pam will most likely be upset about this. You'll probably hear from one or both of them," I said.

"She didn't deserve that money, and Pam certainly shouldn't have any part of it. It should rightfully go to you. This is the right thing," she said before going to bed for the night.

I waited for Kristina's next move, but surprisingly we heard nothing for months. When Claire received her bank statement showing the previous month's allowance check had not been cashed, she tried calling Kristina's number, but it was disconnected. Claire worried about her, but I felt nothing but relief.

One afternoon Cassie interrupted my writing. "Ed, something's not right with Claire. She's in her room resting right now, but she seems a little disoriented," she said.

"Claire, can I come in?" I asked after knocking on her bedroom door several times with no response.

I opened the door. Claire seemed to be sleeping. I tried to wake her, but she was very groggy. When I called the doctor, he recommended putting her in the hospital for observation. The doctor deduced that Claire had been over-medicating herself, forgetting when she had taken the last pill and then forgetting to take others. When we explained to Claire what happened, she begged to be moved into the limited care facility that had recently been built in the neighborhood.

"I swore I would never be a burden to you two," Claire said. "Cassie can't take care of the two little ones, work part-time, and take care of me. Please let me go there. I'll still be close, but I can pay others to watch over me."

With much reluctance, we agreed to her plan and moved her in the next week. She had a few friends there already and even joined a bridge club the first week after her arrival. I gave Claire Pam's address, and she addressed a letter to Kristina, giving her new address and phone number. Soon Kristina was on the phone to Claire.

"What are you doing there, Grandma?" Claire told me Kristina asked when she first called.

"She's going to come for a visit, Ed. She's worried about me," Claire said.

"When is she coming?" I asked.

"Next week."

"I'll make reservations for her at a motel nearby. She can rent a car at the airport," I said.

"Can't she just stay with you?"

"I don't think that's a good idea, Claire."

"Why? I was hoping we could have some meals together, just like old times."

"I don't trust her, and I don't want her around my children."

"I wish we could just be a family." Claire looked at me forlornly. When I didn't respond, she squared her shoulders before continuing. "But if you feel that strongly about it then I guess that's that. We can have dinner together one night though, can't we?"

"We'll see, Claire. I'm sorry if this hurts you, but I have to think of my family. Besides, you two have lots of catching up to do, and you don't need a couple of toddlers and two pushy adults in the way. You'll have a better time without us around."

"If you say so. You know best," Claire said, as I bent down to kiss her good-bye.

He sat calmly on the beach allowing the waves to wash over his feet. The salt water healed his wounds leaving behind the gray slashes that now scarred his skin. As he gazed upon the dead flesh, he found peace.

CHAPTER SEVENTEEN

I KEPT MY WORD and stayed away during Kristina's visit. I'm not sure what Claire told Kristina, but Kristina stayed away from me, too. I didn't hear anything until the morning of her departure when I received a telephone call.

"Mr. Townsend? This is Sally Hines, the nurse at Oakview."

"Hello, Ms. Hines."

"This morning when your aunt got up to go to the bathroom, she became quite dizzy and fell against the tub. She's on her way to the emergency room at Monroe if you want to meet her there."

By the time I arrived at the hospital, they had already admitted her to a cubicle and were working on her wounds. They wanted permission to do a CAT scan since she hit her head pretty hard.

"Sure, do whatever's needed, doctor," I said before pulling aside the curtain to enter the small space occupied by Claire.

"What are you trying to do, get some sympathy or get ready for Halloween," I said as I came close to the bed and saw the bruises and cuts.

"Ed, I'm so glad you're here," Claire said before she burst into tears. Even though Claire and I had been close for years and suffered together the tragedies of losing those closest to us, this was the first time I had seen her cry.

"What's wrong? Hey, don't cry. I was just joking," I said as I patted her back. She grabbed my hand and pulled it close to her face. "Where's Kristina?" I asked.

"We said good-bye last night. Her flight was early this morning. Ed, I thought you were mad at me. I'm so glad you're here."

"Now why would I be mad at you? You're my best girl after Cassie and Tessa."

"Oh, you know, all that stuff with Kristina. And then all week I expected you to call at the very least, and I didn't hear anything. I thought you were mad because I let her come."

"No, I told you why I stayed away. I bet you had a much better visit without me around to mess things up."

"We did have a nice visit. Kristina took me all sorts of places. But that kid, she has such bad luck. All the time."

"Like what?" I asked.

"Last night, for instance. She said she just wanted to buy her grandma a coke, so we drove down to the 7-11 on the corner. She went inside while I waited. When she came out, she looked puzzled as she handed me my drink. I said, 'What's the matter, Kris?' She told me she had given the clerk a $50 bill for the drinks but now she couldn't find the change."

"Didn't she go back inside and ask about it?" I asked.

"No, I guess she didn't. I told her, 'Since you just wanted your grandma to have a drink, I think I can give you fifty dollars.' So I did. But you know, Ed, that's all the cash I had. Do you think you can go to the bank for me?"

"Sure, Claire, don't worry. Where's your purse?"

"I made sure they brought it with me. A lady must never go out without her purse, you know."

"Yes, I know. Is your checkbook there?"

"Yes. Just take it and write me a check for cash."

I took the checkbook and attempted to account for every check written since Kristina's arrival. All I saw was one written out for $350, which Claire told me covered Kristina's airline ticket and car rental. *Not too bad and fairly reasonable*, I thought. When I asked her about paying for the motel, she told me she charged it. I would look over those statements carefully, too. On the surface, it seemed on this visit all that Kristina had managed to scam had been the fifty dollars that Claire could well afford. It was the means she used to get that money that always amazed me.

Claire never fully recovered physically from her fall. Her head wounds healed and her crying, which continued for nearly a week, eventually stopped. Then she was her old self once again. But she had done something to her left leg that left her unstable on her feet. I purchased a walker for her, which she hated and only used for the long walk to the dining room. Nearly every visit to Claire in the next few months resulted in me lecturing her after finding her wobbling around her room without a cane or the walker.

She became the child and I the parent. I hated ordering her around, but I worried constantly that she would break a hip. Even though that's what had brought about her own mother's demise, she didn't seem to heed my warnings. She began physical therapy but that didn't help. Increasingly she became upset about the care center's staff who often times left her stranded in the activities room or card room, which meant after a wait of a few minutes or longer, Claire would attempt the long walk back to her own room sometimes falling but never enough to injure herself.

As the weeks went by, Claire began to tell me more about Kristina's visit, and I discovered the real purpose behind her surprise appearance. It seems Kristina had a plan since Claire was no longer living in her own home.

"Kris thinks I should buy a small house, and then she could come and live with me and take care of me full time," Claire said.

"What do you think?" I asked.

"I think it's a dumb idea. What's a young woman like her want with taking care of an old lady like me. I told her I would think about it though."

"Have you heard from Kristina since her visit?"

"No, and I called after I was released from the hospital to tell her about my fall. I left a brief message telling her what happened, but she never called me back. I did hear from Pam though," she said.

"When?"

"Last week. She called to tell me she was sorry I had to be living in a place like this, as if she knows all about it. Anyway, she said I should move out to Las Vegas to be near my only blood relative. She offered to let me live with her and Oscar."

"That's a surprise," I said.

"Sure is. That woman always hated me. Now she wants me to come and live in her spare bedroom so I can be closer to Kristina? That takes the cake. Then she went on to say that even though you had been very good to me, you weren't real family, and with her and Oscar and Kristina, I'd be with a real family. Can you believe the nerve?"

"How did you handle her?"

"You would have been proud. I was gracious and told her I was very comfortable here and that she shouldn't worry. She's a mess." Claire and I both laughed.

Soon after, Claire became increasingly weak on her feet and was dissatisfied with the level of care she was receiving. When we visited her doctor, he suggested that the time had come to move to a nursing home that would be better equipped to meet her needs. Claire agreed and within the week, I moved her to Magnolia Arms in Ocala, the best facility in north Florida.

When she finally fell and broke her hip, I wasn't surprised. I had expected it since she still insisted in getting up and moving around without assistance. Short of tying her in her chair there was very little to do. When I saw her in the hospital, she explained that she only wanted to move the wheelchair away from her bed a little way.

The doctor told me they would have to perform a hip replacement since the hipbone had come out of its socket. While we waited for surgery to be scheduled, I tried to call Kristina. I eventually called Pam when I had no luck at Kristina's apartment.

"Thanks for calling, Ed. I know Kris will appreciate it," Pam said.

"I just thought she should know. It's pretty serious for an almost 90-year-old woman to go in for major surgery. I'll call when it's all over."

Claire came through the surgery with an excellent chance at recovery. Kristina called me soon afterwards.

"I'm coming there for Thanksgiving, Ed," Kristina said.

"Good, good. Your grandmother will be happy to see you," I said.

"I'd like to see you, too," she said.

I was silent for a long moment. "Cassie and the kids would love to see you," I said.

"OK, if you want to play it that way, Eddie, baby. I'll probably see you at the nursing home. I've really missed you."

"Kristina, please don't do this."

"Haven't you missed me just a little? Don't you ever think about us? Remember taking me Christmas shopping?" She talked soothingly and softly lulling me back into her web.

"For chrissakes, Kristina, stop," I said.

"I will for now. But you'll see me when I get there, won't you?"

"Yes, yes, of course."

"Good, Eddie, you won't be sorry, you know. Remember I've always told you it was bigger than both of us." She paused. "I need to ask you something. Mom and Oscar want to know if the nursing home might have been negligent."

"You mean, could they have prevented the fall that broke Claire's hip?"

"That's right. How could it have happened if everyone there had been doing their job?"

"Kristina, Claire is a very stubborn woman. One reason we moved her to the nursing home was for more supervision, and short of restraining her in a wheel chair or bed, they couldn't have stopped her from doing what she did."

"But was the floor slippery? Did they leave the wheelchair in her way?"

"What are you talking about? They feel awful about what happened. Claire fell. Restraining her is illegal."

"Did you know my mom just started working in a nursing home? She thinks maybe they were negligent and are now covering up something."

"Have you called Magnolia Arms?"

"I made some inquiries, but evidently, you, as power of attorney, are the only one who can request records. So we wondered what you thought."

"Kristina, Magnolia Arms has given nothing but excellent care for Claire. Remember I've had some experience with nursing homes, and this one is the best."

"I'm sure you'd spare no cost for Grandmother's care, would you," she said, the tough girl returning. "Oscar thinks you enjoy spending my inheritance."

"You can tell Oscar to mind his own business. And since when did you start listening to him anyway?"

"He's been very good to me these last few years while I tried to get established in Vegas. He's found me some jobs and sometimes he makes a lot of sense when he starts talking about my money."

"If you are coming here to cause trouble, then don't bother coming," I said. "Claire is very fragile right now."

"OK, OK. I'm just covering all the bases. I just feel so bad for Grandma."

"Good, she needs your kindness. Besides, she's been talking about moving to the place where her mother resided after she broke her hip. It was in a private home, and I've had some people checking on it. Maybe a smaller facility would suit her more."

"Maybe. It might cost less, too. And, Ed? I really miss you, and I respect you and think about you often. Please don't shut me out when I get there. I really need to see you."

"Kristina, you've always known how I felt about you. I just wish you took more responsibility for yourself. Aren't you almost thirty now?"

"Not quite. I'm trying, Ed. So you'll see me while I'm there?" she asked in her familiar little girl voice that still haunted and aroused me.

"It'll probably be a mistake, but I don't see how we can avoid one another."

"Still can't trust yourself?"

"I can't trust you. I think I can handle myself."

"Yeah, you've always handled yourself and me just fine, Eddie," came the seductive reply.

"Good-bye, Kristina. I'll see you at the nursing home on Monday afternoon. Are you going to call Claire and tell her?"

"I already did before I called you. I just wanted to ask you a few questions. I trust your opinion, you know. I'm sorry if it upset you, but now I can get Oscar and Pam off my back."

"Just come here and be kind to your grandmother and don't hassle the nursing home staff. You might not want to mention your mother's name around your grandmother. The two of them never got along very well."

"Don't worry, I'll be her perfect little princess. See you Monday, Eddie."

I walked into Claire's room the next Monday afternoon bracing myself for a face- to-face confrontation with Kristina. Instead, I found a very frail Claire lying flat on her back with a box of homemade peanut butter fudge open next to her on the night table.

"Hi, Claire. Where's Kristina?" I asked when I saw Claire turn toward me.

"She went out for some lunch. She'll be back soon," she said.

"Here, let me roll the bed up some. Why is it down flat?"

"Sometimes I just like it that way. Oh, that does feel better, Ed. Thanks."

"Where's your roommate?"

"She went home for the holidays this afternoon. It makes it nice for Kris and me to visit."

"I'm glad that you and Kristina are having a nice visit."

We sat and talked quietly for a few minutes. Some good friends of hers who had dropped by earlier in the day brought the peanut butter fudge. She told me Kristina had been spoon-feeding it to her during the afternoon. I noticed that little bits had been taken from the fudge, and a spoon rested on the edge of the table.

"I'm back. Hey, Ed, you're here. Sorry it took me so long." Kristina rushed into the room and into my arms before I knew what happened.

"Isn't this nice. My favoritest people in the whole wide world right here with me," Claire said.

"Yes, Grandma. We're all here except for Cassie. Right, Ed? Grandma was telling me how close she and Cassie have become and how your kids are the 'bestest' besides me, in the world. Right, Grandma?"

"That's right, honey," Claire said.

"What's wrong, Claire?" I asked as I looked at her drooping eyes.

"I feel awfully tired. I'd like my nightgown on I think. I'm going to eat dinner here."

"I'll call an aide," I said as I headed for the door.

While Claire prepared for bed, Kristina and I walked out into the hallway.

"I'm worried about Grandma. She doesn't seem herself. Come on, Ed, I need some fresh air," Kristina said as she headed for the front door.

"How do you mean that Claire doesn't seem herself?'" I asked as we began a walk around the building.

"She seems depressed, for one thing. She always told me she was going to live to see the year 2000, but today she remarked that maybe that wasn't such a great thing after all."

"She might be a little down, I guess. You know how active she always was, and her recovery has been slow."

"Also, she has trouble following a line of thought for very long."

"Really? I find her to be as alert as ever," I said.

"I got a list of her medications because I thought maybe that might be a problem. Mom works in a nursing home, you know."

"So you said. Who gave you the list?"

"One of the nurses. Anyway, I'm going to call Mom tonight, and she'll look into the meds and see if anything there might be causing the problem."

We had come to a dark corner behind the nursing home, and Kris stopped walking as she leaned up against the building. She motioned for me to join her. I looked at her standing there in the dark night highlighted by her very tight white jeans. Her equally tight sweater did not conceal her shape in any way. As if hypnotized, I walked toward her.

"Now isn't this better?" she asked as I walked into her waiting arms. "I've missed you so much, Ed." She brought my head down to her waiting lips, and I sank into her body that had already opened itself to me.

I sought her breasts with one hand while our lips locked together for one long drink. She pressed against me until I couldn't stand it any longer. I pulled my face away from hers but locked my hands firmly to her front.

"Please, Eddie, please. I've missed you so much. You're the only one who understands me. Don't be mad at me," she babbled while I lifted her sweater and unsnapped the front of her bra. When I had released her breasts, I no longer heard her continued pleas as my mouth found its way home.

She began fumbling with the front of my pants and as much as I hated losing the cushion of her when she moved her head lower, I no longer cared about anything but the feelings her mouth aroused.

Suddenly headlights came around the corner and lit up the side of the building. When the light hit my eyes, I woke from my trance and saw for the first time what was happening. I moved slightly so the car wouldn't be able to see the squatting body in front of me. They probably thought I was just relieving myself in the bushes.

"Kristina, stop. Stand up. Here pull down your sweater," I said, but only after I had been spent.

"Ed, I want you so much. Can't you come back to the motel with me?" she asked sweetly as she reached up to caress the side of my face.

I looked at her longingly but knew I couldn't do anything more tonight. "Maybe tomorrow," I said. "Besides we need to get back inside."

"OK, but, Ed, do you really think the nursing home wasn't negligent when Claire fell?"

"No, I don't. I've already told you that, Kristina."

"Have you seen the report about her fall?" she asked.

"I don't need to see it. This nursing home is the best that money can buy and is providing Claire with excellent care.

" I have no doubt that you would give her the best possible care and spend her money freely. By the way, Ed, where are Claire's valuables? Oscar told us to ask because he warned us that nursing homes are notorious places for thieves, especially among the employees."

"You and Oscar don't need to worry about her valuables, Kris. Just concentrate on helping her get better."

We walked back into the room. A woman stood next to the bed talking quietly to Claire. She turned around as I came nearer.

"Hello, Ed. How are you?" Pam said.

"Pam? What are you doing here?" I asked.

"Yeah, what the hell are you doing here?" Kristina echoed.

"I wanted to visit Claire. You know I owe Claire an awful lot for helping me get through the early years with you, and I wanted to come and see her," Pam said.

"That's thoughtful of you, Pam," I said.

"I was talking about all the parties Claire used to throw for us in Ann Arbor. Those were the days, weren't they, Claire?"

"Yes." Claire said.

"What's wrong, Grandma?" Kristina asked.

"I miss everyone so much. Philip, Gary, they're all gone."

"We're still here, don't forget that," I said. I was shocked to see Claire weeping. She hadn't done that since Kristina's last visit in September.

My lawyer, Tim Pierce called the next day as I sat before my computer with a major case of writer's block. Kristina always managed to stifle my other passion.

"What's up, Tim?" I asked.

"I got a call from a Pamela Timmons today. Do you know her?"

"She was married to Claire's son Gary at one time. She's Kristina's mother."

"I figured that out," Tim said. "Do you know why she's here now?"

"She says she just wanted to come since Kristina told her that Claire wasn't doing very well. But last night Pam tried to talk to me as I left the nursing home and said she was worried that Kristina might be planning something. I think it's probably Pam that has the plan. She's been pushing for years for Kristina to get money from the Townsends," I said. "And now I get the feeling Pam might be pushing Kristina into filing a law suit against Magnolia Arms."

"Can't be done unless you agree; she doesn't have power of attorney. The reason I called you is because I'm a little uneasy about some things, too," Tim said.

"What things?"

"First, Pam asked to set up an appointment with me. She said it was about Claire's will. My secretary came and got me out of a meeting immediately because we both thought it meant Claire had died. Those requests don't usually happen until after a death."

"That's a little creepy," I said.

"I told her that since we didn't represent her, I couldn't talk about it with her. I probably wouldn't have even called you if it had ended there because I didn't know both she and Kristina were in Ocala at the time."

"What else happened?"

"Next, I got a call from the Clerk of the Court office. Kristina was down there raising hell about seeing your Aunt Susan's will in probate. They called me because I'm the attorney of record, and she was making such a stink. I told them to go ahead and show it to her. She wanted copies, I guess."

"That's interesting," I said.

"They've both been terribly busy. Soon after that, I got a call from a lawyer friend who had a Miss Kristina Timmons and a Mrs. Oscar Timmons in his office. Kristina was claiming that an evil nephew with my help had cut her out of a will. He was calling to get the scoop before proceeding any further. I told him the story, and he agreed that she wasn't entitled to anything."

"Pam and Kristina went to that lawyer together?"

"That's what this guy said. I guess Pam wanted him to draw up an affidavit that stated Kristina was really the daughter of Gary Townsend. That's why I called. Are they at the nursing home very much?"

"Kristina arrived yesterday and spent all day with her; Pam arrived last night. It's difficult because Claire isn't herself."

"What do you mean?"

"She's tired and weepy."

"Doesn't sound like Claire. Make sure the nursing home staff is aware that Pamela was making inquiries about Claire's will today. I would suggest they not leave either of them alone with her.

"Why? You don't think they'd do something to harm Claire, do you?"

"Who can say, but why take the chance?"

"Pamela will be easy to keep out, I guess. She's probably the one we need to worry about. Kristina said Pam would be checking on Claire's meds, but that was before Pam arrived. Kristina seemed quite surprised when we found Pam in the room last night talking to Claire."

"Just put everyone involved with Claire's care on alert. I don't like the things I heard today."

She greedily reached for another piece of meat not waiting to finish chewing before stuffing more bites into her mouth. Juices dripped down her chin onto her naked breasts, and he greedily lapped up the leftovers.

CHAPTER EIGHTEEN

ON A COOL NOVEMBER day, I entered the nursing home where Claire had moved earlier in the year, reluctant to face the troubles that might be in store for me. Troubles named Kristina and Pamela I didn't need right now. My main concern was Claire who had been failing rapidly in recent days.

Claire, weakened from her broken hip that had required surgery several weeks earlier, was not well. Her eyes could not focus, and her heart rate was dropping. The nursing staff greeted me as I walked toward the nurse's station with Claire's updated condition.

"Where's Charles?" I asked the head nurse. Charles Stuart was the director of the home and had been a great help to me ever since Claire had been admitted.

"He's getting ready to hold a staff meeting about Mrs. Townsend right now," one of the aides told me.

"I'm going in to see Claire. I want to see Charles as soon as he's available," I said.

When I walked into the room, neither Kristina nor Pam was there. Claire lay still on the bed. I touched her shoulder lightly as I stood next to her. When I grabbed her hand, she attempted to open her eyes. When she did, I noticed they were covered with a slight film making her dark blue eyes seem light.

"Ed, it's you," she said so softly I had to lean over to hear. "I can't believe you're here." She began crying once again.

"Claire, what's wrong?"

"I'm just so sad. I wanted to spend Thanksgiving with you and Cassie and the kids."

"You will. We're going to come here and bring you dinner," said.

"Pam said you wouldn't be coming." She began crying harder.

"Shush, that's silly. We'll be here."

"Ed, what's wrong with me? I'm so scared."

"Don't be scared, Claire. I'm here now. Cassie will probably be here later this afternoon."

"Ed, did Pam do this to me?" she asked just as I turned to leave and find Charles.

"What makes you say that? Has she said or done something?"

"I can't figure out why she's here. She never liked me much and then she and Philip." Claire lost her train of thought and just stared at me with her dim eyes.

"I don't know if she's done something or not, but if she has, I'm going to find out. Just rest, Claire. I'm here now, and I'll take care of everything."

"Yes, you always have, Ed. Thank you. You're the bestest," and the tears began to run down her cheeks again.

An aide came into the room just then to tell me Charles needed to see me. I asked her to stay close to Claire for as long as possible until I could get to a phone to call Cassie and ask her to find a babysitter so she could come sit with Claire.

When I walked into the conference room, I dispensed with greetings and approached the nursing home director.

"What's wrong with Claire? I've never seen her like this and the nurses tell me her heart rate is dropping rapidly. What's going on?" I asked.

Charles looked at me carefully before answering. "She's not doing very well, and we've been trying to figure out why. We're going to be taking blood and urine samples immediately. Hopefully, we can find something out quickly. We've put a rush order on everything."

Before we could continue, a nurse came into the room.

"Charles, could we see you for a moment?" she asked.

"Sure. I'll be right back, Ed. Make yourself comfortable."

I paced the room and wondered what would happen next. I thought about calling Cassie, but I decided to wait until I had more definite news. I looked up as Charles entered the room solemnly.

"Ed, I'm afraid I've got some bad news. Claire died just a few minutes ago. Probably right after you left the room. The aide said she took a deep breath, turned her head, and exhaled. That was it. It was very peaceful."

"How could that happen? Where's Kristina, her granddaughter?"

"No one knows. She left with her mother about an hour ago without a word to anyone. Some of the staff said the two had been arguing in the courtyard right before they left. The mother looked like she'd been crying. Would you like to see your aunt before we call the funeral home?"

I stumbled out of the room determined to keep my composure. I managed to keep it until the nurse who had been so kind to Claire came up to me and embraced me. We stood holding one another for a long time.

"She was a good woman," she said as she released me.

"Yes, yes, she was, the bestest," I managed to say before going in to say my final

goodbyes to the woman who had always been such a solid part of my life.

After Claire's funeral, I decided to take a long walk around the neighborhood to clear my head. Cassie understood why I left even though she was suffering also. She loved Claire as a daughter loves a mother. She also made Claire's last years joyful and happy ones as she included Claire in every moment of our children's lives. I couldn't help but think back to another funeral in another lifetime. It was natural I would think about Gary as I walked alone remembering the past. For most of my life, Gary walked beside me during these times of strife. I felt his presence today more than ever. I remembered back to the last time I sat beside him at his bedside in New Orleans.

As I continued my walk on the day of Claire's funeral, I began thinking unwillingly about Kristina. She had certainly gotten what she had wanted, and I was left once again to clean up the mess. Claire told me that she had named me as the personal representative of her estate since I lived here, but I knew that Kristina stood to inherit everything once the house, for which I had been paying Claire, was re-mortgaged and the money deposited in the trust. She probably would receive the trust immediately since Claire was adamant after

Philip's death that her estate be simply turned over to Kristina upon her death with no probate.

Kristina and Pam did not attend the funeral. As far as I knew, they didn't even know that Claire had died. When Pam first arrived in town, she made several attempts to talk to me alone. She wanted to tell me that Kristina just wanted Claire's money at any cost. I told her each time that she was mistaken. It was Pam pushing for the money. Kristina only asked for it when Pam pushed her. I thought that maybe Pam had some angle going to get money from Claire herself without Kristina's interference.

The phone rang as I came into the house exhausted from the long walk. I was surprised to hear the voice of Claire's doctor.

"Ed, we just received the final toxicology report on Claire. Her blood showed a fifty percent level of Phenobarbital. Forty percent is toxic."

"How the hell did that happen?"

"We're not really sure, but I've got to report my findings to the police. They'll probably be calling you, and I wanted you to be prepared."

"What do you think?" I still couldn't voice the words.

"I really don't want to speculate, but if you know where the granddaughter and her mother are, it might help in the investigation," he said. "The aides have been coming forward with some suspicious reports."

"What kind of suspicious reports?"

"Aides said that the mother kept rolling the bed down after being told that Claire should be left sitting up. And a couple of other strange things like that."

"Do you think Pam could have drugged her?"

"I don't know, but Claire didn't drug herself, that's for sure. Ed, call me if you have any questions. And I'm sorry. I thought your aunt was a very special woman."

I hung up the phone and went into the living room to pour myself a healthy shot of scotch. I needed time to absorb this information. As I slowly sipped, I felt a welcome numbness enter my limbs as I found the reality far too harsh to absorb.

Almost immediately, the phone rang again. This call gave me no respite from my thoughts and suspicions.

Tim Pierce, my lawyer and good friend, had more news.

"How'd it go yesterday?" he asked after the preliminaries.

"It was fine, Tim. The service was small, just some folks from the country club and Claire's church and Cassie and me. No other family, of course."

"So, Kristina and her mother didn't stay around long enough to pay their respects? I have some news for you, and some for Kris, too. But legally you're the only one I need to contact."

"What news? I'm not sure I can take anymore *news*."

"Why, did something else happen?"

"Dr. Gantt, Claire's doctor, called a few minutes ago to tell me Claire had a lethal dosage of Phenobarbital in her system when she died," I said.

"No kidding? Who do they suspect?"

"He's turning everything over to the police. They'll probably be calling me soon."

"Ed, let me tell you why I called. A month ago, Claire had me come over to the nursing home, right after her first fall, before she broke her hip. Remember? Kris had just visited. She wanted to write a new will. We did it right there with the staff as witnesses."

"She changed her will? Did she name Kristina personal representative instead of me?" I hoped this might be the case so I could finally be rid of Kristina forever. The money would no longer tie us together.

"No, buddy, she doesn't mention Kristina Timmons anywhere in this will, which is her last will and testament, and the one we send on to the court. She told me Kris worried her lately, but she didn't want to concern you. She took her out of the will completely; she won't inherit a thing," he said.

"Then who did she name?"

"Her best friend and confidante, is the way she put it in the will. And, Ed, that's you."

I sat back in my chair, overwhelmed by Claire's gesture. I had felt close to Claire all my life. Sometimes I think she wished I had been her son, even though she loved Gary. She would have liked both of us to be her sons. These past years of sharing the same house had been easy ones for Cassie and me. But for her to go against Philip's wishes of leaving everything to their only grandchild, meant that something more must have happened during Kristina's previous visit. Claire decided to keep whatever it was to herself.

Suddenly I remembered the description of Claire's fall the day Kristina left. The staff had told me that she had become dizzy and disoriented right before she slipped. I made a mental note to ask the doctor if any urine or blood samples were taken in the emergency room when they stitched her up.

However, I still couldn't believe that Kristina would resort to murder. I would believe it sooner of Pam than I would about Kristina. Kristina needed love, that was all. I had tried over the years, but I had always ended up loving her in the wrong way, a way that still gave her the wrong things.

I now realized Kristina and Pam had been working all the angles. I'm certain it was the reason that Pam had shown up in Ocala. I would bet that most of the plans had been devised by Pam over the course of several years, maybe ever since Philip's death. Then they plotted to go for even more money from the nursing home for Claire's fall.

I suspected that Kristina and Pam also wanted a way for Kristina to inherit part of Aunt Susan's estate. Why else had she been asking for her will at the court? Kristina would never receive the thing she wanted most – her legacy in the Townsend family.

I heard through some of the nursing home staff that Kristina had started a brief fling with one of Claire's male aides as soon as she arrived. He gave her the list of meds. The poor schmuck had become alarmed as Claire's condition worsened, so he quit his job the day before Claire died.

However, when he read in the paper that Claire died, he came forward with some interesting information. During the first few days of Kristina's visit, she had been trying to get Claire to sign a document. The aide couldn't be sure because he hadn't read it, but he thought it stated that Kris Timmons was Claire's rightful heir. Claire adamantly refused to sign the paper. Even at her weakest, she remained the strong stoic I loved all my life.

Later the next day the police came by for my statement. They told me they had to do an investigation because of the suspicious nature of Claire's death; everyone who had been around her during the past few weeks would be interviewed as routine procedure. Even Cassie would have to be questioned. I gave them all the information I could about the last days of Claire's life.

"How well do you know the granddaughter, Kristina Timmons?" one of the detectives asked me.

"I've known her since she was born, but there was a gap of about fifteen or sixteen years where no one in the Townsend family had any contact with her."

"Bad divorce?"

"Something like that. Kristina's mother left with her when Kristina was two. She wouldn't let anyone know where they were"

"Do you know where they are right now?" he asked.

"I'm not sure. They were staying out at the Comfort Inn, I think, but I haven't seen her since the afternoon before Claire's death. I'm not sure if she and her mother went back to Las Vegas or not. I can give you some phone numbers, if you'd like."

"That would be good, Mr. Townsend, if you wouldn't mind. We need to ask them some questions, too."

I went into the study to retrieve my address book and carefully wrote down the last addresses and phones numbers that I had for Kristina and Pam.

"We may need to question you again, Mr. Townsend, after we talk to these two women. I hope you don't mind. I know it's a difficult time for you."

"No, no, Detective, I understand. Just call me."

After I showed them the door, I felt swept back into the past, remembering the night of Gary's funeral and how easily I had been seduced by Kristina. I remembered all of the times I had been with her and knew she couldn't have been the one that killed Claire. Despite her tough exterior, she loved her grandmother, and she loved me. I felt certain she wouldn't destroy either of us that way.

When the detectives called, again I wondered if I should tell them everything. At least I should tell them about my suspicions of Pam. Maybe they didn't need to know about Kristina and me. I thought about the last few years and my relationship with Kristina that had never really ended and that continually threatened to pull me under. I decided that no matter what, I would tell Cassie. Maybe by confessing this albatross, I could finally get rid of it. And if she left me, then I would have received only a portion of the punishment I deserved.

Pam's call broke into my thoughts.

"Ed, it's Pam. I want to see you today."

"Did you know that Claire died?"

"Claire died? No, I didn't know, but she wasn't doing very well when I left. I'm sorry. I know how close the two of you were."

"Where did you go and why did you leave without saying anything?"

"I needed to get back to Vegas for some personal reasons. But I'm back now and we really need to talk. I've brought Oscar with me, and we'd both like to meet with you. Soon."

"Pam, I really don't know what you and Oscar could say to me at this point."

"I think we might have some information that you might like to have, too."

"OK, but I'm not crazy about meeting your husband. Kristina hasn't been very complimentary about him."

"No, I'm sure she hasn't. But why don't you meet him for yourself and then decide? How about seven tonight? We can come over there or meet you some place."

I made arrangements to meet them at a restaurant close to their motel out by the interstate.

Later that day, Kristina finally called.

"Ed, is it true? Is Grandma dead like they said at the nursing home?" she asked.

"Hello, Kristina. Yes, she died four days ago. Where did you go?"

"Mom and I had to go back to Vegas. Oscar was sick. How did she die?"

"We're not sure," I said. I didn't know how much I should reveal before the police talked to her. "You went with Pam back to Vegas?"

"Yes, she was really worried about Oscar so I went to give her moral support. Have I missed the funeral?"

"It was yesterday. Where are you?"

"I'm at the Comfort Inn at I-75. Here in Ocala."

"Really? When did you arrive?"

"A few minutes ago. I came back and called Magnolia Arms to talk to Grandma, and they gave me the news. Can you come over, please?" I recognized the voice pleading with me now and felt myself pulled by the vulnerability creeping into her words.

"Why?"

"I need a friend. Just come over, please. You know Cassie wouldn't like it if I came over there. I'm in room 301."

After I hung up the phone, I decided to call the detectives who had been at my house just a few minutes earlier. They asked me for Kristina's and Pam's Las Vegas addresses, but I thought they might like to know that both of them were just a few miles away. As I prepared to meet Kristina, I remembered the last time I had been with her just days before Claire died. I felt relief that the detectives would be there to protect me from the control she always exerted over my mental and physical being.

It came just as quickly as he always hoped it would. The release itself was ecstasy, and then, nothing. Nothing left but the blackness of the abyss and the endless feeling of falling.

CHAPTER NINETEEN

KRISTINA OPENED THE DOOR of her motel room almost immediately after my first tentative knock.

"Eddie," she said as she flung herself against me. "Hold me, please just hold me."

Unwillingly I held her, trying not to remember how vulnerable this young woman had always seemed to me in these moments. She looked at me, and in a life-long gesture, she reached up with one hand to touch the side of my face. I smiled tenderly as I remembered the toddler at my wedding to Kelsey who had done the same thing when I had swept her into my arms.

Almost as suddenly as those unwanted thoughts came, another sensation developed as I realized that Kristina was now pushing desperately against me and moving in a rhythmic pattern. I fought to retain control, but my body once again began responding.

"You can't deny it, Ed. Not anymore. You have always wanted me, and I have always wanted you. We're meant for one another. You loved Gary, and you love me. Quit fighting it." She pushed harder against me, and I tried not to feel her warm breasts crush into my chest.

"See, you think too much, let your body take control. It's OK, baby, just love me," she whispered as she felt my arousal. "Now we can be together all the time. We can leave this place and go anywhere we want. I've been making plans, Eddie. We can go away together, and I'll take care of you just like you've taken care of everyone else all these years." She continued to caress me letting her soft voice work its magic.

"You want that, too, don't you, Eddie? You know you do; there that's right; I've missed you so much," she said.

I began working on the buttons of her blouse, and when I couldn't stand it any longer, I pulled at the material until the bottom buttons fell onto the floor. I soaked up the scent and feel of her. I blotted out the rest of the world from my consciousness. I could hear her voice continuing its litany.

"We'll go to Mexico, first, baby. That feels so good. You always know what's right. Mexico, OK, Eddie?"

"Yes, yes," I managed to mumble between mouthfuls of her ample flesh.

"You love me, don't you, Eddie?"

"Yes, for God's sake, yes, Kristina." I closed my eyes and only felt the sensation of her hands caressing me.

Suddenly Kristina pulled away from me. "Cassie," I heard her say through my thick fog of confusion.

"Cassie?" I repeated.

"Hello, Kristina, Ed," I heard my wife say from behind me. I turned to stare at her standing in the doorway.

"What?" I said.

Cassie glared at me. "Kristina called me and asked me to come over. She said she had something she wanted to share with me. I didn't realize it would be my husband. Ed, really, how could you?"

I looked from my angry wife to Kristina and saw the sardonic grin spread across her face.

"I thought it was time that she knew," Kristina said. "Ed has always loved me, Cassie, long before he even knew you. He only married you because his high standards prevented him from pursuing me. As you can see, he's always wanted me no matter what."

"Kristina, shut up. Cassie, wait, we need to talk."

"That's probably an understatement. I'll meet you at home later," Cassie said as I saw her fight back the tears, and then she left the room as quickly as she appeared, leaving me alone once again with Kristina.

"Why did you do that?" I asked.

"Someone needed to do something. I got tired of waiting for you to move. In the long run, you'll see that it's better this way, Ed. Now everything's out in the open." Kristina stood before me with her blouse still gaping from my exuberance of a few minutes earlier.

"Kristina, you and I . . ." I was interrupted by the ringing of the telephone.

"Hello," Kristina barked into the receiver. "Hi, Theresa. What'd you find out?"

Kristina's body tensed imperceptibly as she listened. Only someone who was familiar with her body would notice the tight ball of steel it had become since answering the phone. She buttoned the two remaining buttons on her blouse while she listened.

"Of course, I want to know now," I heard her say.

I continued my scrutiny of her until I heard a knock at the door. I had forgotten until this moment that the detectives would probably be showing up soon.

"What do you mean?" Kristina paid no attention to the demands of the visitors as she continued her phone conversation.

I knew who I would face when I opened it, and I hesitated slightly in the hopes that Kristina would answer the door herself. Just as my hand touched the handle, I heard her scream, "Everything!? What the..."

When I finally opened the door and faced the detectives I called before leaving my house, Kristina's cursing filled the room.

"Hello, Mr. Townsend. We got here as soon as we could," one of the men said as he needlessly flashed his badge and identification. "This is my partner Detective Winston."

"Is that Miss Timmons?" Detective Winston nodded toward Kristina's back as he reached to shake my hand.

"I don't believe it!" came the scream from the spot next to the bed where Kristina stood tightly holding the phone's receiver to her ear.

I pointed toward the angry form. "She seems to be receiving some bad news."

"Interesting," Detective Winston said.

Kristina slammed the phone back into its cradle and came toward me, her eyes wide and wild.

"Miss Timmons, I'm Detective Larson with the Marion County Sheriff's Department; this is Detective Winston. We'd like to question you about the death of . . ."

Kristina's voice pierced the air and effectively cut off the detective's attempts to engage her attention.

"You bastard! You really won this time, didn't you? She left it all to you, you son of a bitch. First, Gary, and now you, Mr. kiss-my-ass Perfect! I could kill you!" Then she fell toward me, fists flying as she pummeled my chest.

The detectives each grabbed an arm and pulled her away from me. Kicking her legs fiercely, Kristina continued to struggle even as the large men held tightly to her upper arms.

"Please calm down, Miss Timmons." Detective Winston spoke to her as if she was a child. "We need to ask you some questions about your grandmother's death."

Finally, Kristina turned to look at the detectives. First one, then the other. Slowly they released her from their grips.

"Who are you?" she asked as if they had just appeared in the room.

"I'm Detective Larson, and this is Detective Winston. We're from the Marion County Sheriff's Department, and we need to ask you some questions about the death of your grandmother, Claire Townsend."

"What did you say?" She seemed to be struggling to understand the detective.

"Your grandmother. Claire Townsend. Her death is being investigated as a homicide, and we need to ask you a few questions."

I excused myself from the motel room and left the detectives alone with Kristina to ask their questions. I assumed that whoever had just called brought the news of Claire's will.

When I arrived home, I went directly to my study and shut the door. Cassie hadn't arrived yet, but it didn't matter. I wasn't ready to face her. I needed time to think about the events of the past few days. I usually liked to just push those thoughts aside or write about someone else's life during these moments, but I had reached a crucial turning point in my life. It deserved my immediate attention.

I had always taken care of the family. Everyone, including my Uncle Philip in his later years, learned to depend upon me. I didn't question why I took on the role of family patriarch; I just did it. I'm sure if I examined my reasons, I would have discovered that I actually enjoyed having the family come to me for advice.

I looked over at the sea oat sitting next to my computer. Thank goodness everyone had died so they couldn't see how miserably I'd let them all down. I began to lose control when I first had sex with Kristina as Gary lay dying in the next room. I wondered now if the nightmare would ever end for me.

I sat in my study remembering Howard Mickle and Kristina's extortion of his money and how I had seen myself through his experience. Whenever I felt my lowest concerning Kristina, the image of Howard always appeared to remind me of how far I had gone. When the phone rang, I reluctantly reached for the receiver.

"Mr. Townsend? This is Detective Winston. I think we're going to need to speak with you again."

"OK, yes. You said that earlier. When?"

"How about now? Can you come down to the station?"

"Sure, sure. Is everything all right, Detective?"

"Just get down here as soon as possible," he said.

When I arrived at the police station, I was escorted into a conference room where I found the two detectives who had visited Kristina at the motel earlier in the day.

"Mr. Townsend, I'll get right to the point. Kristina Timmons and her mother gave us some very interesting information today, and we'd like to ask you some questions about it. Did you talk with Kristina about going to Mexico?"

"She mentioned it before you arrived this morning. Why?"

"She says that you planned to leave with her right after Claire Townsend's death. She also told us that you had been having an affair for the past seven years. Is that true?"

"Do I need to call my lawyer?" I asked when I realized that the friendly detectives of yesterday had disappeared into these intense scrutinizers of something loosely called the truth.

"That might be a good idea," Detective Larson said.

Once Tim arrived, we sat and talked for a long time before the detectives joined us. I told Tim briefly about their questions, and then I told him a little bit about my relationship with Kristina.

"I'd like to cooperate fully, Tim."

"Are you sure? Some things you don't have to tell them if it doesn't relate directly to Claire's death."

"I know I didn't kill Claire, and that's what they're thinking right now. There's the changed will and then who knows what those two have told the police. I need to tell them everything, then they can decide."

"OK, OK, I don't necessarily agree, but you're the boss here, Ed. I'll be here through the whole thing. Keep your answers focused. And just tell the truth." He looked at me and laughed. "I never thought I'd be saying that to you."

When the detectives returned, they began by telling me that Pam suggested I interfered with Claire and Philip and their granddaughter a little too much.

"Detectives, I'd like to tell my side of the story. I'm not sure what either Kristina or Pam have told you, but I think I should let you know the whole story, at least from my perspective."

They told me to go ahead and only interrupted for a point of clarification or to ask a question. I began the saga of Kristina and me, leaving very little out. I felt they needed to know everything that had happened in the past few years, and they needed to understand how Kristina and Pam had been plotting to get all of the money from the Townsend family legacy.

It began to get easier to tell the detectives everything as I moved through the story. I could even talk about her seduction of Howard without wincing.

I paused to take a sip of water after telling them about the Christmas shopping excursion that ended up at a motel. I also told them what Kristina had said about deserving the money.

"So what year was this?" Detective Winston asked.

"1991, I think."

"Did you ever discuss any of this with Claire or her husband? I mean did you try to warn them about the money?"

"Yes, sometimes at the risk of making Claire angry, but Philip began to suspect that not all was right with his granddaughter soon after that visit during Christmas. It was right after that I suggested putting her on an allowance."

I explained that both Kristina and Pam were angry about it. Kristina did not call for some time after that.

"How long did she stay away this time?" One of the detectives asked me.

"More than a year, until Philip's death."

Then I proceeded to tell them about the trip from the airport on the very day that Phillip died.

"So, you two got it on, on the very day that your uncle, her grandfather, died." Detective Larson shook his head.

"Look, Detective, I'm trying to tell you everything."

"OK, OK. She's some hot number that's for sure."

"What happened after you two arrived in Ocala for the funeral?" Detective Winston asked before Larson could make any more stupid remarks.

"My wife and I decided we would move into the house with Claire after adding an addition for our new baby."

"What did Kristina think of that?"

"She hated the idea; she thought Claire should sell the house. I could tell she just wanted to get her hands on the money, and she thought I was going to have too much control over Claire by living in the same house."

"It would seem like you were moving in on her territory," Detective Larson said.

"Please, Detective, that's an opinion-laden comment. Let's stick to the facts," Tim said.

"All right, then. What about Pam? Do you think she had a motive for calling Claire after the Phillip's funeral?"

"I think it's like Kristina told me. She hoped that when the money became available to Kristina, it would also become available to her."

"I don't understand the hold that Pam thought she had over everyone. Why didn't Kristina just cut her loose? Why did Philip allow the manipulation over a little groping in the garage unless there was something bigger you're not telling me?" Detective Winston looked at me steadily.

"I'm trying to tell you everything I know, Detective."

As difficult as the detectives made it at times, I continued my story. I explained that after Claire broke her hip, I was grateful when Kristina called to say she was coming for a visit. I remained hopeful that she might help me make decisions regarding Claire's life.

"You still believed that after all she had done?" Winston asked.

"I did. It might be hard to imagine, but remember, I've known her all her life. I know there's some good in there. It's buried very deeply, but it's there. Pam's influence really can't be discounted here, you know."

"Is there anything else you can think of Mr. Townsend?" Larson asked.

"No, I think I've told you everything I know."

"Then I think we're done here for the night, don't you, Winston?"

"We'll be in touch. You know the line, 'stay in town?' Remember it, Townsend," Winston said as he opened the door of the conference room, releasing me for the night.

"Thanks, Tim. It was easier with you there," I told my lawyer and friend as soon as we made it outside the police station.

"Anytime, Ed, you know that. I know it wasn't easy. Here's some other advice you probably don't need. Stay away from Kristina."

"OK, good night, Tim." We shook hands in the parking lot before getting into our vehicles and driving away.

I looked at my watch and saw that it was just after seven. I could still meet Pam and Oscar and perhaps get some answers to my questions.

I saw Pam waiting in the lobby with a distinguished looking gentleman wearing a yellow golf sweater and gray slacks. He stood to greet me when I approached.

"Ed, we thought maybe you wouldn't come after all," Pam said.

"I've been at the police station. They had quite a few questions for me."

"This is my husband Oscar Timmons. Honey, this is Ed."

We shook hands and took stock of one another. Oscar looked nothing like the creep I had imagined.

"They had quite a few questions for me as well. I tried to be as honest as possible," Pam said.

"Me, too. Let's get a table, shall we?"

"Is your wife joining us?" Oscar asked.

"No, I don't think so. She's probably had enough of me for one day." They both looked at me. "Kristina tried for a family reunion of sorts that backfired."

Once we were seated at the table, I wasn't sure why I had agreed to meet them. I should have been home trying to talk with Cassie.

"Ed, I know you haven't approved of some of the things I've done in regards to Kristina and her inheritance," Pam said. "But I hope you'll give me a chance to explain."

"I'm listening," I said.

"I know that I wasn't a very good mother in the beginning when I was still married to Gary. I drank far too much, probably still do, but once I went out to Vegas by myself with Kris, I really tried hard to do the best I could. I even started having some of those motherly feelings when I realized that this little kid only had me in the world to depend on. Then I started working in one of the clubs dealing black jack."

"You didn't strip?"

"Are you kidding? No, but I would let a few of the girls at the club watch over Kristina while she slept, and I worked. Why do you think I stripped?"

"Kristina told me you did that until you couldn't anymore."

"One thing you need to realize is my daughter lies. And she does it quite well. Whatever seeds I had sown in the beginning of her life, soon grew and no matter how much I tried to make up for things as she grew up, something must have stuck from her earliest days. I admit that back then I couldn't stand to look at her."

"So, you dealt cards? Is that where you met Oscar?" I asked.

"Yes, Oscar owned the club, and we fell in love. He even liked Kristina, which most of the guys had found difficult whenever I had tried dating before."

"He liked Kristina?"

"Yes, I did," Oscar answered. "No matter what Kris might have told you, I thought the world of that little girl. She was about seven when I married Pam, but she never let me get too close to her. I think she thought I was going to take away her mommy. It only got worse after our son was born."

"You didn't beat her?"

"We've heard all these accusations before, Ed. But, no, we didn't beat her; I didn't rape her when she was twelve; we didn't send her out into prostitution when she was fourteen," Oscar said. "When Kris turned fourteen, we began a round of nightmare experiences with the police and truancy officers and social workers."

"I was so desperate that I begged her to visit her father," Pam said.

"She knew about Gary from you?"

"Of course. I know I told you once that I told her he was dead, but that wasn't true. I was always honest about that."

"And then when she was about seventeen, she tried to seduce me," Oscar said. "She made sure she was kissing me when Pam walked in the door. She told me it was meant to be; she had always loved me; she could take care of me if I would just run off with her; crazy stuff like that."

I felt the bottom drop from under me. The very words Kristina had always used on me. Except this man, Oscar Timmons, sitting before me, had more sense than to believe it.

"Ed, what's wrong? Have you ever heard Kristina say anything like that?" Pam asked.

I just shook my head and motioned for Oscar to continue.

"We threw her out of the house. That was the last straw for both Pam and me. We couldn't handle her, and we didn't want her around our son. We gave her enough money to fly to New Orleans to visit Gary."

"What about all the times you pushed Kristina to ask for money, for her inheritance?"

"I admit that I did want the Townsends to recognize Kristina as their own. Even though it might have been wrong, I hoped if Kristina felt like she belonged to this family, then maybe she would get the other parts of her life together," Pam said.

"Why did you come here last week?"

"I tried to tell you, but you were so certain that I was the bad guy who had created this monster, that you refused to listen. Kristina started asking lots of questions about medications and was acting suspicious around the time she visited Claire in September. I worried then that something might have happened, especially when I heard about Claire's fall. I even called and tried to get Claire to move here where I could watch her. I began to suspect that Kristina might be plotting to get rid of her."

"That's when you called Claire," I said.

"Right, but I knew it was mistake. Claire was loyal to you, and I could tell right away that I shouldn't have mentioned the fact that you weren't a real relative.

"Right after Kristina left for Ocala this last time, they discovered that someone had broken into the med cabinet at my job. I was convinced that Kristina had come here to kill Claire."

"Have you told the police all of this?"

"Yes, but I'm not sure they believe me. I think they might still think I'm a suspect. I'm sure that Kristina didn't try and change that perception when they spoke to her."

"Right now it seems they're focusing in on me. Did you know that Claire changed her will after Kristina's last visit? I inherit everything."

"Why did Claire change her will?" Oscar asked.

"I don't know, but I think I know the person who does," I said as I prepared to leave. "It was nice to meet you Oscar. I'm sure we'll see one another again soon. Pam, I need to see Kristina, and then I think I'll understand things a little better."

I pointed the car toward Kristina's motel. I had no intention of staying away like Tim suggested. I drove there deliberately and with no thought in my mind but to get some answers to questions that had been plaguing me during the last few hours.

Kristina had killed Claire. At least that is what I started to believe as I drove the car toward the motel. The world began to lose its vagueness, and as I drove, my vision began to focus.

Now I knew she could either pull me down with her, or I alone would stand accused if I didn't get some answers pretty quickly.

Kristina, my lover for the past seven years, threatened to take everything from me, and I willingly allowed her to do what she had always done best.

"What the hell are you doing here?" she said when she saw me standing outside her motel room door.

"I wanted to finish our discussion, Kristina."

"Get out of here, you bastard," she said so quietly that I almost didn't hear her.

"You know, Kristina, it would have been all yours if you had just waited. What was so important about that money that you couldn't wait?"

"You couldn't ever begin to understand. It wasn't the money," she said in a different, sadder tone.

"What was it then?"

"It would have meant that I was somebody. I could have bought you, too."

I shook my head. "I would have eventually come to my senses."

"Maybe, but I would have won."

"Won what? I don't get it."

"No, you wouldn't, would you, Eddie? You know we could still leave together. It's not too late. I know the police are torn between their suspicions of the two of us plus Pam. Did the mother or the daughter give her the drugs? Did he? Did they do it together? It was simple to plant those seeds once I found out that the will was changed. Claire had me fooled on my last visit, that's for sure." She sat down on the bed and shook her head with a bemused smile crossing her face.

"Kristina, what happened when you visited last time? What happened that made her change the will?" I needed to hear about the last piece of the puzzle.

She snorted in derision as she looked up at me with haunted and sunken eyes, the eyes of an old woman. I could no longer see her beauty nor could I see any resemblance to Gary as I had before. She had become as ugly and worn as her dreams and desires.

"I decided it was time to come clean. I thought maybe she'd feel a little more sympathy for me. I really thought it had worked. Claire was a good actress," she said with a touch of admiration.

"Come clean about what?" I asked, not sure that I wanted the answer now that I had come so close.

"Come clean about the whole thing. I even cried a whole lot, and she held me. I told her about Oscar and Pam and their little jobs for me as I grew up. Then she cried. It was a real Waltons' moment, Ed. You should have been there. But then of course you would have been feeling me up and getting a hard on, so the moment would have been lost."

"You disgust me," I said as I turned to go.

"No, I don't, Ed. The only reason you say things like that to me is because you know how disgusting you are. You were ready to screw my brains out just a few hours ago even though you had come here to accuse me of murdering Claire. Now that's disgusting."

"So you told Claire that you were a prostitute? That must have killed her. Why did you lie?"

"What do you mean lie? I told the truth, and she was shocked. Let's face it; the country club life hadn't prepared her to hear anything like that about her granddaughter. But that's not the part that really killed her, the part about having a prostitute as her granddaughter." She looked at me for a long time, and I held my breath.

"You better tell me the rest of it, Kristina."

"You don't know, do you? You never suspected?"

"Suspected?"

"Who my real father is? I'll be damned. Pam was sure you knew and were just too much of a gentleman to bring it up. I guess she miscalculated. You were too stupid to figure it out."

"Gary is your father."

"No, I don't think so. Gary never managed to finish the job with old Pam. Can't say I blame him. But now Philip, that's a different story. Twice he managed to knock her up; luckily for everyone, especially the baby, Pam had a miscarriage the second time around."

"You're lying." I stood over her threateningly. The only other time I had been tempted to hit another human being had been when Philip called Gary a queer when I told him his son was dying of AIDs. As I stood there accusing Kristina of lying, I knew that it was all true. For once, she told the truth.

"No, I'm not lying, and you know it. But it doesn't really matter now. Claire pretended that she didn't care when I told her. Said stuff about me always being her granddaughter no matter what. I left thinking all was well. I drew up papers, which said that Philip was my father, and Claire even told me that she would sign them. That way I could inherit Susan's estate."

"But why did you start giving her the pills?"

"That was Pam's idea. She got her med list and then got someone to send her pills, which had more pheno in them than what Claire was already taking. We really didn't see the harm. After all, Claire had lived a long life, and it was only a matter of time before she died anyway. We just tried to speed things along a little."

"That's murder."

"Well, that's what you believe, Ed. I don't happen to see it that way."

"Pam didn't really have anything to do with it, did she, Kris? You stole the pills, and you came here twice to kill Claire."

"Pam, who had been pushing me for years to do something about the money, started acting weird when I talked about the meds. But her place at the nursing home, provided me with easy access. People are pretty easy to seduce, you know." She looked at me with that grin that I thought always resembled Pam, but now I realized that it was Kristina's all alone.

"You've seduced all of us, haven't you, Kristina? For the first time, I'm thankful Gary is dead. If he saw this, it would kill him."

"It would have been so simple if you had just gone along with it, Eddie," Kristina said.

She attempted to come closer, raising her hand toward my face. I stepped back toward the door and took one last look at what had become of this child who had been loved by everyone except her mother. I walked out the door and away from Kristina forever. The fog had finally lifted, and I walked away a free man, even though I still had to deal with the police and my wife.

He fought against the rising tide and swam as if his life depended on it. If he couldn't out swim the current, he would go under and never recover. Soon he rested on the beach breathing in the fresh air and watching the sun rise over the horizon.

CHAPTER TWENTY

WHEN I GOT BACK to the house, Cassie's car was still gone. I parked in the driveway and walked. But I wanted to talk to someone. I wanted to walk and talk with Gary. In my entire life, I had never told anyone my innermost feelings, and now I found myself longing to confess to the one person I had listened to the most. Gary would understand and guide me.

Gary and I protected one another for so long. We stood up against our fathers together. Without his presence in my life, I doubt I could have taken care of the family for so long. I had managed somehow, and I even enjoyed the position that had come to me as the head of the family. But it didn't negate the ache and longing for spending time with Gary.

The affair with Kristina didn't begin until the night I found out that Gary had AIDs. We needed one another at that awful movement. She came to me wounded, and I was in dire need of tenderness. I couldn't turn her away from my bed any more than I could stop breathing. I needed her as much as she needed me. That night it was pure and simple and helped us both survive and face the pain of losing Gary. Funny, but I had never analyzed it much before. I just always felt guilty, but there was something there between us.

I love Cassie, but I never felt the same way about her that I did about Kristina. Cassie doesn't need me. She could survive without me. She would probably even thrive without me in her life. But Kristina always needed me, I thought. I brought her protection and safety. If I had chosen to go to Mexico with her, she would have needed me. But then how could I ever be sure that she wouldn't be out picking up some other jerk who she convinced she needed, too. I had been deceiving myself about Kristina for too many years. Maybe if I had loved her enough and in the right way, she could have changed.

Even as I had these thoughts, I knew I was once again retreating behind my mask. Even when I attempted to understand my feelings, I still lapsed into a great void of unreality. I couldn't shake the feeling that if Kristina knew she was loved, she could be a good person. She had so little acceptance in her life and that caused her to do many of the same things Gary had done. They both ran from the truth and looked for acceptance in the wrong places. How was I any different? The three of us, the children of Stanley and Philip, were not so very different after all.

Suddenly I realized there was one person who would listen to me and make an attempt to understand. I turned around and headed home. As I came to our corner, Cassie pulled in the driveway.

"Where are the kids?" I asked when I noticed she didn't open the back door of the car to begin the ritual of unfastening seat belts and car seats.

"At my sister's. Detective Larson called and asked to come over so he could question me. I thought it would be better if the kids were gone. I'll be less distracted that way. You look exhausted. The detective said you were there most of the night filling in the pieces for them."

"Cassie, we need to talk before they get here."

"I know," she said.

We walked into the house silently, and I wondered how I could ever explain to this kind woman what happened. Confessing my sins to my wife would be the most difficult thing I had ever done in my life.

We sat at the kitchen table, and I began with Kristina's birth. When I finished Cassie looked very carefully at me.

"Did you ever use protection?" she asked.

"What?" I expected her to say many things but not this.

"Did you ever use protection when you were with Kris?"

"Most of the time."

"Most of the time? But not all of the time?"

"No, not every time, at least not the first time."

"Then you and I both need to get tested. I can't believe you would be so stupid in your passion that you wouldn't use a condom, especially after what happened to Gary."

Her indictment of me came as the biggest blow of all. It was no more than I had been doing to myself all these years. Somehow, it relieved part of my guilt and disgust to have a public judgment made about something so tangible and obvious.

"Do you want a divorce?" I asked.

"I honestly don't know, Ed. It's all too much, although I suppose I should have suspected before this. You always looked like a sick puppy whenever Kris came to visit. I could tell she had some type of power over you, but I chose not to dwell on it. When I saw the two of you together today, it was as if I'd been expecting it. I didn't feel the shock you'd expect.

"You're a good father, Ed. I also know that you've suffered all these years. I just never knew the exact cause of the suffering."

"Do you think you could ever forgive me?"

"I guess time will tell. I know that the only time you cheated was with Kris, and I also know that it will never happen again with anyone else." She smiled at me as she reached for my hand across the table.

"You're pretty smart, you know." I squeezed her hand and smiled for the first time in a week.

"But for now, why don't you just move some of your things into Claire's or Susan's apartment? Then we'll see. First we've got to deal with the police; we'll work on us afterwards."

I nodded my head, grateful she wasn't throwing me out like I deserved. I headed back to our bedroom to pack a few things when I heard the detective at the door.

They arrested Kristina the next morning. Detective Larson was kind enough to call me that afternoon to tell me what happened.

"What about bail for Kris?"

"The judge will hold a hearing today. Do you think she can make bail?"

"Probably not. The only person who ever bailed her out of her situations before is now dead," I said.

"That's the shame of this whole thing, isn't it? She probably did away with the only person who could now save her."

"Detective, when did I stop being a suspect?"

"You never really were. Winston likes to play tough, and he thought you might know more than you were telling. We knew it was Kristina all along. We contacted the nursing home where Pam worked and found out the type of medication found in Claire's bloodstream had come up missing from the med room a week before Claire's death. Kristina made the rest easy."

"So, you didn't believe her when she started accusing me or her mother?"

"No, it was too obvious. Believe me, we've dealt with her type before. Pam was pretty forthright, and her story checked out. It really was simple to put it all together, especially when we saw Kristina's reaction to finding out about the will."

After I hung up, I sat for a long time looking at the phone thinking about the irony of his comments. I couldn't help Kristina ever again. She had to face her punishment no matter what form it took.

As for me, my punishment wouldn't be quite so obvious. I would get tested for AIDs within the week. Whether I tested positive or not, my scars were deep and permanent. There would be no surgery or salve that could ever erase my guilt for past actions. I carried with me the strong notion that I could have prevented Claire's death if only I had stopped Kristina earlier.

I knew I had to clear Kristina out of my mind and my life. Then I'd get to work on this novel inside of me. It was time to create and cleanse myself. I needed to make some sense of the horror of the past.

For a few seconds when Kristina asked me to go away with her, I was sorely tempted because the enormity of Claire's death hadn't hit me yet. The murder of Claire was not real, and as I've always done in my life, I was able to sweep it away and not deal with it. That's why I was able to go into Kristina's arms so easily.

When Cassie entered the motel room, I finally woke up. It was as if I'd been wrapped in that New Orleans fog for the past ten years, if not for my entire life, and suddenly it cleared, and I saw myself, Kristina, and Gary all clearly for the first time. I saw what we had done to each other through our fear and selfishness and the belief that we were not worth anything ourselves.

We all shared that quality, and so we did things that hurt others. Even Claire allowed Philip to torment and abuse Gary because she was afraid of him and even more afraid of being alone. Gary never allowed his real feelings to show because he was afraid of the consequences, and Kristina never wanted anyone not to love her first so she made herself as unlovable as possible sometimes.

And me, good old Ed Townsend, everyone's friend; a friend to everyone except myself. I allowed things to happen to me in my life. I went into my first two marriages with little thought. They wanted to get married, and so I married them.

For now, I'll move into Aunt Susan's apartment. It may not be the best situation, but Cassie wants me to stay close to the kids, and so do I. And when I'm writing, I shut myself in and become a recluse anyway so staying in the house is perfect for right now.

I wonder if I'm meant to be married. I like the idea of our family unit, but I'm not sure that's a reason for Cassie and me to stay married. Cassie has to be able to trust me again. I have to be able to trust myself, too. I let myself down more than anyone else. My pain and guilt cut deep but for so many years, I kept it at bay by not thinking about it. A great Townsend family trait. We don't talk about those difficult things, like homosexuality or Alzheimer's.

I never even confronted Philip about finding him and Pam in the garage. In fact, I tried to wipe the whole thing from my memory. I should have been outraged for Gary's and Claire's sakes when I found them. Instead, I pushed it aside. I wonder if I did that because I suspected all along that Philip had fathered Kristina?

When Gary died, instead of dealing with my pain, I fell into Kristina's arms. Then I could concentrate on that guilt and not feel the loss of my best friend.

I believe that within all of us we have the potential for good and for destruction. Sometimes we do both and sometimes one wins out over the other. I allowed my darkest nightmares to emerge when Kristina pulled me into her darkness. She never had a chance to develop the goodness that I would sometimes see glimmer across her face. She never was allowed to develop that side of her. I had plenty of opportunities to work on my good side. Only Kristina saw my other side.

But my darkness, evilness, whatever it is called, hurt only me at first. When I allowed it to continue, it hurt Cassie, too.

I let my thoughts drift to Gary. And to Philip, who had never been satisfied with his son. As a result, Gary was never satisfied with what he had in front of him. The one man he wanted to please the most, his father, could never be pleased. And finally, I thought of the fruition of both Philip's and Gary's demons: Kristina, who searched for something that she had all along. She always had Claire's love and acceptance, but instead of realizing that, she destroyed Claire.

Maybe by writing about it, I could make sense of it all. And in doing so, I would leave a more meaningful heritage to my own children.

I touched the sea oat on my desk, and then looked at my computer screen. A blank document stared back at me. I placed my hands on the keyboard and began to write in an attempt to heal my wounds and leave a lasting legacy.

Life's many twists and turns and ironies bring us to places we never intended to visit. My traveling took me to hell again and again, even though each time I bought a ticket for a destination, I ended up going somewhere else. Even hell would be preferable to the reality of what I had done and what I had almost become. I gently placed my suitcase in the back of the closet and turned to face the walls of my self-imposed prison that would provide me with the penitence and solace needed to heal.

THE END

THANK YOU

Thank you for taking the time to read *A Lethal Legacy*. If you enjoyed it, please consider telling your friends and posting a short review on Amazon. Word of mouth is an author's best friend and much appreciated. Again, thank you.

To learn more about my work, please visit my website at www.pczick.com.

~ P.C. Zick

ABOUT THE AUTHOR

Bestselling author P.C. Zick describes herself as a storyteller no matter what she writes. And she writes in a variety of genres, including romance, contemporary fiction, and creative nonfiction. She's won various awards for her essays, columns, editorials, articles, and novels.

The three novels in her **Florida Fiction Series** contain stories of Florida and its people and environment, which she credits as giving her a rich base for her storytelling. She says, "Florida's quirky and abundant wildlife—both human and animal—supply my fiction with tales almost too weird to be believable."

P.C. writes both sweet and steamy romances. The sweet contemporary romances in her **Smoky Mountain Romances,** are set in southwest North Carolina. Another sweet romance series, **Rivals in Love,** contains seven stories about finding and keeping love alive. The novels follow the Crandall family of Chicago as the siblings find love despite their focus on successful careers.

Her steamy romances go from Florida to Long Island. The **Behind the Love** series, set in a small fictional town in Florida, feature a community of people who form bonds as they learn to overcome the challenges of their youth. Her **Montauk Romances** are set in and around Long Island and feature simple, yet sophisticated beach houses designed with romance in mind. The two books in this set are filled with steamy scenes as love grows and thrives.

Zick offers a variety of nonfiction books, which include a book on vegetable gardening, a compilation of her essays and short stories from her decades-long career as a writer, and a primer for writers on taking an idea and turning it into a published book. She has also published and annotated the journal of her great-grandfather based on his experiences as a Union soldier during the Civil War.

Her novels contain elements of romance with strong female characters, handsome heroes, and descriptive settings. And all of her works express her philosophy of living lightly upon this earth with love, laughter, and passion.

She and her husband split their time between Tallahassee, Florida, and the Smoky Mountains where they enjoy gardening, kayaking, and hiking.

You can keep track of P.C. Zick's new releases and special promotions by visiting her website, www.pczick.com.